What J. Scott Payne's readers say:

"Not what I expected, I expected a good book and got an excellent one."

"I had trouble putting the book down. The authenticity is evident throughout. The combat seems so real, you can smell the cordite."

"This book was very realistic and informative. You felt like you were right there. It was well written. If you like war action you will like it."

"Very well written. Humor, horror and vivid description of war."

"First time reader of this author. I will read anything this author writes! Extremely interesting storyline, well developed characters, kept my interest and it was hard to put down."

"Great book. First book I've read by this author. I am going to read the others."

To David

J Scott Payne

6/21/21

The Orphan

A Novel Of The American Revolution

By J. Scott Payne

ARGON PRESS

The Orphan
A Novel of The American Revolution

Cover design
Deanna Compton

Cover photos courtesy of Shutterstock.com

Published in the United States of America
by Argon Press.
ISBN: 978-1-944815-44-8

For Amelia and Lane
With Love

Author's Note

When setting out to tell of a teenage rifleman in the revolution, I wondered how to imitate the period's speech patterns.

The issue of *Thou, Thee, Thy* and *Thine,* for instance. The words remind me of an old joke about a furious puritan who bad-mouths an adversary: *"I pray that when thou arrivest home thy mother doth run from beneath the porch and bite thine ankle."*

Okay. So, should it be "arrivest or arriveth" home? I haven't checked -- not after learning *thine* is correct regarding "ankle" because "ankle" begins with a vowel while *thy* is correct for "mother" which begins with a consonant.

This sort of thing may fascinate English lit majors, but I suspect not your basic historical fiction reader.

Anyway, by 1775, a linguistic as well as a political revolt was well underway. People in England and many of its colonies, loyal and disloyal, were dropping *Thou* and *Thee* and for the simple catch-all *You.*

So it is that my early Americans speak with something more like our modern vernacular.

British troops in this novel, however, sound much as they do today with accents ranging from those of County Cork to Cornwall.

Another Word

Readers new to eighteenth century warfare may stumble on the word "redoubt."

During the revolution, a redoubt usually was an artificial mound of earth and stone. It could be forty or more feet high featuring very steep sides. the idea being to make it difficult (and costly) to assault.

A redoubt served as a strongpoint from which infantry and artillery could fire upon approaching troops, thus stalling, diverting or even repelling enemy attacks.

Those who designed such strongpoints often girded them with an abatis, an obstacle consisting of entangling rows of sharpened logs or tree branches – the role barbed wire serves today.

J. Scott Payne

Prologue

(October 14, 1781)

Our cannon fire drummed so loud I couldn't hear Lieutenant Colonel Hamilton's words. I read his lips, though.

"Please, Sir! *Please!*" He gestured with raised hands while virtually hopping up and down. General Washington turned a stony face to him.

Now I ain't the brightest candle on the mantle. I haven't the brains of Colonel Hamilton who did some of General Washington's thinking and much of his writing.

But I know damned well you daren't guffaw or cut up around His Excellency. Whosoever affronts his cast-iron dignity suffers a white-hot glare. It pierces...painfully, like a musket ball twixt wind and water.

So to conceal my smirk, I wheeled around to face away from the goings-on in front of General Washington. I also rapped out a quick "About turn!" at my boys because a few started chuckling.

General Steuben probably would damn my eyes for turning the troops' backs to His Excellency. But he and the gaggle of other generals seemed focused entirely on Colonel Hamilton's antics.

Though the scene looked comic, I admit to a trickle of dread. See, this pup of a staff officer actually was begging to lead me and my men to assault and capture a British redoubt.

The redoubt was a steep-sloped earthen mound forty feet high ringed with a tight fence of tree trunks sharpened to fire-hardened points.

Four dozen redcoat regulars manned the trenches atop the redoubt. The royal artillerymen with them served two eighteen-pounder cannon. Blasting out a hatful of grapeshot, one of those guns could butcher a full score of us.

The colonel, though, wanted to risk our lives and his because he ached for fame and glory.

Now we of the light infantry ain't shy about a fight. Oh, our Adam's apples might bob a bit, and before an action our mouths tend to go dry. But we cloak the fear gnawing inside.

When so ordered, we attack with speed and all our strength and fury.

But not for glory.

Not me. No sir.

My appetite for glory vanished at Bunker Hill when a musket ball splashed my face with a comrade's brains.

Forget glory.

Now originally, General Lafayette picked a pair of French battalions to attack Redoubts 9 and 10 on the east approach to Yorktown. The redoubts were our keys to victory.

We couldn't assault Yorktown from west or south thanks to swamps, tidal inlets and their gluey Virginia clay. The York River itself formed the fortress's north side. The dry ground lay east where General Cornwallis's engineers had piled the two redoubts.

Those two strongpoints lay right in the path of our intended parallel – the quarter-mile trench that would shelter our troops as they approached to within assault distance of the British fort.

Personally, I would have been happy for the Frenchies to take both redoubts. They're the Johnny-come-latelies in this war, and welcome to my share of the glory.

But Colonel Hamilton -- desperate to show himself a hero by leading an attack, an American attack – kept entreating General Washington to override General Lafayette.

# # #

"Please your excellency! It happens I *am* senior colonel!"

General Washington suddenly unbent and nodded. Lafayette rolled his eyes and flapped his arms in exasperation. Hamilton's face lit up. He gleefully pivoted toward us.

"We have it! We have it! Redoubt Number 10!"

"Wait!" The order stopped the colonel in his tracks.

General Washington was a man of few words and even fewer gestures. Now he stabbed with a forefinger to buttress his orders to Hamilton and Willie Twobridge – that's our nickname for Wilhelm Zweibruken, the Alsatian count, baron or maybe prince appointed to lead the French attack on Redoubt Number 9.

After listening to the general, the group broke up. Colonel Hamilton's assistant, Major Fish, trotted to us.

As I saluted, the major smiled, "Captain Scot, you may tell your troops to break ranks and relax. His Excellency directs that we not attack until well after full darkness."

He continued. "The general also requires us to attack solely with the bayonet. No load in any musket. No pistols. Only cold steel for the lobsters." A couple of my men groaned about being sacrificial lambs.

I snapped, "Shut up!"

"Men! Men!" the major said. "Rest assured our cannon shall play on both redoubts all the day through. We attack in full darkness. Our advantage! No moon tonight."

I went to Corporal Saddler, a soldier larger and probably stronger than even General Washington. I directed him to draw axes for himself and eleven other men. "Corporal, tonight you and your men will cut entrances through that redoubt's abatis so we can clamber up and get at the redcoats."

He nodded. "We'll see to it, Sir."

"I recommend you make sure those ax blades are sharp."

He looked irked at me telling him the obvious. "They'll be razor sharp...*Sir*."

After that there was nothing to do. We sat down to wait, trying to relax as mortars and howitzers made the dirt fly atop the redoubts.

The boys honed their bayonets. I stoned my sword's edge. We waited. And waited.

The Continental Army has taught me patience. I've been in this army and this war almost seven years since that first damned day, April 19, 1775, in a dingy little house southeast of Lexington, Massachusetts.

Chapter 1
Rob Scot
(April 19, 1775)

Lowering an armload of kindling beside the fireplace, I puzzled at the distant rattling sound – something like corn popping.

"What's that noise?"

Jan VanderMolen lashed me across my shoulders with his cane. "Never mind, you lazy Scotch bastard." He damned me and I dodged as he tried to strike again, but just then two beefy grenadiers burst through the door.

Without a word, the redcoats stamped about yanking open bins and cupboards. They kicked over what little furniture we had.

Then they killed him.

The old devil might still be alive if he hadn't turned his vicious temper from me to them. Waving the cane at them, he screamed, "You damned toss-pot lobsters! What in hell is your business in my home? Damn your eyes, get out!"

The lead redcoat snarled, "We be aboot the business of 'is gracious fookin' majesty, King George III. So shut yer gob and stand aside you auld fool!"

Jan yelled back, "Get your red arses out o' my home or else!" He dropped the cane and reached toward the rifle tilted against the fireplace.

That's as far as he got.

One soldier stamped forward in a long lunge, ramming his musket's seventeen-inch bayonet socket-deep into the old man's rib cage. Then he kicked his boot into the victim's belly to yank the blade out.

When the blade came free, the wound wheezed and Jan's face contorted. He collapsed to his knees and then fell backwards, his white head stricking the hearth with a solid thud.

Blood pooled with frightening speed on the floor beneath his left arm.

The sight so stunned me I could only gawk. The other lobster snapped me out of it. "Boy! Where do 'ee keep thy powder?"

"Powder?"

"Ess, damn you! Goonpowder! In barrels! We be the King's Own Regiment and we're after rebel goonpowder stores."

I shook my head. "We havna powder." I bent thinking to help Jan. He coughed, spattering me with blood and stopping me cold.

With brass-clad musket butts, the soldiers smashed our table and one of the chairs. They kicked the splintered fragments against the north wall and added wads of straw from my bedding.

They thrust a burning log from the fireplace beneath the pile. As the straw caught fire, the murderer grinned at me and nodded toward Jan. "Yon's a right bad 'un, lad. Ah'm glad Ah stook him for 'ee. Noo, best get oot o' this. Place will go up fast."

Maybe he felt sorry because he overheard Jan curse at me. Possibly he thought he saved me from Jan.

Well, he did.

I hated the old man and I think he hated me because, in his old age, he depended upon and was jealous of my strength. He always was caustic and brutal. His flinty stinginess led to my foster parents' deaths. He connived to enslave me. Yet, though I was indentured to him, he still was the closest living human I had as a relative.

The splinters began to snap as the fire spread, flames licking up the wall.

The soldiers skipped out. Jan coughed again and beckoned with a feeble hand.

He gasped, "Rob! Rifle's loaded...kill 'at bastard for me." As I snatched up the firearm he gave me a bubbly red grin.

I often wonder what my life would be had I ignored him. But ever since I was ten I followed his every order. So I hefted the rifle, full-cocked it and aimed through the open door.

The two redcoats, trotting to catch up with their section, were maybe thirty steps away.

Crack!

My shot struck the base of the murderer's neck and sent his powdered wig and pope's cap flying. His corpse slammed into two files of his comrades, knocking them over like so many nine pins.

"Jan," I called, "Got him! He's dead meat!"

Jan's face still had a grin, but his eyes now were dry just like those of the deer I so often shot for him. He was dead.

The redcoats' corporal rose to one knee. "Dirty barstid!" He fired his musket at me, but the smoke from my shot spoiled his aim.

I snatched up the rifle's powder horn and its leather bag of balls, and dashed for the woods behind the house. Several more redcoats fired. The shots zipped by me, spurring me on.

Some redcoats even started to chase me. But burdened with boots, packs and heavy uniforms, they hadn't a prayer of catching a terrified, long-legged 17-year-old in rags and moccasins.

Further discouraging them -- more popcorn sounds, much louder outdoors -- shots erupted behind a stone wall bordering the woods. Several men in farmer's togs now plied ramrods to reload their muskets.

At first I thought they came to rescue me. Actually they were among several small groups shooting at the redcoat column.

I joined the farmers behind their wall and reloaded the rifle, a slow, painstaking process. Most folk need thirty seconds or less to load and fire a musket. A rifle takes a minute or more.

The wall from which we fired lay parallel to the redcoats' marching column. Two or three of the farmers at a time rested their muskets on the wall to fire at the British. As they reloaded, others in the group fired, too.

It excited me to copy them. I had no idea why they shot at British soldiers. Didn't care, either. It just warmed me to hurt people who'd murder a scrawny old man, even one mean as sin.

Maddened by our sniping, a line of British soldiers took three steps from the column and fired a volley towards us. Most of their balls thudded among the sprouting corn plants to our front, but two of our company cried out and fell.

As the English troops loaded for a second volley – they were incredibly fast at it -- we ducked behind the wall. I found myself face to face with one of my companions. He didn't look as old as Jan, but his hair in its neat queue was iron gray.

He mopped his sweating face with a cloth said, "I'm Isaac Fletcher, lad. Who are you?"

"I'm Rob, Sir."

He looked askance at me in my ragged clothing. "What's your family name?"

"Dinna really have one, Sir. They sometimes call me Scot on account of I'm from Scotland."

"No family name?"

"No. Just an orphan indentured to Jan VanderMolen. Or was, any roads."

"You ran?"

"Well, yes Sir. Lobsters killed him."

I pointed. "That's his place ablaze over there. A redcoat soldier skewered him and fired the house. Just afore he died, he ordered me to take his rifle and kill the redcoat.

"I did. Then I took out fast as I could."

Fletcher nodded approvingly. "Our men who just got hit now -- Will Parker and Stephan Rice – they're goners. If you care to, you can fill one vacancy in the Sandbury Militia."

"I dinna ken what that is."

"We're Minutemen."

"You're what?"

"Minutemen. We stand ready on the very minute to drop our plows and pick up our weapons to defend our liberty. That's why we're scourging these lobsters today."

"Oh."

I was experiencing liberty for the first time, but had no idea what it was. My thoughts instead dwelt on Jan's dying grin. It was the only smile I remembered the old man ever bestowing on me during the years he owned my indenture.

When I had time to reflect, it made me proud. It was hours before I could reflect, though.

We kept busy picking off troops in that redcoat column as it retreated from Lexington back to Boston. I was proud to knock three officers from their horses.

Chapter 2
The Fleeing Mob

Thanks to Jan's dying order, I was the only rifleman in our little group. The rest of the men carried either muskets or fowling pieces.

Fletcher told me he and his men ran almost ten miles from their village to join in the battle. He advised me to stay in his troop's spread-out line, keeping at least thirty paces from the Redcoats and at least five paces from the other Minutemen.

"We daren't cluster together," he explained, "and we always shoot from behind walls or trees."

"Why, Sir? The lobsters surely stand side-by-side."

"Right! Makes them easier for us to hit, you see. And we don't care to return the favor.

"Look you, lad, the redcoats fire but in volleys. If just one shoots at you with his musket, he'll almost surely miss. Them Brown Bess muskets have no rear sights and one redcoat usually can't hardly hit a barn.

"But mark you -- if two dozens of them fire at you in synchrony, chances are a ball or two may hit you. It might splinter your thighbone or gore right through your belly. You'd spend the rest of the day screaming afore you die."

My eyes must have bulged.

He nodded solemnly. "I know whereof I speak, boy. I fought beside redcoats in the Indian War. You're pretty safe long's you stay at least thirty paces distant and even better if you're behind cover…"

We heard footfalls and equipment rattling behind us. Four redcoats were pounding towards us, bayonets at chest level.

"Damnation!" Fletcher yelled, "Lobster flankers! Light infantry! Defend yourself!"

He fired from the hip and I saw where the ball smacked dust from the lead redcoat's chest. The shot bowled him over backward, giving me clear aim at the next soldier.

My shot struck the redcoat's midriff, dropping him into his comrades' path. As I started to reload, Fletcher yanked a pistol from his belt and shot the third lobster.

He hurled the empty weapon at the fourth, but the soldier ducked. Snarling, the Redcoat repeated the same bayonet lunge I saw earlier that day, spiking his blade deep into Fletcher's chest.

Before the redcoat could withdraw the weapon, I slammed his face with my rifle butt.

Seven years of cutting and splitting timber, hauling water and digging and plowing for Jan had built hard ropy muscles in me. I was tall, strong and cat-quick.

As the redcoat fell, I bashed the rifle butt again and again down onto his skull crushing it like a pumpkin.

Someone grabbed my arm, arresting my frenzy. A voice said, "Whoa! Eeeeesy, lad, easy! He's dead…most deadest redcoat I ever seed."

"Good," I snarled, and yanked my arm from his grip. "Filthy bastard deserved it!"

Fletcher's other men gathered, looking down at him as he coughed blood. "I'm done," he said. "This orphan boy avenged me."

One of the men watched me wipe blood and brains from the rifle butt. "Orphan? A raging orphan, I say."

"Truly," Fletcher gasped. He craned his head around, "Dan Marshall? You here?"

A very tall man knelt beside him. "I be here, Cap'n."

"Danny, you command now. Take this lad under your wing. Name of Rob Scot. Good soldier…got no home or family.

"First, though…" he coughed again, spewing blood that now ran freely from his mouth and nose, "…you boys keep torn into them lobsters. They're fleeing. And notice? Flankers didn't shoot."

Fletcher coughed again. Voice fading, he said, "Couldn't shoot. Out of cartridges. Much fatigued…sweated clear through them thick red coats. We're defeating them. Don't go home yet…not long's you got powder and ball."

We carried on under Marshall's lead, continuing to pick off the lobsters as their column processed past us.

Marshall called me aside and said, "Look, lad, it takes you a long time to load that rifle, but you can hit from much greater distance. So please to shoot officers and sergeants. Without leaders, the lobsters get confused.

"If the lobsters charge toward you," he added, "we'll come to your aid. Our muskets ain't near so accurate as rifles, but we're all much better shots than redcoats."

Just then one of our company fired and yelled. "Yeeeha! I hit another. Good lobster hunting today!"

# # #

The redcoats never did charge us. Their column rather broke into a shuffling trot, some officers now in panic, racing out of the column, trying to get ahead of their men, trying to escape.

They found no quick escape. Fresh Minutemen companies kept arriving to swarm the column, taking them under fire from behind stone walls and trees on both sides of their route. The British column steadily shed a bloody trail of wounded and dead. Many redcoats in the column limped badly thanks to buckshot wounds from fowling pieces.

The lobsters' return shots often were wild and un-aimed. They didn't seem to know to use stone walls or trees as aiming rests for their weapons.

Our main worry was their patrolling flankers. Though the light infantrymen now lacked ammunition, they still had wicked bayonets and knew how to use them. We had none.

It was near dusk when the tail of the British column crossed the narrow land neck into the Charlestown Peninsula overlooking Boston harbor. They had reinforcements so we couldn't follow.

Besides, open gun ports frowned up at us from Royal Navy ships in the harbor.

The British troops, once safe, must have collapsed from exhaustion in the farmland above Charlestown. The poor devils began their march to Concord and Lexington late the night before.

I certainly felt like collapsing and I was only in the fight for three hours. But it was my first fight and it felt like it lasted a week.

We used captured British horses to carry our three dead back to Sandbury.

Chapter 3
A Home

A gaunt white-headed matron holding a candle opened the door when we clumped wearily up the steps onto her front porch.

The instant Captain Marshall doffed his hat she knew she was a widow. She put her fingertips to her mouth. "Where's my Isaac …?"

"Madam Fletcher," Marshall said, "it grieves me to relate that your husband died today at the hands of the King's soldiers. We delivered his remains to the pastor over to the meeting house."

"Dear Lord." She coughed deeply. The candlestick trembled in her hands. "Pray tell me how it happened."

"I don't know. This lad, Mr. Scot, was present with him when…"

She turned her haggard eyes to me.

"I'm very sorry," I said, "but I…" Another word wouldn't come.

Having seen two men killed so brutally, and having killed a third with equal brutality…well, it suddenly was too much. I burst into scalding tears and turned to hide my face. I kept trying to say, "I'm sorry," but through my blubbering I couldn't utter even those words.

"Oh, dear," she said, "he's but a boy. Come, lad."

She embraced me, the first hug and comforting woman's touch I'd felt since Momma died when I was ten. I pillowed my sobs into her knobby shoulder. "There, there," she kept saying, "God love you poor boy. More's the pity to see such horrid things." I felt her coughing return.

Marshall clucked his tongue in irritation and her soothing tones became crisp.

"Dan Marshall, you march right along home now so Dolly will know you still at least are among the living. Alice and I will look after Mr. Scot tonight and then he can join his family.

Marshall said, "Trouble is, Ma'am, he has no family. I was going to put him up with us. He was indentured but lobsters killed his master. He killed the redcoat what did that and he also did for the one what killed Isaac."

The widow now burst into her own tears. Clinging to me, she at length was able to speak again. "Well, then, Mr. Marshall, he can stay here for the nonce. Nobody can replace my Isaac but at least we'll have a man in the house."

By now I partially recovered my composure. "Mrs. Fletcher I don't think it would be right…"

Her eyes drooped in sorrow, but she held up a commanding finger. "Wheest! I vow you must be famished after such a day."

Holding the candle to light my face, "And just behold you! Powder burns all over your cheek. Dust and blood on your clothing which is so tattered. What would your mother . . . ? Never mind all that. Just come in."

Weeping silently, she led me into the home where, beyond the candle's light, I made out a dim form gliding down stairs from the second floor. "Momma, what is amiss?"

"Alice, your father is dead. The redcoats…"

"Oh, good heavens…" Alice embraced her mother and began crying. The widow dropped her candlestick and the flame blinked out. In the dark I groped for it on the floor.

I stood apart from them until at length their sobs and tears subsided. Widow Fletcher said, "Come. Let us to the kitchen. We have food for you, Mr. Scot, and you can relate what transpired."

Alice led us to the kitchen where she began lighting candles from the fireplace.

I followed. A candlelit halo of lace and blond curls framed Alice's lovely face, taking away my breath. Her upper lip also had a curl to it. "Oh, Momma, can one so filthy sup at our table?"

She was right. My ears burned as I looked down at myself. The candles revealed not only blood and grime, but also the wretched state of my garments. I looked to be a rag-picker; a grimy homespun shirt missing half a sleeve, several rips and tears in my pantaloons, muddy moccasins. And bare shins, for I owned no stockings.

"She's right," I said. "I should leave."

"Nonsense," Widow Fletcher said. "I won't hear of it. "Please to wash off at the well out back. Isaac just yesterday repaired the windless handle . . . or were it this morning? Dear Lord!" She dropped into a chair and began weeping again, resting her head in her arms on the kitchen table.

Alice pointed out the door. "That way," she ordered. She sat down to hug her mother, patting her shoulder gently.

Steps beyond the kitchen door guided me in the dark down to the well. Winding up the bucket, I divested myself of my filthy garments and rinsed them thoroughly.

I scrubbed my face in the icy water and then poured a final bucket over my naked body. The cold set my teeth to chattering and I shrank from the prospect of donning my sopping rags.

Light flared behind me and I heard Alice giggle.

"Mister Scot, I have draped two blankets on the railing. Please to cover yourself and bring your clothes inside. They'll dry before the fire."

I didn't turn back toward the stairs until I heard her close the door, giggling again.

Chapter 4
Rob's Tale

Garbed in the blankets and reveling in heat from the kitchen blaze, I wolfed down cold beef with johnnycake and honey.

The women sat across the table from me, each dabbing at her eyes as I tried to tell of our fatal encounter with British flankers.

My tale emerged awkwardly. I knew nought of women. Jan had lived almost as a hermit, keeping me from the community claiming I owed him every minute of my time. So I only saw ladies at a distance. I had hardly more than nodded to a woman since Momma's death.

Having glimpsed Alice's face, I wanted to see more of her. To feast my eyes on her, as they say. But I was too shy even to glance her way, let alone meet her eyes.

So, keeping my gaze down on my platter, I said, "I wish I could have acted to save Mr. Fletcher. In the few minutes we spoke he seemed most kindly."

Both nodded and wept anew. Finally Widow Fletcher said, "Pray, tell us of yourself. Your speech says you hail from Scotland."

Still looking down, "Aye, but there's no much to tell. I come from a city they call 'Carol' but is spelt 'Carlisle.'"

"Oh, then you can read and write?"

I glanced up and smiled briefly.

"Aye an' I can reckon. See, just after we took ship from Scotland, a storm swept my true parents overboard. It so stunned me I couldna even remember the family name.

"Angus and Mary took me then, treating me as their own. They were older folk. And kindly. 'Twas their notion that since I'm from Scotland I was a scot and, therefore, ought be of the family Scot.

"Angus MacDonald, a clark, taught me my letters and sums during that four-month voyage. He and Momma Mac also taught me reading in their Bible. Even after his death she kept me at the Bible.

"I recollect he wished to be a teacher," I said. "But first they had to work out their seven-year indenture to pay for their passage.

"When the voyage ended at Boston, Jan bought their paper. He took Mr. MacDonald on as a laborer and her as cook and weaver. Momma said Mr. MacDonald did not know such work. And, sure enough, when splitting logs for Jan he sliced the ax deep into his own foot. Jan wouldna send for a surgeon. The wound mortified and Angus died soon after.

"So Jan told Momma she must work for him fourteen years since he'd paid for a seven-year indenture for each of them."

Widow Fletcher shook her head. "How wicked and cruel some folk can be."

"Well, then Momma sickened. She died in our second winter here. I think 'twas mainly grief what killed her. But Jan was so very tight. Except on the very coldest of nights, he bade us live, eat and sleep in his shed.

"It had no fireplace so the cold added to her illness. Then when she died, Jan said I must work nineteen years because my family was indebted to him for passage for three people. God how I hated him!"

Alice's eyes became enormous and, for an instant, I felt as if drowning in them. "What a monster," she said.

Her mother nodded. "Bless his soul, but good riddance. The man was a miserly devil." She paused to cough again, a long, wracking cough. "Do you remember your mother clearly?"

"Oh, aye, the both of them." I chuckled. "When I think on them, the auld accent cooms back. I remember her -- Momma Mac that is -- tellin' me, 'Soom day wee laddie, ye'll oonderstand. An' when you're all growed up and worked oot o' your contract, they'll gie you land and a musket. Ye'll find yoursel' a fine lass an' then...'."

I bit my tongue, fearing they would think I had designs on Alice.

Maybe with the same thought in mind, Alice abruptly jumped up and went to examine my clothing drying before the fire. "Have you other garments? Mother and I can sew some of these rents, but most of the fabric is threadbare."

"What?"

"I mean it's near worn through."

"Well, I havna others, so they maun last me." I explained that my few possessions, including my parents' Bible and copy of *The Pilgrim's Progress*, undoubtedly burned to cinders along with Jan and his home.

I said I hoped to loot some togs from dead redcoats.

"I doubt their breeches would fit," Alice said. "From what I saw of them in Boston, the lobsters were such short fellows." She grinned, "But you're terrible long in the legs."

The widow snapped, "Alice!" My ears started burning again suspecting that, in the light of her candle, Alice probably saw me bare-assed naked.

"We can worry about raiment tomorrow," the widow said. "For now we all must bundle to bed. We all need our sleep because on the morrow we must start preparing for Poppa's burial."

"I'll help any way I can," I said. "I'm very grateful for you letting me into your home. And for giving me a wonderful meal."

They talked of arranging a straw pallet for me. I pooh-poohed it, saying I could simply roll into the blankets on the floor. I'd slept years on the shed's earth floor. They went upstairs and soon I was toasty and snoring in front of the fireplace.

Redcoats and Jan came to me in the night, all skewering me again and again in the right shoulder.

When I awakened, realizing it was a nightmare. I understood my shoulder's pain. It ached not because of specters' bayonets but because of the hefty kicks I received each time I fired Jan's rifle...*my* rifle, my only possession.

Unable to get back to sleep, I got up to wander and nearly jumped out of my skin when I felt a touch on that same shoulder.

"It's just me...Alice. I'm so saddened I couldn't sleep."

I couldn't speak

She touched my chest. "Please," she said.

She pushed the blanket off my shoulders. "Please," she whispered, then put her lips to mine.

Pure lust overcame me and I clumsily reached for her.

All I seized, however, was her shawl. She whirled out of it and practically flew back up the stairs.

I never got back to sleep…mainly because of Alice, but not quite entirely. Fearing the nightmare might return, I spent the rest of the night cleaning the rifle.

Chapter 5
The Mourning

Before dawn, I pulled on my dried and badly wrinkled garments...carefully, so as not to widen their rips and tears.

Then I just sat in the kitchen. A large tabby cat curved back and forth against my leg as I day-dreamed about Alice's "Please." Her kiss lingered, a cool spot centered on my lips.

I held her shawl to my face, inhaling her scent and praying that she'd awaken and descend to the kitchen before her mother.

With sunrise, the sound of footsteps upstairs brought me fully awake. My notion to tease Alice with the shawl ended, however, with a hard rap on the front door.

As I swung the door open, a thick-set young man on the porch turned to doff his tri-corn hat. His buff coat looked a bit worn around the elbows, but his neck cloth was neatly tied and his shoe buckles gleamed. He obviously took pains with his attire.

Seeing me, he said, "Oh!" and clapped the hat back on his head. "Who are you?"

"Who wants to know?" Over his shoulder I observed a rider approaching. Pointing, I asked, "Is that a friend of yours?"

He glanced. "No." Then he ran his eyes down my ragged clothing. "Who are you?" he repeated. "*What* are you? Why are you here?"

I braced myself as tall as I could and looked down at him. "I'm Rob Scot. I'm here because I killed the redcoat what murdered the man of this house."

His eyes widened. "Isaac Fletcher is dead?"

I nodded. "Yes. By redcoat bayonet."

"Wait! Redcoat? My God, man, you killed a King's soldier? God damme if you ain't one of these rebels then. You are a felon. A traitor, in fact! You'll hang for it, sir, and rightly so!"

His statement rattled me to the core, but I tried not to show it. "Well, I doubt Mr. Marshall and his Minutemen would let lobsters hang me. So, again, just who are you? And what is your business?"

He stiffened. "My name is Simpson. I come to see if Mistress Alice is safe."

"At dawn?" Widow Fletcher spoke from behind me.

He bowed to her. "What with all the fighting yesterday, I feared for her safety…and yours, ma'am."

Widow Fletcher moved to my side. "Miss Fletcher is quite safe, Mr. Simpson, thank you. Perhaps it would be best if you departed for now and called at another time. We're in mourning, you see."

He bowed again. "I understand," he said, "and I proffer my commiserations."

He took a deep breath. "But now," he added in frosty tones, "I apprehend the true nature of events leading to these most unhappy circumstances. Indeed, I wasn't aware this family was in rebellion against the Crown."

The rider, Mr. Marshall himself, spoke from his steed. "This is no rebel home, sir!"

He dismounted and ascended the steps to the porch. "This is the home of a courageous man who gave his life rather than be a slave to His Majesty's corrupt ministers. Perhaps you should heed his widow and depart. Forthwith, sir!"

I stepped through the doorway toward Mr. Simpson. "Perhaps you need some help leaving, sir."

Simpson backed away from me. "Oh, rest assured I shall depart," he said. "And I shan't return…at least not for any social purpose." He began to descend the steps.

"That has the sound of a threat, Mr. Simpson."

"Take it as you will, Mr. Marshall."

"Jonathan Simpson, it would be wise for you to bear in mind that this home and its occupants are under militia protection."

Simpson snorted, took his reins and mounted his horse. He rode a short distance and then stopped. He yelled, "This will not go well with you people. Nor with that felon you harbor nor yet your claptrap militia."

Marshall shook his head as Simpson rode away.

Then he doffed his hat. "Ma'am? Miss Alice? I come bearing the commiserations of the Sandbury Militia. We regret Isaac's loss very deeply. He was a fine man, a good friend and a fine soldier."

The widow and Alice, both wearing black, nodded and gave shallow curtsies.

He looked at me. "Mr. Scot, perhaps I could induce you to accompany me. I could use your help on my farm. I'd pay you, of course."

"I think I should stay here for now," I said. "I promised the ladies I would help them with Mr. Fletcher's burial."

Marshall said, "He was *Captain* Fletcher, Sir, and I serve in his stead until we have elections. As for his funeral and burial," he gave a disparaging glance at my rags, "our company is pleased to arrange the services and provide a uniformed guard of honor."

The widow said, "We welcome your help, neighbor. What time have you appointed for the funeral?"

"It is to be eleven of the clock tomorrow, Ma'am, along with the services for our other casualties, Parker and Rice."

"Of course," she said. "For now Alice and I shall get together decent attire for Mr. Scot whom the redcoats burned out of house and home."

Marshall said, "But . . ."

"Daniel, we feel a special responsibility to Mr. Scot since he helped defend our blessed Isaac. We will come to services in our trap."

Chapter 6
Boston

When Captain Marshall mounted and left, Widow Fletcher sat down suddenly and began coughing into her handkerchief. This time it turned a bright red.

When the paroxysm passed, she smiled sadly.

"Your pardon, Mr. Scot. I have a lung flux and I believe God will fulfill His plan by joining me with my husband this winter or perhaps even sooner. I hope we can trust you men of the militia to look after our Alice then."

"Why certainly . . ."

"For now," she ordered, "you must stand stock still for us so we can measure you."

I smiled because she smiled and because Alice approached me with a measuring cord. She blushed as she measured.

It transpired that I was two inches taller than Isaac had been, but he and I had similar breadth of shoulder and length of arm so that with modest alterations, the ladies fitted some of his clothing to me.

"I fear it may not be suitable for me to wear Mr. Fletcher's clothes."

Bent over her sewing, Widow Fletcher said, "Stuff and nonsense, young man. He has no use for these garments now so what else should we do? Burn them?"

"You defended Poppa against the redcoats as best you could," Alice said. "'Tis only right that you should have them." Then she dimpled. "Though I own it is a trial to refashion the legs to be long enough."

Her mother snapped, "Alice!"

"My apologies, mother."

Widow Fletcher looked up at me with a smile, giving me a glimpse of the beauty that certainly attracted Isaac years before.

"Mr. Scot, might we prevail upon you to harness General Gage to the trap? Except I suppose now we should change the general's name to something else. I know! Alice, what if we instead name our horse King George, him to be a monarch who now will do *our* bidding?"

I didn't understand who General Gage or King George might be. It took the ladies a few minutes to explain they originally named their horse, a gelding, for the governor-general commanding the British garrison in Boston.

As for the King, they explained George III was a fat German whose corrupt London ministers were taxing loyal Massachusetts subjects to ruin.

As they described the monarch's ministers to me, I couldn't help but picture Jan VanderMolen.

# # #

I'd attended no funeral since the burial of my step-mother, a tiny affair at which only a parson, his wife and Jan himself were present. I believe Jan attended only to prevent me from fleeing.

Services for Captain Fletcher and his fellow casualties were much longer and more elaborate and attended by more than forty people. I'd not seen so many people since my voyage from Scotland. Marshall and his men paid me the honor of asking me to serve as a pall-bearer.

The pastor gave a long sermon praising the Minutemen and militia for defending the lives and property of the colony. "We all are loyal subjects of the divinely anointed King," he said, "but each man's home is his castle and we cannot permit guttersnipes in uniform to invade and destroy them."

His words made the hairs on my neck stand, bringing back my fury over the murder of Jan in his own parlor.

After we lowered and buried the caskets, Marshall invited me to join the Minuteman company.

"Mr. Scot, we head back to Boston tomorrow as part of the Army of Observation. Being's how well you fought, we'd welcome you to join us."

"And your rifle," somebody added. "Be sure you bring her along too."

That crack generated a gust of friendly laughter warming me with a feeling that was entirely novel. For the first time ever I felt as if I belonged, and as if I had friends.

"You said we're an Army of...?"

"Observation, Rob. We're to watch over the British garrison in Boston. Should they venture any further invasions into people's homes and land, we shall stop them. We have a very able commander..."

Chapter 7
Siege

During our march to Boston, I figured we might shoot redcoats again. But at the end of a fourteen-mile hike our little company merely joined the Army of Observation posted on the hills and bluffs above Boston and its harbor.

Our group's position overlooked the Charleston peninsula that juts into Boston harbor. At first I thought we simply were standing around gawking. The only other scot in our group, a red-headed banty named Samuel Liddle, explained that we now were engaged upon a siege.

"Well, what's that?"

"Near as I can say, Rob, we Minutemen keep the redcoats penned oop inside o' Boston while them redcoats keep us oot."

When I asked how he knew so much, Liddle explained he had deserted last year from a British brig where he served first as a powder monkey and then as a part of a gun crew.

For my part, I'd never been among such numbers of people. I remember being bewildered. I didn't so much seem like an army as kind of a county fair – except it was spring instead of harvest time.

Some men built huts and raised tents. A few lined up as sentries. All seemed much elated about driving the British back into Boston.

But with no rhyme or reason I could see, most Minutemen simply milled about. Rather than fighting the British, they seemed content to brag, booze, lounge, cook, chew, spit and gamble.

Our lieutenant, Andrew Duncan, spent much of his time trimming the men's hair. It was his means of paying fees at that Harvard College where he studied for the ministry.

Once we got up onto the heights I saw Boston itself for the first time since I was a child. It was almost an island in the bay, only a narrow stem linking it to the land. The sight of the town itself overwhelmed me. It looked to me like thousands of houses packed together. And if I saw one, I believe I saw a dozen church steeples.

Somebody laughed and nudged me.

"Quit gawking, Scot. Here's a shovel. General Putnam wants us to start digging."

"Just who in the hell is he?" If I learned one thing from Jan VanderMolen, it was swearing. But I also knew how to dig and got right to it.

Temporary Captain Marshall explained that during the Indian war General Putnam fought as one of Roger's Rangers and that he was tough as boot leather. Supposedly he survived being captured and tortured by Indians.

"So," the captain said, "when he says, 'Dig!' we best start spading and piling up the earth."

We Minutemen – officers and foot soldiers alike -- all dug, day after day. Officers told us we cut trenches in the earth and built redoubts to protect us from British cannon balls. Meanwhile, the positions would give us at least some concealment from which to shoot lobsters when next they attacked.

First we dug trenches commanding the Charleston neck, the strip of land connecting that peninsula to the mainland. Then they hiked us a few miles south and east so we could throw up earthworks facing the Boston neck near a settlement called Roxbury.

We still did no fighting and before long Minutemen began disappearing.

"Why're they leaving?"

"From what Ah hear," Liddle said, "they drift back home so as to plant muir crops, do their chores and diddle their women."

Eighteen of our thirty-man company departed. I thought it would be nice to visit Alice and Widow Fletcher but the Army decided it needed us back north near Charleston again.

A couple of days later, one of our generals came striding past the new trench that two dozen of us were digging.

"Ssssst!" one of the boys said. "Here comes the general, Isaac Putnam hisself."

I held up digging to get a glimpse. He disappointed me at first. He was a short round-faced stump of a fellow. Old, too. With his big frizz of white hair, he looked old as Jan VanderMolen, maybe. But his shoulders were wide as a cargo wagon.

He glared at us and exploded like a white-haired cannon.

"Why in God's name are you men piling dirt to the rear of your damned trench? Pile it to the front to create a parapet! Gives you better cover and a rest to aim your muskets. So some idiot officer went and changed my instructions? Maybe he supposed this to be your company's turd pit? My God Miss Agnes, what whoreson organized this rabble?"

Still cursing, he stamped away, his big jaw snapping open and shut hard as a bear trap.

As I returned to digging, I told Sam Liddle, "Well, I don't think old Putnam is such a much. I sure don't need no dirt pile rest for aiming to shoot a damned lobster...not even at a distance."

"Big talk, Rob," Liddle said. "Ah'd admire to see ye do it."

"By God, Sam, I believe I'll show you."

"You bluidy well better keep on digging, man. Putnam's coming back."

"Sir?" I held up a hand.

Putnam said, "What, young fella?"

"Sir, I think I could pick off lobsters with my rifle. I dinna need a dirt pile...maybe to shit, you might say, but no to shoot, that is."

"You have a rifle?"

"Yessir. They killed my master, so I used his rifle to kill some of them."

He frowned. "Well, come on up here and let's see if you can shoot good as you talk."

I took great care loading. First the fine-grain powder down that five-foot barrel. Then I laid a cloth patch greased with bacon fat over the muzzle, placed the ball on it and, with the short staff, shoved ball and patch down inside the muzzle.

"What size ball?" Putnam asked.

"Pretty small, Sir," I said. "Not quite a half inch. But it does the job."

He grinned.

With the full-length ramrod, I then shoved patch and ball all the way down the barrel. Then a pinch of powder into the flash pan.

You always load the pan last because if the flint happens to spark when you ram the charge down the barrel, it'll blow your hand and half your face toward the sky.

Once I was loaded, Putnam said, "Lad, see if you can hit that rock over there." It was a white rock about the size of a man's head more than a hundred paces away.

Jan's rifle had been our pride and joy – mine and Jan's.

He loved it because its fiddleback stock was beautiful and it was a prize he won at cards with a drunken woodsman. Jan's eyes were bad, though, so he couldn't shoot it for shit.

I loved it because my eyes were good and the barrel was true and it shot beautifully. I could hit with it at long distances. Jan had me use it to bag deer. He made money selling most of the venison to folk around Lexington.

He also made me spend half my time cleaning and oiling the barrel and lock and trigger before reassembling them back into the gorgeous waxed stock.

I started to aim.

"Wait, young fella," Putnam said. "My mistake. Get yourself back down in the trench first so's the lobsters can't see what we're about here."

Breathing hard as a race horse, he climbed down to stand a few feet to my left.

The day was gusty, with mist-filled salt air whipping to us off the sea and across the harbor.

I sighted on the rock, held off a tad for the wind, took a deep breath and gently eased back on the trigger.

The rifle cracked and its smoke clouded my view. Liddle, looking on from my right, whooped. "Ye hit yon rock square, Rob! That ball smacked oop a big puff of dust off'n it!"

Putnam grinned, "Good shot, young man. Good shot! Think you could do it again?"

"I could do it all day long, Sir. I been shooting this piece two years now and I nailed some lobsters back around Lexington."

"Is that so?" He grinned and punched my shoulder. "Well, mayhap we can find you a place in a company what's coming here from Pennsylvania. Supposed to be all backwoodsmen – all of 'em sharpshooters with rifles."

"When do they get here?"

"Oh, it'll be a while, likely. Depends on them limp lilies in Congress and their damned olive branch to London."

"What?"

"Never mind that, young fella. Just keep on with your digging for now. And keep your powder dry."

Chapter 8
Muddling

The Pennsylvania sharpshooters didn't arrive. In fact not much at all happened except the generals kept us digging trenches. Of course, it often rained, converting our earth works to brown slop.

Occasionally we'd shout friendly insults back and forth with redcoat sentries.

"Why don't you go back to England you bootneck bastard?"

"You daft bugger, Ah'm nut from bloody England! Ah'm Welsh."

Something foul awakened me one dawn. One of our hut mates was groaning. Using flint and steel, I finally got the glim lit and found Johnny Wheeler mumbling and all tangled in his blanket. His eyes were vacant and his face pale and sweaty. He was hot to the touch and stank of vomit and shit.

We dragged him outside and sloshed him off with several buckets of water. The bath cleansed him and his blanket, but he only mumbled and seemed half-conscious.

Glyn Owens, our sergeant and a Welshman who himself was once a redcoat, said it looked to him like Johnny had the ague.

"I first saw it during the siege of Havana back in '62," he said. "Surgeons called it 'mal air' because they said bad air caused it. Treated it with a tea they made from some kind of bark. Johnny will either pull through in a week or he'll die of it.

"Leastways he ain't got blackwater fever. It kills everybody what gets it."

Johnny wasn't the first. The entire Army of Occupation seemed to sicken. A dozen at a time, either ague took them or they got the shits, which the surgeons called the bloody flux.

As temperatures rose, the trenches stank worse than any barnyard. Some of the men either couldn't wait or wouldn't bother to squat and do their business in the proper places. Flies were thick.

Sergeant Owens was easy-going with us except about where we emptied our bowels.

"Damn your eyes! Don't just drop your load outside the hut or behind some bush! That spreads the ague. Do it in the pits provided for you or I'll bloody well throw you into the pit with your own turds!"

We heeded him, but many other troops infuriated him by squatting any convenient place. He became volcanic the day we discovered some lazy bastard shitting upstream in a creek where we draw our water. He almost shouted himself hoarse.

"You peawit buggers can be damn sure none of this sickness is afflicting our enemies! The King's Army gives you three hundred lashes with the cat if they catch you fouling the grounds. They don't act like babies still in their nappies!"

# # #

We heard a lot of shouting about other matters because we actually had several armies, one from Massachusetts, others from New York, Connecticut, and so forth.

Each colony had its own general who bickered constantly with other generals in their councils of war.

One day we dug next to some negro soldiers from the First Rhode Island Regiment. They were slaves who received their freedom upon enlisting. Like everybody else, they'd take orders only from their general.

We liked Old Man Putnam. He actually was a Connecticut general and he wasn't supposed to give orders to us Massachusetts men. But he cussed best so we obeyed him anyway.

He had a lot to cuss and shout about because things were so disorganized. They'd drive in cattle taken from some loyalist's farm and pretty soon we'd hear a brawl erupt about which colony's troops would butcher and which would get the beef.

It shook me.

"I tell you, Sam, I get to wondering if I joined the wrong side. Old man VanderMolen was bitter and cruel. But organized!

Everything had a place and there was a place for every damn thing. And if I didn't get tools put back right, he'd whale me with that cane of his. But I opine that this Army's just a big muddle."

"Aye," Liddle said. "We've all kinds of generals, but Ah think naebody is in charge."

At one point I even got the impression we were fighting separate wars.

After one shouting match in mid-May, General Putnam called his Connecticut troops to attention and marched them – five hundred men all told -- right across the Charlestown neck down onto the peninsula's hills and farmland overlooking Boston Harbor.

We heard he was daring the redcoats to ferry a force across that half-mile harbor from Boston to attack his men

Meanwhile, the New York, Rhode Island, New Hampshire and Massachusetts generals quarreled about whether to join Putnam, or, if the British attacked him, whether to go to his aid.

I asked Captain Marshall, "Why the hell would Putnam do that?"

"Hard telling, Rob. I suppose he wanted to lure the lobsters into battle and maybe force the rest of us to cooperate. Maybe he feels the lobsters would break on charging us."

"You think they'd break?"

"Well, Rob, you remember we outshot them when they were retreating from Lexington and Concord."

Chapter 9

Furlough

I worried because The Army of Observation – or armies, I should say – lost men daily to ague or malaria as some sawbones called it.

The queasy feeling crept upon me that if we kept running low on men the lobsters could walk all over us. Then they could strike inland again.

For sure, the number of lobsters in Boston swelled. Every day or two a new British ship tied up at Boston's wharves.

"I canna see that well. Muir lobsters?"

"Aye, Sam. It takes no spyglass to spot a fresh load of soldiers in them scarlet coats coming off the ships."

It didn't help my morale, knowing that more Minutemen drifted away of a night to help their families with crops and livestock.

I finally drifted too. I admit disappearing twice to visit Widow Fletcher and Alice. I pretended an interest in whether they needed help around the farm.

Both times the two ladies welcomed me like royalty. They also came up with labors as tough as anything Jan ever demanded. After I split two cords of firewood and repaired a pair of foot bridges over their creeks, they awarded me sweet praise. And meals.

They were far better cooks than Jan.

When her mother wasn't looking, Alice even bestowed a kiss on my cheek.

Slaving for those ladies surely beat slaving for old man VanderMolen.

# # #

Late one day after splitting logs for some hours, I enjoyed a very thorough sluicing at the well. It being mid-June now and so hot and muggy that the cold water was much more welcome than it was on that first night in April.

I just finished toweling myself dry and dressing when Alice called through the back door.

"Oh, Mr. Scot, please come to table. Supper is ready for us."

"Thank you Miss Alice." I bounded up the steps three at a time and popped into the kitchen.

The widow Fletcher was absent, leaving us alone together.

"Where's your mother?"

"Mother begs your forgiveness. She's nursing at the sickbed of an elderly neighbor lady who mightn't live through the night."

Alice served our stew plus fresh bread that smelled so damned good and tasted even better with butter and honey. But without the widow's genial talk, we ate in silence, neither looking at the other.

Back then, I was helpless at talk.

Finally, eyes still lowered, Alice whispered, "Mr. Scot, when must you return?"

"Tomorrow."

After a moment she whispered, "I shall miss you."

My food seemed to catch in my throat. Without looking up I managed to mumble. "I'll miss you, too. Very much."

Then I forced myself to look at her. I met her eyes and some dam inside me broke.

"Miss Alice, I miss you all the time. That's why I come here to do chores. When we're over to Boston I think about you. I even dream about you."

She turned a smile on me. "You do?" She leaned forward and slid her hand across the table toward mine.

"Oh, yes, yes," I said, looking into those eyes. I gently covered her little hand with my big rough paw.

I don't remember how it happened, but suddenly we were standing, fully embraced. I kissed her. Not on the cheek, neither.

She gave a little whimper when my tongue, unbidden, searched for and found hers. My heart slammed inside my chest. I pulled my face back and laid my cheek upon hers and the pounding continued, getting so strong I actually heard it.

Alice gave a sudden start. "Oh mercy," she said. "It's the door."

"What?"

"It's the door, silly. Someone's knocking at the door."

We ran together to open the door. It irked me to find Sam Liddle there.

He gave a half bow. "Evenin' to ye, Miss Alice," he said. "Ah'm sorry to barge in so, but Rob, you maun coom. The bluidy bastard English are on the move anytime and they need us all. An' …beggin' your pardon again, Miss…we're to collect all the shovels we can from farms."

"Confound it," I said. "Wait here, Sam. I'll be with you in two minutes."

"Rob, do you hurry noo." I slammed the door in his face.

I grasped her shoulders, "Miss Alice?"

"Rob, can you not at least just call me Alice?"

"Yes. Yes! Alice, I wanted to say…"

"What?"

"May we have the lend of two of your shovels?"

She stamped her foot. "Oh! Shovels? You want *shovels!*"

"No! Wait! Yes, shovels. But Alice of course I also beg you to please bide for me. Please!"

Those enormous blue eyes fixed on mine. "Why?"

"You know very well why, Alice. I long for you. I miss and love you and want you for a wife. When next I can see your momma, I will beg her permission . . .

She interrupted. "You want me for *A* wife?"

"Uh, I want you for *my* wife. I havna money now, but I shall do anyth. . ."

She interrupted again. "Rob Scot, one minute you are shy, the next you babble. Of course I'll bide! God bless you!"

I tore myself from her and raced to get my rifle and pack.

"Cannot you at least finish supper? Mr. Liddle could come in to share it."

"No Alice. No time. How's about a departing kiss? And no sharing with Mr. Liddle, neither."

She giggled. I shut off her giggle with a long kiss and a bear hug. Then I bolted through the door.

Chapter 10
Digging In

Sam had ridden and brought a second pony with him.

"Where did you get these critters, Sam?"

"Bluidy well borrowed 'em, Rob. Maun have you and them back by roll call or we'll both be in big trouble."

"Sam, what are the lobsters doing?"

"Spies say they're going to land a large force at Charlestown tomorrow and attack our lines. So we're rounding up extra muskets and militia from the countryside.

"Old Putnam and some colonel – man name of Prescott – want to block them Sassenach devils. Massachusetts is buying muir muskets, so all the men can be armed.

"Oh, and like I said, shovels, too."

# # #

Shortly after dark June 16, a thousand of us Massachusetts Minutemen, firearms on our shoulders and spades and picks in our hands, filed in three columns across the narrow neck of the Charlestown peninsula.

We weren't much for marching in those days. But sergeants and officers bullyragged us to speed the pace and close the gaps in our column.

General Putnam and two or three hundred Connecticut troops came along with us.

About midnight they had us stack our firearms and began digging in a field.

In six hours, thirteen hundred men can move a hell of a lot of dirt and rock.

Dawn's light showed us we had piled up a square redoubt atop a hill more or less in the center of the bell-shaped peninsula.

Our miniature fortress was thirty foot high and a hundred thirty paces along each of its four steep sides. Manned by four hundred troops and a pair of light cannon, it would be a deadly, fire-spitting obstacle for redcoats if they actually landed.

Looking around as I spaded, I saw that the peninsula was mostly farmland, cut here and there by fences and stone walls.

The peninsula itself was a mile long from its two hundred pace neck to its mile-wide base. Charleston itself, a fishing village, lay along the south shore facing Boston across the Charles River.

The peninsula's north side was the shore of the Mystic River, the Mystic and the Charles merging in Boston Harbor.

As the sun rose, two companies stamped back and forth atop the redoubt to tamp it flat. The rest of us kept wielding picks and spades on two other structures.

We in Captain Marshall's troop helped dig a rampart three hundred paces long just east of the redoubt and commanding the crest of the bluff overlooking Charleston. We piled up a rampart with the dirt and rock from the ditch plus logs and old fencing.

Yet more men built a redan – a spur extending from the redoubt's south face. Men firing east and west from the redan could make life hell for soldiers trying to attack up the redoubt's steep sides.

Shortly after dawn, a man working on the redan shouted down to us, "Hey, boys! Some English ships be moving this way!" Boats were towing three sloops toward the Charlestown waterfront a quarter mile downhill from us.

I chuckled as I dug. "Ships can't sail up on this hill, by God."

Captain Marshall said, "Quite correct, boy. But I wager ten shillings that their cannon balls can reach us. Did you think about that?"

I had not. He was right.

The little vessels began firing toward us. At first it made us jumpy. But the cannon balls – nine and twelve-pounders – usually thumped into our earthen breastworks without doing damage.

Sometimes, though, the cannon balls bounded up the slopes towards us looking harmless as children's toys. One of our party tried kicking a ball to stop it from rolling along the ground.

It ripped his foot clean off.

He howled as much in surprise, I think, as pain. After tying off his leg, four of our party carried him north across the neck to our camp.

Minutes later, another shot cut a furrow in the ground and bounded upward to strike the head of a Minuteman in the party next to ours. The impact spattered his hair, bone and blood among us.

We all recoiled in disgust, trying to wipe hands and faces clean but General Putnam launched a tirade.

"Damn your eyes, keep digging! You four! I want a grave for him over there! Come on, you lickspittles, ain't you ever seen a dead man afore? I'll be bound he won't be the last you see today.

"The rest of you ninnies, keep digging that trench. We want to be able to pay back these lobster bastards. When they come at us, we'll kill ten of them for him. Maybe a hundred, even! But we need that rampart! Dig, Goddammit! Dig!"

We dug.

Plying his spade next to me, Sam whispered breathlessly, "Did ye see that Rob?"

"See what?"

"See how he just stood there after that ball bashed off his heid? He just swayed, like, blood spewin' intae the air. And then he toppled, slow, like a tree."

"I dinna want to recall it, Sam, so shut yer gob!"

Chapter 11
Sniping And Payback

We hunkered down behind our rampart to take a break. Despite the slamming British naval guns, many of us dozed off and began snoring. We had worked a long, hard night.

Captain Marshall brought me awake by kicking my feet. He yelled, "Men! Wake up and grab your weapons! We're going down into Charlestown to do a little target practice."

"Rob," Sergeant Owen said, "be sure to bring that rifle of yourn."

"Oh, aye. What will we be shooting?"

"What do you think, you peawit? Lobsters, o' course."

As we filtered into the village, the sergeant said Colonel Prescott spotted what looked like an entire redcoat regiment forming on Boston's wharfs across the bay from Charlestown.

Ships' boats were meeting them there.

"Likely, they'll ferry those lads over here," Owen said. "We'll start picking them off. You'll be wantin' that rifle for sure."

# # #

Maybe fifty of us sheltered in buildings along Charleston's waterfront. Sam Liddle and I picked what seemed like good aiming points, windows of adjoining rooms in the second story of a house.

I loaded the rifle and peered out to look for boatloads of redcoats.

Sam yelled, "Hey, Rob! Look ye at all the roofs over there in Boston! Folk be squatting atop the roofs like waiting for a raree show."

Through smoke drifting from the ships' cannons, I made out what looked like entire families clustered on roofs of houses and perched beside church steeples. People crowded windows, and I even spotted some brass spy glasses.

The thought of people eager to watch men kill each other soured me. I was glad Alice and her mother were more than a dozen miles away.

As we watched the watchers, the first boatloads of lobsters pulled into view, oars rising, dipping and pulling in perfect unison.

he redcoats sat rigid and held their muskets upright, sun glinting on the barrels.

Captain Marshall yelled, "As soon as you can hit, open fire!"

Within seconds, smoke puffs bloomed around us and the sporadic popcorn rattle of individual musket fire came to our ears.

My first two shots must have missed, going into the water or hitting a boat's gunwales.

The third shot, however, struck a sailor who was pulling an oar. The injury seemed to cause confusion because the boat rocked and slewed around into the course of another.

As I reloaded, others fired, whipping the water around the boats into a froth. You'd often see a lobster jerk when a ball struck him. He and his musket would fall creating a scramble in the boat.

At that point, the British command decided wink was as good as nod. It was time to for the Royal Navy to make life uncomfortable for us Charleston snipers.

Two ships shifted targets and began firing point blank into the village's waterfront.

Now a twelve-pound cannon ball may not do much damage to earthworks, but we soon learned that a wooden house is different.

A loud crash and storm of splinters and plaster dust made me flinch and duck. The ball bashed away half the wall between my room and Sam's.

Through the dust and dangling lath fragments, we exchanged sickly grins and commenced shooting at the boats again. "Sam," I yelled. "How the hell do those anchored ships change the aim of a whole broadside?"

"Oh, 'tis simple, Rob. They fix a spring from an aft gunport tae the anchor cable. Then 'Yo He Ho'. A few turns on the capstan swings her from nor'west to nor'east, either way, in about three minutes."

More round shot impacts caused the entire house to heave. We felt it beginning to crumble around us.

Trying to sound casual, Liddle said, "They seem tae be getting' pairsonal aboot this. I deem it impairtant we get the hell oot. What do ye think?"

"Aye, man, you're making sense."

I beat him to the stairs, praying we could get outdoors before the building collapsed upon us.

My first notion was to resume shooting from one of the wharves. The ships' gunners quickly changed my mind, however, by blasting grapeshot right into the waterfront. Screeching batches of those iron balls shattered docks and pilings while splintering the fronts of houses and stores.

One ball did some real damage to me.

Something struck my rifle, knocking it from my hands. When I picked it up, I found the hammer snapped off, leaving the weapon useless.

Captain Marshall told me to keep the rifle because he said a good smith could repair it. Meanwhile, he gave me a stolen Brown Bess musket.

The bayonet's weight made it feel clumsy compared to my rifle. And was vexing because it had no rear sight, I had to aim it By Guess and By God.

It was better than no gun at all, though. I found later that at close range it was murderous.

We kept shooting and changing positions until British cannons in Boston began lofting heated, red-hot shot across the harbor into the shattered village. The glowing cannon balls started a number of fires and the Charleston waterfront soon blazed from end to end.

Rather than roast alive, we hightailed back up to the redoubt.

Now unimpeded, the Royal Navy's boats ferried redcoats by the hundreds onto the base of the Charleston Peninsula. By noon, it looked as if they delivered at least two battalions of redcoats. More kept coming.

Myself, I didn't see them. I was digging.

See, it suddenly had occurred to Colonel Prescott that we had a gap in our defenses, so three of our companies got busy with picks and shovels again.

The gap was that the Mystic River's bank – a beach, actually, because of the tide – lay beyond effective musket range of our redoubt. Nothing could stop the British from marching a whole battalion along the beach clear past the redoubt and all the way up to the peninsula's neck.

If they seized control of the neck, they'd not only cut our supply lines, but also be able to attack us from behind.

So our job was create the new obstacle, a wide wall of earth, fence rails and stone extending right to the water's edge.

Chapter 12

Bunker Hill

By midafternoon, we completed our chest-high Mystic River rampart. Dripping with sweat and stooping in weariness, most of us were ready for another catnap.

The sudden rattle of drums snapped us wide awake.

The two cannons mounted atop the redoubt began firing. The bluff screened their redcoat targets from our view, but the gunners cheered and waved their hats. Their little barrage must be doing some damage.

Nonetheless, the redcoats very deliberately marched into view, slowly cresting the bluff.

They came in three forces, each with its own set of flags.

Two units marched in wide, three-deep lines. One climbed the bluff and proceeded directly toward the redoubt. The second headed toward the rampart we dug east of the redoubt.

The third outfit, a quarter-mile column of fours, emerged into view along the Mystic River, coming straight toward our new rampart.

Sergeant Owen spat. "I can't believe they're attacking this way. Maybe they think they'll scare us into running."

They certainly scared me. The drums' driving rhythm and the redcoats' deliberate pace was so frightening I broke out in a cold sweat. It was hard to breathe.

I couldn't see the enemy faces clearly, but the column was impressive -- men in scarlet coats four abreast, tall pointed black caps, two broad white straps crisscrossed every chest, muskets vertical, a steel hedge of very pointed-looking bayonets.

The column looked like an unstoppable machine.

Some new officer named Stark paced behind us. "Men, make sure you're loaded, but keep your pieces on half-cock for now.

"We want to give them a very good volley, all of us together, but only at my command! And I want them close enough that every shot counts! Any man fires early and I will shoot him myself with my own pistol."

Under his breath, Liddle muttered, "Ahh, go and shoot yer bluidy pistol up yer bluidy arse."

Sergeant Owen snapped, "Liddle! Shut your mouth and look to your front!"

Normally, I'd laugh. But the approaching column gave me the impression it would barge right through us, bayonets stabbing, impaling, piercing between ribs, turning us into blood-dripping sponges. I feared the sharp agony both Isaac and Jan suffered.

It seemed mad to think of fighting when we were so tired. I wanted to run. But I feared doing even that because the others around me stood fast, looking impassive.

Sergeant Owen muttered to us. "Steady, men! Steady."

Now the column was close enough that the redcoats' grim faces were visible. I imagined hearing their boots swish through the thigh-deep grass.

The column broke into a trot toward our rampart, equipment jingling in perfect rhythm.

Behind us the officer's voice. "Now remember, men -- aim low. Aim for those handsome coats."

"Readdddy!"

Seventy muskets rose and clicked as we pulled the hammers to full cock. I aimed at the silver gorget worn by an officer keeping pace beside the column's lead company. He raised his sword and turned his head toward the column. He inflated his chest as if to shout an order.

The voice behind us boomed, *"FIRE!"*

A crashing explosion cloaked the target with gray smoke, transforming the lobster column into a dim jumble.

Fear disappeared.

I was frantic to reload before the shine of bayonets speared through the smoke. I ripped open the paper cartridge, trickled powder into the pan, snapped the frizzen shut, poured the powder down the barrel, shoved paper and ball into the barrel, twirled the ramrod above my head to ram the charge home. I wanted to fire before the redcoats hit us.

"Keeping firing, men!"

We aimed into the smoke and fired again and again.

"Cease fire! Cease fire!"

Smoke drifted from our front.

It revealed a butcher stall.

I suppose I should've cheered. I felt like vomiting.

The column's lead company lay twenty paces from us. Some redcoats -- the unlucky ones still living -- screamed, tossing and twisting in agony, spines arched, arms waving, eyes bulging. Many others sprawled motionless, heads crushed, white shirts and trousers now as scarlet as their coats.

A killed deer looks clean, somehow. Even pretty.

But a butchered man, intestines caught up in his ripped uniform, is an ugly, repelling sight. The officer I targeted writhed on his back in the grass. The sun glinting off the sword lying across his heaving chest.

The bulk of the redcoat column was in disarray, It retreated back along the river as fast as it had come.

The voice again behind us. "Very good, men! Now clean your muskets and reload."

"You think they'll come again after that?"

"They're regulars," Sergeant Owen said. "They'll be back." He pointed to our right. "Look over there. Those lobsters are attacking the redoubt."

Drums beating, the lines of British troops marched slowly in perfect step, only hesitating here and there to clamber over farm fences or stone walls.

The redcoats came closer to the rampart. Closer. Closer.

"By God," Liddle breathed, "now it looks like they're in touching distance. Look! They leveled their musk..."

Lightning flared and smoke billowed along the rampart, the roar reaching our ears an instant later. The men atop the redoubt fired too.

The volleys chopped lobsters down like cornstalks, clawing big bloody gaps in the redcoat lines.

The surviving lobsters sidestepped inward to close the gaps in their lines. Then they retreated, firing uphill toward the redoubt and its rampart.

The voice behind us said, "Ahh, fire and be damned! They can't hit our troops from that distance."

The redcoat officers apparently felt the same, because the line stopped shooting and backed down the bluff out of our view.

Chapter 13
Defeat And Retreat

Captain Marshall called out, "Rob, you've got grand eyes, right? Do you trot over to the crest of that bluff. Take a looksee at what the lobsters are about.

"Take Liddle along," he added. "Don't tarry. Just take a glimpse and come back and tell us."

As we started to run, he yelled, "Don't go that far if you spot redcoats wanting to fight."

The only redcoats we found along the bluff's crest were dead or dying. They lay, some still twisting, in thick piles where volleys had slashed them by the score.

A wounded corporal reached up to me. "Gives a swig of water, lad. Ah'm perishin' thirsty. You ain't 'elping an enemy, like, 'acos Ah'm done. Ah'm past 'urting you fuckin' rebels now."

I knelt and handed him my water bottle. He took a big swig. Returning the bottle, he looked down toward his wounds giving a bitter chuckle. "Ahh, no damned odds, were it? I feel t' drink comin' out 'oles in me guts."

He raised his forearm to cover his eyes. "Thanks, lad. Kindly of you. Sorry for the waste of it."

Liddle called to me from the bluff's crest. "Rob! Get yersel' over here! They ain't giving oop. Muir boats with redcoats." I joined him to see fresh troops come ashore. Each boat then retracted from the beach to ferry wounded back to Boston.

The new troops lined up with the remnants of formations of the first fight.

"Coom on, then. Let's gang back to the captain."

# # #

The next attacks began and ended much the same as the previous ones. Formations came within thirty paces. The lead ranks fell to our volleys. Survivors retreated, leaving behind screaming welters of bloodied, gutted, dying redcoats. Long gouts of blood streaked the grass around them.

This time, however, our adversaries retreated more slowly, falling back, half-concealed in smoke from their own volleys.

When their shots did strike amongst us, the damage was ghastly. A ball hit Eddie Peckham's thigh ripping away one leg of his pantaloons and a chunk of flesh the size of a healthy cod.

He tried to crawl away using his elbows but collapsed face-down right in our line.

A ball hit Arthur Craven's left breast, knocking him flat and blasting a hole big enough to hold a fist.

Then I had to sweep brains, blood and bits of bone from my face when a ball caved in Albert Simms' head.

Thank God most redcoats' aim was poor. Having backed downhill from us, they fired too high. Though most of their fire passed above us, they still inflicted the wounds that defeated us.

Most of their shots thudded to earth in showers forty or fifty paces behind us. Our ammunition bearers happened to be there in their race with empty cartons toward the supply point on the far side of the neck.

Later we heard three of the ammunition party escaped injury. Two of them – seeing those three-quarter inch lead balls butcher their comrades -- ran away to never return.

We in the line were elated at the collapse of the second British attack. We also were nearly out of ammunition and didn't realize that no more powder and ball was coming to us.

Captain Marshall sent Liddle and me forward again to scout at the bluff's edge. The scene on the beach changed.

"What the . . . ? Ho, Sam, look! The lobsters is shedding their shells!"

Still more troops disembarked from boats.

Now, though, the British soldiers clustered at the foot of the peninsula removed their heavy packs, stacking them in neat ranks along the beach. They removed their peaked caps and leather neck stocks and then lifted the crisscrossed white belts over their heads.

Finally, they doffed their heavy scarlet coats and folded them over the packs. Then they draped the cartridge belts back onto their shoulders.

Now in shirtsleeves, again holding their muskets pointed to the sky, they formed line to assault again.

"Come on, Sam. Back to the cap'n."

# # #

Fifteen minutes later the lobsters surged toward us, this time in larger numbers, this time trotting rather than marching.

We fired, knocking down maybe two dozen of them. But when I reached into my ammunition pouch, I discovered it was near empty. I was down to three cartridges.

A few scattered shots later and our rampart went silent. An oncoming redcoat bellowed. "Yer out, are ye? Naah ye'll taste cold steel!" They clambered over the rampart and burst in among us, a hedge of flashing, stabbing bayonets and slamming musket butts surmounted by furious empurpled faces.

Instead of rattling gunfire, now all I heard were snarls and gasps, thudding impacts on heads, curses, growls, screams and calls for mercy.

Two men in front of me gasped and spasmed as triangular bayonet tips came poking out their backs.

Sergeant Owen yelled, "Can't fight! Get out of this, men! Now!" He stumbled and fell.

He turned over to rise when a bayonet pinned his left leg to the ground. He yelled in rage and shot the soldier with his pistol. Two more lobsters raised their muskets high, butt upward, and stabbed their bayonets down into his chest and belly again and again, changing his yells to screams.

I screamed too, gripped my empty musket by the barrel and gave a long swing, braining an officer as he hacked at me with his saber. I dodged two grenadiers jabbing bayonets toward me and used the musket to club one of their comrades.

The impact broke the stock, so I swung the naked barrel smashing more lobsters with the iron breech end. Some of them backed away. I hurled the musket at another grenadier, picked up my broken rifle, and did what everyone else did.

I ran.

British bayonets broke us into a panicked mob.

General Putnam and I raced together across the neck. We halted twice to let cannon balls fired from the ships bound across our path.

As we found our way into our own earthworks, I noticed something had clipped off two joints of the little finger on my left hand.

"Damn!" I said, staring at it. "How'd that happen?"

General Putnam slapped my shoulder. "Don't worry, lad. That little fleabite won't sour your shooting."

That's when I noticed he was missing three fingers.

Chapter 14
A Victory Of Sorts

I stayed beside the general as he and other officers succeeded in stopping the retreat near the trenches just beyond the Charleston neck.

General Putnam yelled, "Rally here, boys! The bastards ain't giving chase. You give them enough for one day. They don't want no more.

"There's no sign of them," he added.

At first, I didn't believe him. But when I looked back across the neck toward Charleston, it was true.

The only redcoats visible through the smoke drifting from the burnt-out village were maybe a dozen pickets, all in shirt sleeves. They were maybe two hundred paces distant and staying put. Beyond them, other redcoats – also now in shirt sleeves -- carried wounded men and dug graves.

We saw no formed British troops.

Captain Marshall helped calm us. His face was grave, but he acted calm and relaxed.

"Men, let us proceed to the supply magazine for cartridges. We can give the lobsters a warm reception if they dare to come. But they daren't."

After we drew ammunition, the captain lined us up for a depressing roll call.

"William Anderson?"

"Here."

"Adam Bristol?"

"He's wounded," Liddle said. "Got a ball in the arm. Left it danglin'."

"Andrew Jones?"

"Here."

"Sam Liddle?"

"Yep and ready to take 'em on again."

"Rob Scot?"

"Here with a broke rifle and missing finger."

"John Franklin?"

Nobody answered.

"William MacEvoy?"

Anderson said, "I think he run…long before the rest of us."

"Eddie Peckham?"

I raised my hand. "Prob'ly dead, sergeant. A ball took off half his thigh. Last I saw he was layin' in the dust."

"Johnny Ryan?"

No answer.

"Albert Simms?"

"Dead. A ball blew his brains out."

"Willard Thompson?"

"Lobsters bayonetted him."

"Did anybody see Sergeant Owen?"

"Bayonetted about two dozen times. I'm sure he's dead."

After calling a dozen more names, Captain Marshall stood silent, shaking his head.

Then he looked up. "Men, don't lose heart. They beat us today because we ran out of powder and ball. But we Minutemen showed we can take on the best of the King's regulars. They're only men, after all. Musket balls cut them down same as anybody else.

"You know, they came at us stupidly. In fact, I think they believed they could cow us into running without a fight.

"Well twice now, we've showed the redcoats that we can fight and that we *will* fight."

His words perked us up a bit, but nobody felt like cheering.

# # #

The lobsters had, indeed, suffered enough.

Over the next week, depending upon who you'd believe, spies in Boston said that in three hours of fighting, we'd killed and wounded more than a thousand redcoats, compared to four hundred of us.

We also heard that their commanders – General Howe, who led the assault, and General Gage – were deeply discouraged about the battle. Howe himself came out of it uninjured, but our musketry supposedly wiped out his staff.

We started feeling a bit cocky because some lobsters were deserting to us. I was on sentry duty when one redcoat came racing across the Charleston neck.

He was a rangy fellow carrying his musket butt upward. When I aimed at him he pleaded, "I surrender! Far the love o' God, man, don't shoot! I surrender!"

He dropped the weapon, threw up his hands but kept running toward me.

He stopped three paces away, unlaced and tore off his leather collar, then his cross belts and then his scarlet uniform coat. "I surrender," he said again. "Please."

I yelled for Captain Marshall.

When the captain arrived, he told the deserter, "You're safe now, lad. So, bring the musket with you and tell me, what's it like in Boston."

"Ooch, sure and it's horrid, Sir. You rebels kicked the bejaysus out of us. Most officers is dead or wounded or after dyin'. Wounded troops get no help, don't you know, 'cause ain't surgeons enough. Commanders is posting sergeants to serve as lieutenants."

"What about captain and majors?"

"Mostly dead. Nobody reckoned you Yankees would fight. Nt like that, by the saints."

"So, they're not going to attack?"

"Holy Mary, mother of God, Sir, what would they be attakin' with? By the saints, I swear that far every soldier standin' another pair is layin' on straw or bein' put 'neath the sod. And they don't even say burial service if you're Catholic like me."

"What?"

"Oh, it's true, Sir! If you ain't Church of England, nobody takes your confession or says last rites or nothing for you. So, an Irishman like me gets killed with no confession or final unction, he goes straight to hell.

"It's the God's truth," he added. "That's why I come over to you."

"Lad, what's your name?"

"Patrick Hannon."

"Well, Pat, welcome to join the Army of Observation. How long was you a lobster, anyhow?"

"I donno for sure. Three years, maybe."

Chapter 15

The Commander

July 2 dawned with a great to-do, nearly the whole army gathered at the big parade ground in Cambridge near that Harvard school.

They were lined up to welcome to the Army's newest and biggest general.

I wasn't part of it, being on sentry-go at the nearby bridge over the Charles River.

Our sweat beaded and ran free that morning because it was the kind of broiling sticky day that often brings on a storm. And it did just that. Dark clouds rolled in, thundering to beat hell. Then came the downpour and the assembled Army scattered to its tents and huts.

Lightning scared the boys in our squad and they scampered down to shelter on the riverbank beneath the bridge. I stayed put on the road because our orders were to guard the bridge no matter what.

So along comes a big four-wheel coach accompanied by a dozen uniformed riders, heads tilted into the rain. I recognized General Putnam on his horse talking through the coach window to the passenger, a huge man who nodded to his words.

Glimpsing Putnam, I figured I must look pretty stupid just standing there all alone with a dripping musket that probably couldn't fire. So I called to the boys under the bridge, "Looks like officers coming. Better get up here."

Liddle yelled back, "I'll no coom up there to get drenched or lightning struck."

That answer burned me. Why the hell should I be soaked or risk getting fried because everyone left me to do the duty all on my lonesome?

So I bellowed, "Officers coming, damn you! Get your arses up here! In line! Do it now, by God!"

I guess they suspected something big was up because they scrambled up to the road. We all stood at attention, muskets grounded by our right feet. We tried not to blink as rain slanted into our faces and dripped off our chins and noses.

The carriage stopped and its passenger looked down at me. He held papers in a huge right fist, but his face caught my attention first.

His steel-colored eyes were level as a ruler. Mouth the same, chin jutting just a bit. His face bore all the expression of a piece of granite. He looked rough, ready to bash anybody in his way.

"You a sahgeant?"

"Nope...ahh, sorry. No Sir."

"Just now y'all sounded lack one."

"Only a rifleman, Sir."

He quirked an eyebrow. "Well, that's shoah no raffle y'all carryin' there."

"Sir, my rifle was broke in the fight. Ain't found nobody to fix it yet."

"What fight?"

"That fight we had here two weeks back when we cut up the lobsters so bad."

He nodded. Then, "Do you know about salutin'?"

I held his gaze. "Sir, I do not. But I sure as hell know how to shoot."

General Putnam grinned. "He's right. Lad can shoot. Seen him. Dead on at a hundred twenty paces."

The big man told Putnam, "Maybe he should be a sergeant."

"I'll see about it," Putnam said.

The officer gave me a curt nod. "Go on, driver," he said, and led his party across the bridge.

As some of the following riders passed, they glanced down at us contemptuously.

After they passed, Liddle asked, "Who in *hell* was that?"

"No idea, Sam. Maybe he's the new general we hear tell of. I sure wouldn't want him mad at me. Big fellow. Big enough to give you a real thumping."

After a minute I said, "If you've a mind I guess you boys can go back down under the bridge afore the rain melts you."

"Sergeant Scot," Liddle said, "I think t'would be better to stay up here."

I snorted in derision because now the rain let up.

The Army paraded again the next day.

That's when I found out the huge fellow was a Virginian, name of George Washington.

The snooty riders with him were his personal guard, also Virginians.

Chapter 16
Organizing

Captain Marshall just shook his head. "So now we have a pouch filled with forms enlisting us in the national army...the Continental Army.

"Yet it's just as in Genesis," he added. "The army is without form, and void."

Lieutenant Andy Duncan, the former barber and divinity student at that Harvard place, quipped "No firmament, either."

"Right," I added, "but what really matters is we're very low on powder and ball."

It soon became clear, though, that General Washington intended to give the army form. First, he ordered the creation of badges of rank.

We had nothing like real uniforms so, outwardly, you couldn't tell General Putnam from Private Nobody.

Most of us just wore farmers' clothes. Some had stiff tri-corn hats, others like me wore hats with floppy brims, good enough to keep off the sun and some of the rain.

Now headquarters ordered us sergeants to wear a strip of red cloth along our right shoulder, corporals green.

Company grade officers wore cloth cockades on their hats, yellow for captains, green for lieutenants and ensigns. Majors, colonels and up wore sashes of various colors.

One morning they transferred Captain Marshall to command a company because our platoon was too small for a captain.

Meanwhile, Lieutenant Duncan would run our platoon which was folded into a company of ninety men led by a Captain Munro. In turn, Captain Munro's company would be one of eight companies comprising Colonel Paul Archer's Regiment.

It confused the hell out of me. But then came a big change -- General Washington's order to elevate officers.

Captain Munro told us we'd no longer be allowed to call officers by their first name.

"In accord with His Excellency's orders," he said, "hereafter we shall use military courtesies. You'll refer to officers by their rank and last name, no matter if you was neighbors or known to each since you was kiddies.

"If one of you wishes to speak with me, first you must salute by raising the hat from your head. Then you must request permission to speak."

I found this insulting, but an old hand from the Indian war brought me up sharp. "It tells me General Washington knows his business," he said. "'Tis the onlyest way an army can operate."

"Well, I don't like it one damned bit."

"Don't matter if you don't like it, lad. We can't fight lobsters if all soldiers ain't in full subordination to their officers – and to their sergeants and corporals as well. Otherwise, it's a mob that will fall apart just like at Bunker Hill.

"Ask our new boy, Private Hannon. In the King's army you daren't speak to officers at all. Correct?"

"Only if they speaks to you," Hannon replied. "Sergeants told us we oughtn't even say 'Yes sir' to an order. That might sound like you think you have a choice, that you could choose to say, 'No sir' which could get you five hundred lashes.

"So we was only to say 'Sir!' and then look sharp about followin' the order."

Our Lieutenant Duncan turned out to be very shy. I'd just turned eighteen and was two years his junior. But he was so guarded and unsure of himself that he sometimes deferred to my suggestions and often sought my advice about dealing with the men.

That was awkward. General Washington wanted officers to end all familiarity with the men. No more officers cutting the men's hair or cobbling their boots or vice versa; no more men doing chores on officers' farms; no more backslapping or company elections; no more whiskey-drinking with the men.

The general cashiered several officers, including some who were found to be stealing pay intended for their own men.

Meanwhile, we heard that His Excellency was petitioning the Congress for uniforms like he and his Virginia Honor Guard wore – blue coats with tan facings and tan waistcoats and breeches.

We didn't start getting uniforms for three more years. Even so, General Washington was beginning to create the Continental Army of the United Colonies and -- the next year -- of the United States of America.

So I officially ceased to be a Minuteman and became a soldier in the Continental Army...or simply a Continental.

Meanwhile a wonderful rumor boosted our hopes. We heard detachments from three colonies captured Fort Ticonderoga from the British and were hauling dozens of cannon from there to Boston.

"Cannons?"

Lieutenant Duncan said, "Yep. Some three or four dozens of them. Heard so from my cousin at General Putnam's headquarters.

"Once the cannons arrive, we'll start firing on all the King's ships down there in the harbor. We can even start pounding Boston itself where the lobsters are quartered. It'll be a big lobster trap."

"How far away is that fort we captured?"

"I'm not sure. Up near Canada. Maybe three hundred miles. "

"And they're hauling all those cannons here?"

"That's what I'm told."

"I hope the lord looks after us meanwhile."

Chapter 17
Promotion

It was a cold November afternoon and Lieutenant Duncan was seated on a camp stool in front of his tent, face in his hands. He seemed to be shaking.

At first I thought the noise of the British cannonade might have spooked him.

But that couldn't be. After weeks of hearing the desultory bombardment, nobody minded it more than a flea – less, actually, because fleas tortured us day and night.

I doffed my hat. "Sir, permission to speak?"

He looked up, his face white. "Yes, of course, Sergeant Scot, what is it?"

"Just wondering, Sir, is the ague afflicting you."

"Oh, I wish it were." He gave me a morose look. "I'm bid to His Excellency's headquarters. I fear he'll cashier me like he has so many other officers."

"For what cause, sir?"

"I can't say. Maybe because I hardly know this calling. He's summoning officers from all over the army and 'tis terrifying." The lieutenant stared at me for a moment. "Sergeant, please come with me to the general's headquarters."

"Me, Sir? But I know nothing about being an officer."

"Yes, perhaps. But sergeant, you do know about the men, all that kind of detail. So I need you there with me if His Excellency has questions I cannot answer."

Late that afternoon, we climbed the front steps of General Washington's headquarters, a two-story mansion that earlier served as a surgery. Lieutenant Duncan wore a heavy greatcoat. Having none, I wrapped myself in a grimy straw-flecked blanket.

Two splendidly uniformed sentries flanked the mansion's door. I took off my hat and announced the lieutenant.

A sentry opened the door to Duncan. I donned my hat and turned to leave but the lieutenant paused in the entrance and said, "Please, Sergeant Scot, wait out here for me."

"Yes, Sir."

As the door closed behind him, the sentries gave me down-the-nose looks. Their uniforms were spotless with gleaming brass buttons.

As the Quakers like to say, my garb was Plain, very, *very* plain indeed, showing much wear and soil from three months of heavy labor, plus blood spatters from battle. The sentries' uniforms made me feel like a hog in a church meeting.

One sentry tried to needle me. "Y'all look mighty young to be a sergeant."

"Ain't too young to kill quite a few lobsters," I retorted.

"Oh. Was you in that Bunker Hill fight?"

The question temped me to brag, to show these fops that deeds make a soldier, not pretty uniforms and shiny muskets. I reckoned, though, that being in front of headquarters it might be wise to use restraint.

"Yep, I surely was fighting at Bunker Hill."

They glanced at each other. One asked, "Bad, was it?"

"Yes. At the end…when we run out of powder and ball. Had no bayonets, neither. But up to then we made mincemeat out of them."

"So you say."

That burned me.

"Mister Virginian, I don't know if you have looked around, but after that fight those British built all kind of redoubts and entrenchments across the Boston Neck and the Charleston Neck. And they fire cannons at us all day long."

"So?"

"But don't you see? They don't attack. They daren't. I think they fear *we* will attack! And maybe we would if we had half the damned powder they waste."

Just then the door opened and a man stuck his head out. "Is Lieutenant Duncan's sergeant here?"

I answered, "Right here, Sir."

The man looked me up and down skeptically. Finally he said, "Come with me, sergeant."

The man, a lieutenant, led me down a long corridor past several offices. Then we turned through a door into yet another office. He seated himself at a small table covered with stacks of papers.

Remembering our lobster deserter's words I stood to attention and said, "Sir!"

He dipped a quill into his ink bottle. "Your name, sergeant?"

"Rob Scot, Sir."

As he wrote, he asked, "How many men in your platoon?"

"Twenty men ready for duty. Four more ailing – with the smallpox. Seven are wounded and four of them will surely die."

"Why?"

"Two belly wounds, from the English shelling, Sir. They won't live. Two others have wounds that the surgeon says have gone morbid."

He gave a slight grimace. "Now, sergeant, of the platoon's twenty men ready for duty, how many have been vaccinated for smallpox?"

"All of us now, Sir."

"And how many of your troops have powder and ball?"

"All of them, Sir, but not enough for a real fight."

Frowning, "Why so?"

"Sir, we have only three made cartridges apiece. I have another fifty made cartridges stored...hardly more than two apiece. Not enough for another Bunker Hill fight.

"If we go into a fight we should have at least fifty cartridges in reserve for each man. Seventy would be better. And if we're going to fight over two or three days we'd need at least two hundred cartridges."

"Do you have cartridge papers?"

"Only enough for maybe a hundred, Sir. We've ordered all the men to preserve cartridges safe from weather. And we don't allow the promiscuous shooting that goes on in other platoons."

"Really, sergeant. How do you stop them?"

"Sir, I purely kick hell out of them. Only takes once."

He snickered. "Good. Some companies have no ammunition at all because of random shooting."

"I heard that," I said. "I don't want to go up against redcoats again without powder, ball or bayonets. Nossir."

"Yes. Now, how are you coming on your gun carriage?"

Each company was building a wooden carriage and limber for the cannons coming to us from Fort Ticonderoga.

I was pretty handy with an adze, shaping timbers into slabs making up a gun carriage. A blacksmith also allowed me to work with him fashioning ringbolts for the carriage and iron tires for the wheels.

He had me spend most of my time charging his fire which at least helped me keep warm. But he also showed me the rudiments of working cherry-red iron.

"Sir," I said, "we finished one carriage…"

"Including wheels?"

"Yessir, and we started on the limber. But we haven't wood enough for an ammunition wagon. Sir, is there any telling when the cannons actually will get here?"

"Soon, I'm told."

"That's good to know, Sir. And sorry for speaking out of turn, but I worry about garments for the men for this weather."

He nodded as his quill scratched. "That's my worry, too."

Eyeing my blanket, he questioned me about shoes, foot cloths, clothing, cooking pots, food and firewood. The sound of a step in the doorway stopped him. He looked up and shot to his feet. "Your Excellency!"

I turned. General Washington virtually filled the doorway. Lieutenant Duncan, pale with strain, stood just behind him.

I dropped the right side of my blanket and held my hat over my heart.

Recognition awakened in the general's grim face. "Ah, the sharp-shooting sergeant. Is your rifle repaired?

"Not yet, Sir."

"Well, at least you have learned saluting."

"Sir!"

"How about drill?"

"Your Excellency, we've practiced a great deal on getting from route column into double line, Sir. Getting smoother. But so far we're not fitting very well into regiment drill."

"You must improve." The general looked at the captain. "Well?"

"Your Excellency, Sergeant Scot seems to have competent knowledge about the people in his platoon…and their needs. He also is literate."

The general nodded. "Sergeant, how old are you?"

"Just turned eighteen, Sir."

"Sergeant, you're no gentleman and I'd say unlikely ever to become one. But knowing your platoon…maybe you should be an ensign. What do you think, Duncan? Would he be of use to you?"

The lieutenant bobbed his head vigorously. "Sir, he already is of inestimable value."

"Good. Better get this new ensign a green cockade for his hat. Who knows, Ensign Scot? Should you continue to progress you may command a company one day."

"Sir!"

Trudging in the snow after leaving headquarters, Lieutenant Duncan said, "Congratulations."

"Sir, I ain't so sure I want this job."

He laughed gaily. "I know exactly what you mean."

Chapter 18
Trying To Learn

Day-to-day, I think I did more to run the platoon than Lieutenant Duncan.

He was smart, though. He studied French military texts telling about regimental maneuvers. He would read several pages and we'd discuss how it all applied to a platoon. Then we started drilling the troops.

At first, even getting the troops to march seemed impossible. Half of them didn't know left from right.

"So, Private Tisdale, which hand do you use when you piss?"

"This 'un, sergeant."

"Good! That's your right hand. Tis on your right side. T'other side is your left. Remember it!"

"Yes, sergeant."

"Damn right, yes!"

Once we got that settled, the men learned to march fairly well, and soon we were able to shift ourselves in a clumsy fashion from a column into a skirmish line or even a double firing line.

But when it came to joining other platoons and companies in those same maneuvers on a regimental scale, we were hopeless – or, actually, the regiment was.

Its officers didn't seem to grasp the French prescriptions for company oblique marches that enable a regiment to quickly transform itself from column into battle line. As for wheeling a line of companies pivoted on one flank or the other, it was bedlam.

During drills, regimental and company officers sometimes became confused and countermanded our orders to our own platoon. As a result, the men often stumbled into each other, muskets clattering to the ground. Sometimes the men cursed. Sometimes they broke out in laughter. Occasionally they fought.

Captain Munro gave Lieutenant Duncan several vicious tongue-lashings. "Honestly, Duncan, you possess the command presence of an insect!" The verbal attacks shattered Duncan for hours. Then he'd get his courage back.

Once, he pointed out the regimental officers' translations were, er, not quite correct. To prove it, he showed them a French-English dictionary which soon had senior officers screaming at each other.

On one such occasion, unfortunately, General Washington happened to ride up. He stopped the argument by shouting "Silence!" His tight-lipped expression seemed only to further tighten. He looked at the officers and shook his head.

It became more and more apparent to me that some majors and colonels not only didn't know their business but also relied on bad-tempered bluster to conceal that ignorance.

With winter's onset, we turned the bulk of our attention away from drill to finding heavy clothing for the men, not to mention blankets. Our other big problem was finding wood for our fires for warmth and to cook our rations.

By late December not a tree was left standing on any bluff overlooking Boston, Charleston and the harbor.

Our new position in the center of the line placed our right flank behind the houses of Roxbury opposite the Boston neck. Already damaged by British shelling, those residences looked to be in a state of slow collapse. Wood parties snuck during darkness to pilfer broken shingles and siding, splintered beams and shattered stairs and stringers.

The lobsters down in Boston itself also seemed desperate for wood.

Red coated work parties – actually, coats now weathered to pink -- cut down several stately trees a day. From a distance looking like so many ruddy ants, they swarmed around a fallen tree, hacked off the branches, split the trunk and cut the resulting rails into firewood.

In three hours an entire seventy-foot tree would disappear.

# # #

"Hey, Rob?"

"Dang it. Sam, you're supposed to call me Ensign Scott."

"'At's right," Private Hannon said. "You must pay respect to your officers."

"Aye, forgive me!" Liddle said. "But have ye heard the latest story coom up from Boston?"

"I ain't. Tell me."

"The story is that the lobsters have only enough food for a month. I hear tell they're already on half-rations."

"Oh, I doubt that."

"Oooch, I think he's right," Hannon said. "The rats in Boston was startin' to look good to us even before that battle."

Liddle swallowed and said, "Rob – oops, sorry, I shoulda said, 'Ensign Scot' – have ye never done any time in ships?"

"Hell yes, coming here from Scotland..."

"No. What I mean is that have you sailed before the mast."

"No."

"Well, I did for four years. And let me tell you, in summer it usually takes no muir than five or six weeks tae sail here from England. In winter, what with those storms out on the Atlantic, you're blessed if ye can fetch any of these colonies in fifteen weeks or even sometimes twenty. Fact is, you're fortunate if your ship even survives some of them storms."

"Sam, I think you're doing a lot of wishful thinking instead of splitting those logs."

"Think so? Well, Mr. Ensign Scot, do you remember us seeing troop ships come in to Boston Harbor every day back in July and August, right?"

"Yep."

"Well, now in December maybe one ship a week gains the harbor. Some of 'em even looks partially dismasted, too. I think the Atlantic winter storms is our greatest ally."

The next day a rumor made the rounds that a whole brigade of redcoats was lost in an Atlantic storm.

I doubted that tale, but there was no gainsaying stories about one other ally. We received an issue of ammunition amounting to twenty cartridges apiece – a windfall, though not near enough that we'd need for a battle.

Its source was an American privateer that captured one of His Majesty's supply ships loaded with muskets, bayonets, powder and ball.

Then came the greatest news of all.

It was during a blizzard that an enormous cheer moved along our trenches. Men were dancing and cheering because they learned Colonel Henry Knox arrived from Fort Ticonderoga with the first of fifty-five cannon on sleds.

Chapter 19
Artillery

The army set about mounting its new artillery and our regiment's share of the work was two guns. Captain Munro's company drew the toughest task.

Most of the Ticonderoga artillery pieces were one and a half-ton bronze or iron field guns. They fired balls weighing either six or nine pounds. Some, the howitzers, were much shorter and lighter.

Sweeping the snow from atop our job, however, revealed an enormous 24-pounder naval cannon.

"Holy Christ," Liddle said, "the damned thing looks mayhap ten or eleven feet long."

Even with Captain Munro bellowing, "Put your backs into it!" twenty of us couldn't stir the cannon from its sled, let alone lift it onto a wheeled carriage.

As we stood up stretching our backs and shaking our heads, the captain snapped at Lieutenant Duncan to take charge. He stalked away.

So, working amid of almost horizontal snow squalls, we followed directions the lieutenant translated from a French artillery manual. We erected a stout timber tripod above the gun and used block and tackle attached to the tripod to lift the gun from its sled.

The tripod creaked ominously as we raised the massive weight. We pulled the sled from beneath the gun and replaced it with our newly-completed carriage. We gently lowered the gun onto the carriage and let out a cheer.

Whereupon the carriage collapsed.

We tried to raise the gun from the wreckage. Blasphemy joined obscenity when the tripod itself collapsed onto the gun.

"Ensign," the lieutenant told me as he disappeared into a fresh snow flurry, "please take care of it."

Shivering and stamping their cold feet, the men grinned and asked. "Now what, Ensign Scot?"

I had no idea.

I could not imagine how Colonel Knox and his men dragged guns such as these to Boston – let alone hundreds of cannon balls, barrels of flints, bars of lead -- over three hundred miles of lakes and rivers and up and down some very steep snow-packed Catskill slopes.

Obviously, though, they had the know-how.

"I'm going for help," I said. "Return to your shelters and try to warm yourselves."

# # #

Hoping to find Colonel Knox, I trudged through the snow to General Washington's headquarters. When I arrived, the building was in a swirl.

Sentries and servants were toting bales of baggage into the house. I stood in the doorway looking for the colonel when a tap on my shoulder startled me. A feminine voice drawled, "Excuse me, suh, please may I to enter?"

Startled, I turned and slipped in the slush on the tile floor, falling full length.

"Good gracious," the voice said, and I found myself looking up at a small, pretty woman garbed in a heavy cloak. I sought to apologize as I attempted to scramble to my feet, only to slip and fall again.

A sentry asked, "Lady Washington, is ought amiss?"

"Heavens no," she said. "'Twas not I who fell."

I asked, "Lady Washington?"

"The same," she said with a dazzling smile. "And youh name, suh?"

From behind me came His Excellency's voice. "My love, it appeahs as if yet anothuh young officer has thrown himself at yoah feet."

She laughed aloud as the general reached down to me. "I was the first young officer," he said. "And I recall your face, Sir, but disremember your name."

I grasped his hand and, showing his immense strength, he yanked me upright. "Ensign Scot, Sir, of Colonel Archer's regiment. I beg pardon for this intrusion. I came to seek advice from Colonel Knox."

He cleared his throat, but she interrupted, "Mr. Scot, You are poorly dressed for such weather."

"The entire army is poorly dressed," General Washington said. "So much presses on Congress that it is desperate slow to address our needs."

"Then, sir," she said, "you must enlist the ladies' help for our soldiers and their cause."

"Pray how, madam?"

"We women spin and sew and knit. It would be strange if we could not begin providing at least a little where Congress cannot or will not."

"Sir? Ma'am?" I said, "Again I apologize. I merely came to find Colonel Knox."

"He is off to Philadelphia to meet with Congress," the general said. Pointing to an office doorway, he added, "Mayhap a member of his staff can help you."

# # #

One of Knox's sergeants came with me to our bivouac. He burst out laughing when he saw the gun and the ruins of tripod and carriage.

"Good Lord, mister! Do you know a 24-pounder weighs five thousand pounds? You loaded it onto yon poor little 12-pounder carriage. Even had the carriage supported the gun, it would have collapsed at the first shot."

It took us two days to manufacture a heavy-weight carriage according to the sergeant's specifications. Then, using a tripod with massive timbers, we mounted the gun onto its carriage. We cheered when we locked the iron squarecaps over its trunnions.

The Big Iron Devil – that was the name we gave the gun – was ready to fire.

We wanted to use the cannon to pound entrenchments which redcoats had dug across the Charleston neck, but headquarters had other plans.

We raised the gun's trails onto its limber and used a team of oxen to haul the 24-pounder to Roxberry. They ordered us to mount the gun in a redoubt covering the British fortifications on the Boston neck.

# # #

Our army's own cannonade started poorly.

Two cannons burst, killing the crews that overloaded them. Soon after, however, our artillery began repaying the British for the shelling they had inflicted upon us.

But truth to tell, our artillery's main effect did little more than deny us sleep. Our barrage didn't seem to hurt the British any more than their shelling injured us.

In fact, the passage of time did far greater damage to us than British cannons.

On December 31, 1775, many enlistments ended and much of our army simply disappeared.

Chapter 20
In Distress

Despite pleas from our generals – not to mention sergeants and mere ensigns like me – regiment after regiment of the Army of Observation marched home.

Lieutenant Duncan and Captain Munro were among the deserters, leaving me -- an "old timer" -- the sole officer running a platoon of seven. I appointed Sam Liddle to be our sergeant and promoted Private Hannon to corporal.

"Can you believe it Sam?" I said. "I hear barely six thousands of us Continentals remain. Our camps look like ghost towns. And if we get new men, can you imagine how many hours of training we'll have to do all over again?"

"Aye, Rob, but even worse, we now face twice our number of redcoats."

Hannon, his face gloomy, nodded.

We soon merged with two other fragmented platoons, now amounting to eighteen armed soldiers.

At first, most of them stayed on duty because -- like Sam, Pat and me -- they had no other prospects.

Then a change occurred. Among the new recruits who started dribbling in to our camp, many seemed excited. They kept talking about "independency".

Finally, one of them gave me a pamphlet entitled *Common Sense* that was circulating in Philadelphia. I needed a full day to read it and one statement kept coming back to me.

> *...Britain is the parent country, say some. Then the more shame upon her conduct. Even brutes do not devour their young, nor savages make war upon their families.*

Those words twanged my memory of two redcoats bursting into our home. I remembered their exact words: "...we be aboot the business of 'is gracious fookin' majesty, King George III!" I still foamed at the memory of how they bayonetted the old owner when he objected.

Up to this moment, I participated in the war because I disliked lobsters and enjoyed soldiering. But Mr. Paine's words turned me into a bit of a crusader. I was all for slashing the bonds between the colonies and "'is gracious fookin' majesty."

Once I found the time, I located a Pennsylvania rifleman who showed a smith how to fashion and properly quench a new hammer for my rifle.

After that, when free of paperwork, I joined other riflemen in picking off redcoats along the Boston lines.

Some riflemen avoided shooting sentries and would only target officers.

As far as I was concerned, ordinary common soldiers were as much my target as any lobster ensign or major. Such were the men who murdered Jan VanderMolen and who knows how many other citizens. For me they were fair game.

At times it did seem like a game.

"No, wait Rob! I spy an officer peering through his glass. He's all stuffed up and proud as a peacock. I don't know. 'Tis quite a distance. See if you can pick him off."

I slowly slid that long barrel through a gap between two logs, aligning the sights on the target's cocked hat.

"Mind, Rob, the wind is from the left!"

"Tell me something I don't know, dammit! I feel it on my cheek. Now, shut your gob and leave me be."

As I brought the hammer to full cock, my fingers told me the flint was clamped tight. I took a breath and gently stroked the trigger.

"*Crack!*"

"Whoa, Rob, you got him! A real gusher. It threw that cocked hat of his a good ten feet! Now get back. It's my turn."

Word got back to us that the lobsters called us riflemen "orphan-makers." They quickly learned to stay under cover.

One day I won ten silver shillings as the only rifleman able to pick off a redcoat dancer. We named the officer The Dancer because he walked or trotted in spasmodic patterns, apparently delighting in fooling us.

He'd jog out into the open, stop, lean to one side, take three steps in the opposite direction and suddenly stop again. Or he'd swing right for three more steps, stop, step backward three and veer right again. Or left. His pace and path were impossible to predict

Five or six riflemen took up the game, taking turns trying to shoot him. Over three days they wasted perhaps twenty shots, one finally coming close enough to knock the tricorn from his head.

The Dancer ducked out of sight to retrieve the hat. He popped into view to make a rude gesture and then disappeared the rest of the day.

Firing the near-miss was Otto Klempt, a surly and boastful Pennsylvania dutchman, who bet he could hit The Dancer if the man dared appear next day.

The Dancer did appear. Klempt missed him four times in an hour. He then folded his arms in disgust and said, "Ach, him no man can hit!"

"I can," I said.

Klempt spit in contempt and bet two shillings that I couldn't. Though I had no money I took the bet. Several of the other men bet with him.

I cocked my rifle just as The Dancer wobbled his way into view, paused, took two steps and waved his hand.

My bullet went right through his palm. Hearing his scream of pain and fury, we laughed.

Klempt tried to welch on the bet, saying the wager specified killing The Dancer. One of the other rifleman exploded in scorn. "You bark-tight Dutchman! Your exact words were 'Ach, him no man can hit.' Well, Rob sure as hell hit him."

I settled for half the wager. Inwardly, I was a bit glad I hadn't killed someone so crazy brave even if he was a lobster.

The Pennsylvanians suggested that I do as they did and give my weapon a name. Klempt's rifle was *Die Hexe*, the witch. Another called his rifle *Sugar Lips* and another settled on *Widow Maker*.

I named my rifle *Lobster Claw*.

It amused us a few days later to hear that the Redcoat command wrote a complaint to General Washington's headquarters about our sniping.

They believed picking off officers to be unfair – as if bayonets, grapeshot, cavalry sabers or .75 caliber musket balls were fair, or somehow gentlemanly.

We heard His Excellency immediately sent a courteous note back to General Howe averring that, like any other soldiers involved in war, redcoat officers must take their chances.

Meanwhile, since I worked with infantry, I committed myself to carrying a musket slung on my left shoulder. But owning a rifle, I always managed to keep *Lobster Claw* and all its impedimenta close at hand.

The impedimenta presented a problem.

A man with a musket can fire three and sometimes four rounds a minute because all he needs is paper cartridges and a ramrod.

A rifleman can't use cartridges.

Oil on the patch wrapping a rifle ball would contaminate the powder in a cartridge. A rifleman therefore must measure out powder from a horn for each shot. He also must use two ramrods.

I'll explain. Push a ball into the bore of a musket and it may rattle half-way down the barrel on its own.

A rifle ball, however, must fit very tight. It takes considerable effort with a short staff to force the patch-wrapped ball into the rifle's muzzle. Then you need the barrel-length ramrod to push the ball all the way to the breech.

That's why most riflemen only get off one shot every minute or two.

Chapter 21
A Damsel In Distress

The only thing I truly regarded as unfair about our war was that though the army shrank, paperwork seemed to expand. It still ruled my life.

We subalterns had to execute enlistment forms for all the new recruits, literate or otherwise. So with a splintery old quill I'd copy their names into the following form.

> I _____ *do voluntarily enlift myfelft into*
> *Captain*_____ *'s Company of foot belonging to*
> *Colonel* _____ *'s Regiment in the service*
> *of the United Colonies of America to continue during the War,*
> *and to be fubject to such Rules and Articles as are or fhall be*
> *established by Congrefs.*
> *Witness my Hand this* _____*Day of* _____ *, A.D.*_____

And I dare you sometime to try filling out such military paperwork with freezing ink.

After writing only a soldier's first name, it was necessary for me to blow repeatedly into the bottle to thaw a tiny puddle of ink, then dip the quill and scribble the enlistee's last name before the fluid turned ice-hard again.

It was just as well that for now we had no real companies or regiments, so I was saved the trouble of thawing ink to fill in captains' and colonels' names.

It was enough of a pain to fill in the enlistment dates. Even with me crouching on a stool near the little fireplace didn't help the ink flow.

That's why a tiny tapping on the door of our platoon hut provoked an explosion.

"*WHAT?*"

A child-like voice said, "Rob?"

"Good God in heaven above, what now? Come in, dammit!" I blew onto the quill, hoping my breath would thaw its coat of black ice.

"Rob?" again.

I looked up to behold Alice Fletcher. She was bundled in a heavy coat and wore a scarf over her blonde hair. But her lips were trembling and her cheeks were scarlet.

She said, "Rob, I'm sorry to…"

Dropping the papers, I jumped up from the stool. "Alice! Good lord, you're freezing!"

Her teeth chattered as I enfolded her in my arms. "Why are you here?"

"Oh, Rob," she sobbed, "they burnt us out!"

"Who burned you out?" What happened?"

"Tories – royalists -- attacked us last night and fired the house and the big barn, everything. Stole our livestock.

"We hid in the thicket out back. But it was all too much for Momma. She suffered an apoplexy and now is with father.

"I have kinfolk in Connecticut," she added. "I am going there, but I wanted to see you first."

"Alice, who did all this?"

"Tories from western Massachusetts. Maybe a dozen of them on horseback. Supporters of the King. I know I saw 'twas Jonathan Simpson who led them. He was urging them on, yelling 'Burn! Burn! Burn!'"

"Simpson! That's the man who came to the door the morning after we met?"

"He's the one."

"He's a filthy coward, using a mob to attack helpless, unarmed women…"

Tilting her head defiantly she said, "Oh, we weren't entirely helpless, sir.

"We had Papa's pistols. Momma winged one of those arsonists, and later I knocked another right off of King George."

She sniffled. "I don't know if the ball killed him...the rider, I mean. I was able to catch King George and ride him here."

She shuddered. I pulled her before our little fire and threw fresh kindling onto it. I tried to warm her cheeks by covering them with my ink-stained hands.

"Well, in this weather you cannot ride to Connecticut. And certainly not alone with such things happening," I said. "I've a notion how you perhaps can stay safe with us."

"Here? With you?"

"No, not here with me. I mean with the army, right at its headquarters." I didn't tell her how damned little army was left.

I knelt beside her and we talked as she warmed in the fire's glow.

"Dear sweet Alice, I still want you for my wife. I should have asked your momma's permission long ere this."

She smiled. "Momma already granted permission. She saw much in you. She told me she believes you're like Poppa -- that you have the strength and the wit to go far."

"I hope she was right," I whispered.

# # #

By the time she stopped shivering, I helped her back up onto King George and led them to His Excellency's headquarters.

The guards admitted her when I pointed out that her witness of royalist raiding might be important to General Washington's staff.

I listened in as she described the raid. One of the general's aides said, "Simpson's people might be that same group we heard was raiding around the environs of Rutland."

I immediately headed back to our bivouac and my frozen ink and the platoon's enlistment forms. I felt certain that once the officers finished questioning Alice, they would take her to Lady Washington.

As Alice told me weeks later, Mrs. Washington at the time was entertaining a neighbor, Abigail Adams, the wife of a very important member of Congress.

The two women convinced Alice that as a seamstress she could do as much as any soldier to help the cause and to avenge her mother.

The trio began knitting stockings that same night.

Within two months, Lady Washington and Mrs. Adams had organized a sewing circle embracing eastern Massachusetts and eastern Pennsylvania plus parts of New Jersey and New York.

They even recruited several seamstress allies living down in British-occupied Boston.

Chapter 22
Retribution

When I returned to the bivouac, the sight of paperwork and frozen ink was too much.

Staring down at those forms…some blank, some already filled in, I called, "Hey, Sam!"

Liddle looked up. "What?"

I said, "Do you spose we could get five or six of the boys to come with us on a little patrol?"

"Aye, but for what? And where?"

I told him what Simpson and his loyalist raiders had done to Alice's home.

"I think Cap'n Marshall knows Simpson," I said, "…or at least knows about him. So he might be able to give us some guidance."

When Liddle and I met with Captain Marshall, he not only told us a great deal about the raider – whom he called a rich, spoiled brat -- but he also insisted that he and four of his men join us.

"I hear from home," he said, "that Simpson's gang has become bolder and bolder with their threats. They've extorted funds from some families and stolen from others. But now knowing what they did to the Fletchers, it sounds like they've becoming outright barbaric. Makes me fearful for my wife and little ones."

He pondered.

"We'll need horses," he said. "'Tis much too far to hike in a night or two. And we'll want sabers and pistols. Carry your muskets slung on your back."

I said, "Cap'n, we have no horses."

"Not to worry," he said. "I'll take care of it."

"Second thing," I said, "is where ever I go, my rifle *Lobster Claw* comes along for the ride."

"I don't know how you'll carry it, too, but do as you wish. Whatever you do, don't forget to tie your saber to your hand. Otherwise, you lose it first time you stick somebody with it.

"And whatever you do, at first contact, give 'em the point. No slashing."

Liddle said, "Why no slashing, Sir?"

"Because you are tyros. New men often slash so carelessly and promiscuously that they cut off their own horse's ears or utterly unbalance themselves and wind up falling off and getting trampled in the mud.

"Another thing to remember. Most wounds in cavalry actions mean death. If you're knocked from your saddle to the ground, a kick in the head by a horse finishes you. That's why "

# # #

It was just after the third dawn of the patrol that our scout spotted Simpson's little troop camping in a wood near Rutland.

Captain Marshall had us dismount two hundred paces from the trees. We crouched as we moved forward through the morning snowfall.

Somebody among the loyalists was building up a camp fire. Stupidly, as I crept forward, I kept my eyes on that crouching form rather than my own path.

So I blundered into a burrow or some declivity and fell my full length. Thank God our weapons were half-cocked so that I didn't shoot a comrade by accident. The noise I made, though, was enough to alert the camp.

Captain Marshall hissed at me. "Damn your eyes, Rob!"

Then he yelled, "Up! On your feet! Cock your pieces and fire!"

Our ragged volley knocked down several raiders who were barely awake. It also sent their horses into squealing, bucking pandemonium.

"Simpson!" Captain Marshall yelled. "I see you! Surrender! We have you surrounded."

"Never, neighbor! I'll never surrender."

We were cocking our muskets for our second volley when a flash and a bang in the camp knocked down the one man who had managed to mount his horse.

Somebody else clambered onto the mount.

Marshall yelled, "Goddammit, that's Simpson. Fire!"

We fired but didn't hit him.

At two hundred paces distance, he stopped and turned his horse toward us. "I'll see you in hell, Dan Marshall, and all your pathetic militia!"

I leveled *Lobster Claw* and fired.

He half fell from the mount. After pulling himself upright in the saddle, he yelled something incoherent and rode off.

Captain Marshall said, "Good shot, Rob. Almost makes up for your clumsiness. Now did anybody make out what those last words were?"

Liddle grinned, "Ah'm fairly certain the word 'king' was part of it and also 'bastard'. But Ah canna say they were connected."

We hanged the three survivors of Simpson's raiders.

I would have favored treating them as prisoners. But Dan Marshall went white with fury when he recognized many neighbors' possessions – including jewelry and portrait miniatures -- in the raiders' leather satchels.

We found a blood spatter in the snow roughly where my shot may have wounded Simpson.

We had no way to tell whether it was human blood or horse blood.

We returned as much personal property as we could. Our patrolling also revealed the raiders had stolen cattle from five farms.

We didn't return them.

We herded the beasts to headquarters. Seeing that tiny herd, the officers there were inclined to overlook our five-day desertion of the lines around Boston.

Chapter 23
Rebuilding

At first, I found it depressing that only a few tiny clusters of recruits showed up to replace entire regiments that had marched home.

But as more and more people read *Common Sense* the trickle of new faces became a modest flow. Our miniature platoon grew enough that Sam and Pat and I could begin again with the left-right, left-right basics.

Then on the heels of Paine's attack on royalty came a victory which boosted General Washington's efforts to rebuild the army -- the liberation of Boston.

That victory began with the arrival of March 1776 and the commencement of our around-the-clock artillery bombardment of Boston. The shelling did little actual damage to the British who, as usual, replied with two or three shots for each one of ours.

What the barrage did accomplish on its third night, however, was to cloak the noise made by another thousand of us foot soldiers turned diggers.

Overnight, our teams of pick and shovel-men created a covered way. It lead from Roxbury across a half-frozen tidal swamp up onto the crests of Dorchester Heights, two tall hills commanding both Boston and its harbor entrance.

As we worked to corduroy the road, one of the new men in our platoon tapped my shoulder and whispered. "By God, Ensign Scot, do you see who that big fella is?"

"It's dark. I can't make out anyone's face."

"Well, by the gun flashes I *can!* It's General Washington hisself."

"No!"

I stood and turned. He was right. The general was standing right behind us. I yanked off my hat in salute.

He nodded. "Ah, ensign. Keep your men pressing ahead. We only have this night, sir."

I got back to work. So did he. The general spent the entire night among us, striding back and forth along that mile-long line of toiling soldiers.

He encouraged us. He tried to joke. He sometimes wielded a pick or shovel, and when he did, let me tell you, that man made the dirt fly! He lent a hand piling shovel after shovel of earth into the fascines, the big deep wicker baskets that intercepted musket balls and cannon shot fired at us by the British.

His example put so much fire in our bellies, that even though it was a chilly night, we ran with sweat.

By dawn we had emplaced our few 24-pounders – including my old company's Dirty Iron Devil – in dug-in batteries square atop Dorchester Heights.

We couldn't help laughing in glee at the shock the lobsters must have felt that dawn. Suddenly our artillery now boomed from the heights -- plunging fire from ship-battering siege-size guns.

For the next two days, we watched in anticipation as the redcoat command massed troops and boats for a cross-harbor assault to recapture Dorchester Heights.

We were ready for them. And eager.

Having learned much from Bunker Hill, we made certain our men were well-rested. We also built up a vast store of musket ammunition right at hand.

But then a week-long tempest roared in from the Atlantic, wrecking most of the British boats and all of their plans.

The storm also gave General Howe an excuse to reconsider launching another frontal assault against us.

At any rate, a few days later, General Howe struck a deal with General Washington.

He proposed that if General Washington stopped shelling British vessels, the Royal Navy would evacuate the British Army from Boston. In return, the British would leave Boston unharmed. They also would take along as many loyalists as they could.

The alternative? They would burn the town and fight to the last man.

I had hoped they would attack us on Dorchester's hills, for I believe we would have slaughtered even more of them than we had at Bunker Hill.

But still, it was wonderful – especially for old-timers like Sam and Pat and me who'd been there almost a year -- to stand up there on the Heights jeering and waving our hats as they warped their ships out of the harbor.

We paraded into Boston late that same day and found it to be a horrible mess.

The British had turned at least one church into a filth-filled riding stable. They scattered crow's feet – sharp-pointed four-pronged iron versions of children's jacks -- on the streets to impale horses' hooves and soldiers' feet.

But they also left behind hundreds of wagons. Within a week, His Excellency had the army loading those conveyances with food, ammunition and artillery.

Like the British, we also left Boston.

The general was sending at least five regiments south through Connecticut to New York City. We were taking all the cannon, too, on a trek of more than two hundred miles.

I learned that a regiment of Pennsylvania rifleman was ordered to lead the way.

Sam asked, "Ain't you going to join them?"

"Maybe once we get to New York," I said. "But I think we need to train these new boys of ours and we can try to do it on the march."

# # #

At first, it was a march in the mud and slop which the storm created. Churning it knee-deep, of course, was a thirty-mile column of hooves, wagon wheels and soldiers' feet.

"We canna drill in this," Liddle said.

"Yep, we can. Have them drill on loading their muskets."

"What? When they're hiking?"

"Why not, Sam? We both saw the lobsters do it on the road out of Lexington. And Bunker Hill, too. Maybe they couldn't shoot worth shit, but I sure'n hell saw them load their muskets when they was marching.

"Isn't that right, Pat? You told us lobsters practice loading blindfolded."

"Roight you are, Sir. Sergeants or corporals call off each movement by number. In practice they can get off four shots in a minute. In the field, they demanded firing at least three to the minute."

On our next break in the march, I told the platoon the drills we would undertake. They growled and complained, of course, claiming it was impossible.

Hannon yelled, "What? You bastards think you can't do as good as a fucking lobster? Sure and if we get into battle d'you think you'll only fire muskets when you're standing stock-still in a nice flat field?"

Still cussing beneath their breath, our boys followed orders. We did a good deal of musket drill while hiking in the mud.

Their progress surprised Liddle, me and themselves. Hannon said, "I told you, did I not?"

The drill added to our general feeling of cockiness. After all, us Continentals had defeated the British three times now.

A day later, the sun came out. Soon our column's wheels, hooves and feet kicked up so much dust you could hardly see the muzzle of your own musket.

"Hey, Ensign Scot! You needn't blindfold us now! We can load in the dark"

But then the cockiness ended.

Chapter 24
Defeat

Like a whirlwind, the story seemed to spread back along the column to us from the lead elements just arriving in Brooklyn.

Liddle was the one who passed the word to me.

"Way I'm hearing it is that smallpox, Indians, militia and redcoats destroyed the entire Continental Army in Canada."

"Oh, bollocks!" I said. "Just more rumors. And anyway, why would Congress send an army to invade Canada?"

"Tae take those colonies from the British, Rob. The folk in Canada dinna like lobsters any more than we. Or so Congress was thinking."

I snapped at him. "Like I told you Bollocks! I bet it's just more campfire stories."

But it wasn't.

In fact, over time we learned the northern Army's remnants began straggling back to into upper New York and Vermont even before we forced the British to abandon Boston.

Despite that ill news, we continued our trek south toward the city of New York which lay at the tip of a long hilly island called Mannahatta.

As we arrived on the island, General Washington's orders immediately put us to work fortifying the city.

We worked like dogs to barricade the streets, to set up batteries to shell British ships, to create redoubts, to sink obstacles in the Hudson River which would block British ships, and to entrench the approaches not only to New York City itself but also the city of Brooklyn immediately to the south on Long Island.

Meanwhile His Excellency also ordered more than a thousand troops to start constructing Fort Washington.

The new fort was supposed to crown a towering granite escarpment ten miles up the Hudson, and it was to be studded with cannon brought from Boston.

On the whole, I avoid the memories of the ensuing summer and its running series of defeats.

Oh, I recall a few high points. I marveled at the city itself because the townfolk actually kept it lit at night with big lamps hanging outside every seventh building.

The highest point in our New York stay came Monday, July 8. That was when General Washington ordered the officers to read the Declaration of Independence to the troops.

Some clauses in the declaration's attack on the monarch's conduct struck me then and still ring within my mind:

> *--He hath ... sent hither swarms of officers to harass our people, and eat out their substance. -- He hath abdicated Government here, by declaring us out of his Protection and waging War against us. -- He hath plundered our seas, ravaged our Coasts, burnt our towns, and destroyed the lives of our people.*

I don't know who first got the idea, but right after the reading, somebody announced that the statue of the King in Bowling Green Park near the New York City waterfront was cast in lead.

"Well, hell," Liddle shouted, "dinna we need musket balls?"

That afternoon, a mob of soldiers, slaves and townspeople looped a dozen stout ropes about the statue's chest and neck.

Heaving, yanking and pulling, they eventually broke the statue from its stone pedestal. It landed on the surrounding stone pavement with a disappointingly dull thud.

It was lead indeed.

Somehow, toppling the statue of George III with his crown and Roman toga sealed it for me.

He no longer was our sovereign, but just another powerful fat rich man. We no longer were England's colonies, nor even the United Colonies.

Now we were fighting for our own country with its new name, the United States of America.

It was a heady, exciting time.

I heard tell that one of the quartermaster crews immediately started melting sections of the statue.

The story was that by the time they were done with the king's statue, the quartermasters had cast nearly fifty thousand musket balls for our troops.

Unfortunately, within a month our army's fortunes cascaded downhill.

And I suspect -- beggin' your pardon -- the redcoats probably ended up capturing His Majesty's balls.

Chapter 25
Defeat And Retreat

I won't go into all the sorry details.

Suffice it to say that as summer progressed, several hundred British ships carrying tens of thousands of British and Hessian troops arrived off Long Island.

Meanwhile, when wind and tide were favorable, two British frigates patrolled at will up and down the Hudson River past New York City's batteries.

Neither our cannon nor the underwater obstructions upon which we labored so hard deterred either vessel.

But then in late August came the worst.

When the British and Hessians began assaulting our lines on Brooklyn Heights, my platoon was stationed far to the east as a flank guard.

I could see no details from our distant position, but we plainly heard musketry and cannon fire off to the east. Smoke billowed over there, a wide gray fog giving me the impression that our troops were holding their line.

For hours they fired from their trenches and redoubts, seeming to repel repeated Hessian and redcoat attacks.

Then one of my pickets, a new farm boy, came running to me.

He yanked off his hat in salute. "Begging your pardon, Ensign Scot! If'n you please, I be seein' bunches of them redcoats."

"Where?"

He pointed to the north. "Off that ways apiece. Kind of like, as you might say, they be behind us."

His report shoved icicles through my gut. I was about to order Sergeant Liddle to investigate when I got another nasty chill – the sudden *brummp, brummp, brumpety, brrrrump* of British army drums.

The drumming came from behind us.

I ran to look and saw a redcoat force marching well past our own flank, circling behind us headed straight to the rear of our army.

All I could do was attack their column with my thirty-man platoon.

I spread the platoon into line and marched them north. At least, I hoped, we could give the lobsters a brief surprise which might alert the rest of our army.

I had the men carry their muskets aloft, loaded and at half-cock.

We crested a small rise and there – not thirty paces from us – was a thin line of surprised skirmishers.

Beyond them were two dense parallel columns of redcoats, regimental flags flying, all marching straight west toward Brooklyn.

I yelled, "Halt!"

"*Present!*"

The men lowered their muskets and tugged the weapons' hammers to full cock.

"*FIRE!*"

A few redcoats fell.

But our little volley was hardly more than a pinprick to the battalion we attacked. As we started to reload, a company of British soldiers – four platoons – faced left towards us, forming a firing line.

As our ramrods clattered down our musket barrels, we heard their captain.

"Comp'ny will advance five paces!"

I ordered our second volley, which knocked down perhaps a half dozen lobsters in mid-stride. As we started to reload, the redcoat captain intoned, "By platoons! FIRE!"

Smoke burst from one section of their line. Seconds later another. And another.

Balls zipped and whined around us, hitting my men right and left.

What amazed me was the precision and speed with which the British troops loaded for their volleys.

Though our shots knocked some men from their ranks, the surviving redcoats didn't so much as flinch. Blank-faced and acting as sergeants roared the orders, each redcoat at the same instant reached his right hand into his cartridge pouch.

By command, all in unison raised their weapons level at their right sides, half cocked the hammer and tilted the frizzen forward to open the powder pan.

They tilted their heads at the same angle to bite off the end of the paper cartridges.

Simultaneously, each trickled powder into the pan and snapped the frizzen back, shutting the pan. Each grounded his musket's butt beside his right foot. Then each poured powder from the cartridge down the barrel and, using their right hand index fingers, shoved the ball and remaining paper into the barrel.

As one, they raised and twirled their ramrods to ram the charges home. Returning the rods to their sockets, all raised their muskets.

Still in mechanical unison, each raised the musket to his shoulder and pulled the hammer to full cock.

Each platoon fired in a single ear-piercing bark.

With every volley, forty musket balls either tore through our ranks or threw up dust around us.

When the big lead balls thudded into men, they produced grunts of surprise and pain.

Then came the sounds of men falling, their firearms clattering onto the little rise on which we stood.

As the first lobster platoon reloaded, the second fired, then the third, then the fourth by which time the first platoon was nearly ready to fire the next volley.

To us on the receiving end, it felt like a continuous rolling blast – two volleys each from four redcoat platoons – three hundred-some shots fired in two minutes at my thirty men.

As the smoke cleared, I stood almost alone beside a line of the wounded and the dead.

The British sergeant called the company back into route march order.

As they double-timed to rejoin their battalion, their captain gave me an airy wave. *Later, old chap!*

The lobsters shrugged off our tiny futile attack and resumed their places. The rest of their column, drums rattling, never stopped marching toward our army's rear.

We delayed them not by so much as a minute.

I was numb, looking stupidly at what remained on the ground where they stood when butchering us -- a loose scattering of paper fragments from their musket cartridges.

Chapter 26
The Long Retreat

We survivors ran to cover in a nearby wood, hiding until that half-mile column of lobsters passed – perhaps a full brigade of them.

The rhythmic rattle of more approaching drums told us a second column would cross behind us soon.

So five of us – Corporal Hannon, Sergeant Liddle, Privates Taylor and Swift, and me – sprinted through the gap between brigades and kept going north toward the East River.

I told the men that once we reached the river, we'd follow it south to Brooklyn, hoping to cross to New York City before the Redcoats crushed the Brooklyn defense.

Liddle pulled me aside to protest.

"Rob," he whispered, "we daren't hie tae New York. It'll be racin' from the stewpot intae the fire."

"Sam, what the hell are you talking about?"

"Will ye kindly recall that Ah'm an old sailor. Ah knows the towns and harbors hereabouts."

"So what, Sam? I'm talking about New York's streets. We blocked all the streets in the town and loads of musket men are waiting behind those barricades. We dug miles of trenches outside the city and threw up redoubts with redans. When the Redcoats attack, we'll bleed them dry."

"No, Rob. There will be no battle in New York," he said. "They'll no attack it. No need. It's a trap. Just like Brooklyn."

"How do you reckon, Sam?"

"New York is like Brooklyn -- it sits at the south tip of a long narrow island – Mannahatta. The island extends at least ten miles between the Hudson River and the East River…and, Rob, the British navy controls both rivers.

"They can cross two dozen regiments from Long Island to Mannahatta any place and any time, trapping all our troops in the city.

"In my way of lookin' at it, our men in New York either will starve or surrender. And if we gang tae New York with them, we'll end up rotting with them in one of those bluidy prison hulks."

I doubted him until we came upon a wild-looking company of riflemen, most of them dressed in buckskin. Leading was a hulking red-bearded captain. "Name's Pfennig," he grinned, "but I go by Penny 'cause most of these bastards can't pronounce t'other."

He immediately demanded my rifle's name.

The query sort of shocked me. But since it came from a man with legs like tree trunks and a chest deep as a hogshead, I quickly answered.

After introducing me to his *Devil Spit,* he explained that the lobsters had blasted a gap between his little company and the rest of its rifle regiment. He and his men escaped.

"We aim to cross to Manhattan..."

"Where?"

"Manhattan. That island – it's the same as the Indian name, Mannahatta. Anyhow, when we get there we'll head north up to Fort Washington."

I asked, "Why no into the city, New York itself?"

"Because, Mister, the lobsters will pinch the city off and capture all the troops there."

Liddle nodded. "I warn ye, Rob. Heed the man."

Penny went on. "They've got the frigates and sloops and boats and can cross either river anywhere they like and our troops in the city won't be able to do a damned thing except wait to be netted.

"Well, by God, Sir," he added, "My boys and I shall not be netted to feed George Hanover."

"Who?"

"The goddamned king, George III."

"Oh! Right. Well, Cap'n Penny, given you'll have us, we'll put ourselves under your command. Lead on."

# # #

It cost us ten shillings to get a fisherman to ferry us in his dory across East River to Turtle Bay on Manhattan. It took four trips. For most of the time during the passages, we heard cannon fire and roaring musketry to the south.

By nightfall, though, it was all over. The redcoats captured Brooklyn.

When halfway into the river on the first crossing, I felt the boat change course.

The fisherman now steered his craft north...until Captain Penny put a bayonet to his throat. He hissed, "I'll slit your gullet if'n you don't turn back west and set us safe on Manhattan Island."

The captain turned to me. "Bastard figured to maroon us on one of the islands in the mid-river. Then I suppose he'd tell the Redcoats about us so's to collect a bounty."

The fisher squealed a protest. "I wouldn't do that, Sir! I just fear the lobsters would catch us and put us in a prison hulk."

Captain Penny kept a knife to the skipper's throat for the first trip. It was my job on the second and I delegated it to Bill Taylor on the third and fourth passage.

Luckily, the only other traffic on the river that evening was small boats. They all seemed to carry refugees like us. Seeing our troops' rifles and muskets, they steered well clear of us.

When we pulled into the bank at Turtle Bay, I demanded that the skipper return my half my money. He still whined about it as we climbed up the bluff onto the island.

Shortly after our last boat load came ashore, we threw in with a regiment of weary Continentals. They also headed north for Fort Washington. Like us, they were depressed at how easily the British had won the day.

Fortunately, the British command gave us a wonderful gift.

Time.

Chapter 27
The Longer Retreat

As I recall it, the lobsters seized Brooklyn at the end of August.

Thanks to a very thick fog the night of that capture, several thousands of our troops – and General Washington himself – succeeded in escaping across the East River to New York city.

Had the British attacked New York the next morning, they could have bagged most of our army and probably its commander.

Instead, they frittered away almost two weeks refitting and reorganizing.

It wasn't until September 12, with nights becoming chill and maples beginning to turn, that General Howe ferried his brigades across the East River onto the east shore of Manhattan.

Making a north-bound forced march along the island's west side, General Washington and the bulk of his dispirited troops barely escaped being cut off and captured.

When I say "dispirited" I don't exaggerate.

By that time I think most of the army – and possibly even His Excellency -- feared the war was over, that the British had won.

With traditions and procedures going back two hundred years, the British Army was far better organized than us. Moreover, it far outnumbered us. Most British troops were hardened veterans. Those who weren't veterans were far better trained than us.

Perhaps the most telling contrast -- their soldiers were trained as members of long-established regiments each with its honored history and traditions. We still were organizing and had no history..

They had outmaneuvered us, driving us from two of our nation's biggest cities.

Our sagging morale was especially visible at roll call. When I awakened each morning, I usually found that two or three -- one day five -- more men deserted during the night.

# # #

Captain Penny and I were stubborn.

"Damn your eyes, Sir," the captain said, "my command will not take a single step inside of Fort Washington!"

The colonel said, "I insist!"

The captain's red beard seemed to jut straight into Colonel McGraw's face, "Insist and be damned, Sir."

The officer yelled, "For God's sake, captain, your troops will be safe in this fort! Fort Washington is impregnable. The British never will seize it."

"Nonsense, Sir! Your fort has neither a well nor cisterns to hold water. Thirst alone will force you to surrender in a week."

"But we're right on the Hudson River!"

"Wrong, Sir. Your fort stands three hundred feet *above* the river. How many hundreds of buckets and miles of rope do you need to haul up water enough to slake the thirst of a two thousand-man garrison?"

"We're working on that…"

"No," the captain snapped. "You're working on yet further defeat. We've had too many defeats and you, Sir, have no authority over my command! Good day!"

He turned on his heel and I followed him out the sally port.

The fort looked impressive because it was huge. But that was part of the problem. It was far too big to be defended by a mere two thousand troops.

Worse, while dozens of cannon had arrived at the fort -- even some monster 32-pounders – no means existed to fire them. The garrison had no place to mount the cannons because it never received powder to blast battery positions out of the solid granite on which the fort stood.

Consequently, British ships repeatedly sailed untouched past the fort.

Neither Captain Penny nor I wanted to be captured when the fort capitulated. Besides, we already joined with two senior officers to arrange a hot reception for lobsters on Harlem Heights.

About a mile south of the fort, Manhatten Island narrows to a funnel hedged with heavy timber, brush and cottage-sized boulders. As the British infantry regiments approached the Heights from the south, Continental officers asked us to join their plan for an ambush.

Captain Penny and our riflemen along with two companies of light infantry were to demonstrate at dawn before the redcoats' advance guard.

Still being fairly new to war, I assumed "demonstrate" just meant an act. We'd pretend to attack the redcoats. Then we'd pretend to retreat in panic, trying to lure them into the ambush.

I quickly learned that though a demonstration might be an act, but musket balls weren't. Nor the screams of the wounded…nor the deaths. As soon as we riflemen picked off redcoat pickets and patrol leaders, the British directed platoon-by-platoon volleys at us.

Those volleys knocked six men out of our skirmish line. We'd hear an "uff!" as a ball cracked into a thigh bone or shoulder. Then came the crackle of the brush in which the wounded fell.

Often they'd say, "Ah! Ahhhh!" Screams and pleas for help came a bit later when the shock wore off and waves of pain surged in.

Feeling actual terror, not pretend panic, I yelled for my men to retreat, fast.

As we headed for the rear, the redcoats shouted in triumph and charged after us, loading and shooting their muskets as they advanced.

Backtracking, I panted to Liddle, "Christ almighty, we've got to learn how to load and fire while moving."

"Later, Rob," he puffed. "Right noo let us gang outa range."

As the lobsters came near us, Captain Penny's compatriots launched their ambush by firing a heavy volley from behind a large granite outcropping. They followed up by charging with swords and tomahawks.

Later the captain and I agreed they attacked too early. They should have assaulted into the lobsters' rear rather than their flank.

Even so, the volley and charge stunned the British. Their attack collapsed and they prudently fell back as we counterattacked, now accompanied by yet another force fed into the fight from the left.

I still was terrified, but it still was exhilarating to see the lobsters' backs for a change. We pushed the shocked redcoats almost a mile before a fresh British regiment arrived to support them.

We in turn fell back into a series of earthen trenches. The British assaulted the positions repeatedly, but never managed to budge us.

After one fruitless redcoat attack, Captain Penny laughed and yelled aloud, "Right! You boys just showed yourselves, man for man, to be as good as the world's best army."

He received a chorus of cheers. And I agreed.

In fact, I think the pride arising from our stubborn little defense on Harlem Heights sustained us through the next dismal weeks. The men were laughing again and acting cocky. Perhaps that lift kept our army from disappearing altogether.

Eventually, of course, the Royal Navy landed a large force of marines and redcoats north of Fort Washington.

Just as Captain Penny predicted, the fort fell in days like a rotten apple.

The redcoats marched two thousand prisoners, together with Colonel McGraw, to languish and sicken and many to die in New York's jails or aboard prison hulks in New York harbor.

Chapter 28
Autumn 1776

When Fort Washington surrendered, we abandoned Harlem Heights and escaped across the Hudson into New Jersey.

If I'd had my way, we would have turned north and retreated toward Massachusetts.

But the British Army crossed the Hudson north of us, barring any flight in that direction.

Captain Penny said, "Take heart, lads. The lobsters may have captured New York and one day they might even take Philadelphia, too, but they never can take our homes."

"Where's your home?"

"Our homes are the mountains and woods of Pennsylvania and New Jersey. There's deer and fish aplenty to feed us And when the invaders come out to loot our provender" -- he raised *Devil's Spit* over his head and shook it -- "we'll scythe them down like so much wheat."

General Washington ordered the army to disperse into small companies forcing the lobsters to pursue us in relatively small detachments.

Their pursuit was vigorous, even so. They pushed us south along the New Jersey shore of the Hudson toward Pennsylvania.

We made them pay for it. Day after day it was a running skirmish.

At a little riverside town called Hackensack, it was my turn to lead the rear guard -- eight riflemen.

It was sleeting and gloomy, but those bright red coats made it easy to spot approaching lobster skirmishers. Liddle and I posted the men in three houses.

"Damn," I said. "Sure glad they wear red and not green."

I fired first, hitting their sergeant at seventy paces. My shot spun the man, but he immediately was back on his feet.

As I reloaded, I had to admire him.

Wrapping a cloth around his arm, he yelled for his men keep their distance. "You bastards look to your front keep your bloody spread."

A ten count, and one of Liddle's men fired next, knocking down a second redcoat.

We fired slowly and deliberately. We wanted our adversaries to feel in the dark about whether they faced just one or a hundred of us.

As the second, third and fourth rifle shots cracked -- and the second, third and fourth targets fell – the skirmishers slowed their advance.

One of my boys said, "Them lobsters show themselves to be a little shy."

Wrapping my next ball in its linen patch, I said, "So would you, Billy, were you losing a mate every three or four seconds."

I grunted as I shoved the tight-fitting round down the rifle's muzzle. Then I dropped the short ram for the full-length ramrod.

The skirmishers, now within a fifty paces, started firing toward us with their own short-barreled rifles. Occasionally a ball rapped against a wall of our house or zipped through a window.

Our rifles' smoke disclosed our general locations. But we made poor targets because the smoke cloaked us from easy view and, thank heaven, we weren't wearing red.

Our fire thinned their ranks and brought them to a temporary halt. An officer came forward on horseback to confer with the wounded sergeant. Two shots from Liddle's men toppled him from his steed.

The sergeant briefly peered down at the officer, gave an order to a corporal and trotted toward the main body of the British column.

Soon after that, the lead British company – they looked to me like grenadiers – shook out into a line came toward us at the double.

It was too big a force for my boys, so we all fired quickly, bringing down a half-dozen lobsters. We pulled back through the village and linked up with Captain Penny's company.

"You and your boys lead," he said. "We'll take rear guard in the next town," he said.

"How far is it?"

"Oh, four or five miles. Place called Newark."

Backpedaling as we fired from behind walls, trees and buildings, we picked off light infantry redcoats and sometimes even green-coated Hessians.

We kept harassing the enemy as we retreated. In a way it reminded me of my first day of combat near Lexington, except now the weather was bone-chilling cold and we were the pursued, not the pursuers.

Through Elizabeth, Perth Amboy, Piscataway and New Brunswick, we paved our retreat with their wounded and dead – and too many of ours.

It was in Elizabeth that a flying unit of Light Infantry got on our flank and nearly trapped us. We escaped, but one of their musket shots hit and killed our giant bearded Captain Penny.

We never held an election. But because Penny and I worked closely – he actually was teaching me -- his surviving men seemed content for me to serve as their leader. They started calling me "cap'n" and it stuck.

Not that it mattered much, because we had little choice about what to do. The only direction to go was south. The boys remained cocky, making the lobsters pay for their pursuit of us,

As we neared the Delaware River – which splits New Jersey from Pennsylvania -- we heard that Congress fled bag and baggage from Philadelphia. They resumed their talking in some burg I never heard of, Baltimore.

Then General Washington sent orders for the army to concentrate. We more or less came together in Princeton and marched ten miles south to Trenton.

While doing so, we either commandeered or destroyed every boat along the river.

The British would have to work hard to follow us beyond Trenton toward Philadelphia.

At the time I didn't understand what His Excellency was doing. I really didn't care, what with being half-frozen and fretting about supplies. I was distressed at how small the army now looked.

I kept it to myself, but I again began to fear the British had all but won.

Chapter 29

Harrassing

My fears about the army were slightly misplaced.

True, soldiers continued to desert our ranks in droves. Likewise, those whose enlistments expired.

Yet the countryside itself seemed to be in a fighting mood and it was fighting the British.

Until one skirmish, we didn't realize what was going on.

Once morning we surrounded a small lobster patrol after a shot from one of our men broke the leg of a British officer's horse.

The fallen animal pinned the leg of its rider, a fresh-faced lieutenant.

As we approached, the officer's face turned as white as his powdered wig.

He raised both hands. "I pray that you refrain from chopping me," he said. "If you must butcher me, I beg that you do it after killing me with my own pistol."

"Why would we kill you?" I asked. "You're our prisoner to be held for exchange with an American officer."

He closed his eyes, expelled a shaky breath and lowered his hands.

"Thank God! I'm most relieved to hear it. We've discovered some of our officers and troops slaughtered with battle axes. I believe you Americans call them tomahawks."

We helped roll his struggling mount from his leg and then killed the suffering beast.

As he got to his feet, I said, "Sir, I think you should understand that General Washington has enjoined the Continental Army to treat all prisoners with complete kindness. Those are His Excellency's exact words."

"Then I am grateful to be in your custody," he said. "Some of our poor fellows haven't been so fortunate."

One of his men, a sergeant, said caustically, "Aye, maybe at least we'll get some rest now."

Corporal Hannon said, "Ah, you lads been feelin' that you have a target on your back, have you now?"

"It's the bloody truth!" the sergeant said. "Our foraging parties cannot go out without they be guarded by at least a company of infantry. Otherwise, they mightn't come back at all.

"So we been marchin' constant. And even then, riflemen shoot at us from the woods. We leave of a morning with a hundred men and get in at night with mebbe ten less."

"Aye, mayhap," Liddle chimed in, "but Ah doubt those snipers be soldiers…more likely farming folk attacking Hessians who raped their women or British troops who stole livestock and grain."

"Right," I said, remembering a grenadier using his bayonet to spit Jan Vandermolen's chest. "…or murdering common people in their own homes."

The lieutenant started to speak. "Why have we come to this? Why are you men at war with your king?"

"*My* king?" Liddle rode over his words. "Ah refuse to bow to a man who set his troops upon us.

"You lobsters take cattle and food from farms whose folk need them for winter. And do 'ee recall of late one of your admirals burned the town of Falmouth entire? Some homes a hundred years old, eh? Folk dinna take kindly to that.

"Georgie boy might be your king, sir," he added, "but he isna mine."

The lieutenant shut up.

# # #

In the ensuing days, we became aware of brief skirmishes occurring in the woods and hills around us…militia or perhaps just farmers attacking the King's troops.

One thing became obvious to me.

No matter how many lobsters and Hessians King George and Lord North might send to these shores, they'd never have enough troops to scour the forests and mountains for all of us rebels.

After meeting some of the farmers, we learned that another war was occurring: loyalists versus rebels, former friends and neighbors now were burning each other's homes and even murdering each other.

Just as in Massachusetts where Simpson and his party destroyed Alice's home.

Just as we retaliated.

Chapter 30
Winter Upset 1776

When we gathered to cross the river at Trenton on December 7, it looked to me as if no more than two thousand men remained in the army.

Admittedly, some or our troops were hard at work upstream and downstream on both banks of the Delaware, confiscating boats and weapons and destroying bridges.

Even so, we heard tell that an entire Continental brigade from New Jersey and another one from Pennsylvania simply took their muskets and hiked home.

As the story spread, Corporal Hannon said, "You can see why. Talk about temptation! They give us no pay for weeks. Our clothes is falling to bits. We freeze at nights and rain and sleet makes you numb during the day. Some of the lads is walking barefoot in this half-froze mud."

"Do pipe down, Hannon," I said. "If our conditions are so terrible why don't you do what so many Americans have? Why not just desert to the royal army."

"Occch, nivver, Sir. Desertion would be madness. If I went back to the King's army, they'd trice me to a triangle and give me a thousand lashes. I'd rather starve than die thus.

"Besides," he added, "I'm a soldier. Tis the only trade I know aside from rag-pickin'."

I was fortunate. Liberal applications of pig fat preserved Isaac Fletcher's boots for me. As long as the soles didn't wear through, my feet stayed dry if somewhat rancid. And inside the boots, a pair of heavy socks – which Alice knitted for me -- provided some warmth.

Some of my men cut out doubled sheaths of untanned cowhide for shoes and used sinew for lacing. The hide wore out quickly.

As if the twin miseries of cold and hunger weren't enough, we heard one evening around our fire that the lobsters captured one of our senior generals, Charles Lee.

The story was that the general was dallying with some lady at an inn when British cavalry surrounded the place, shot his guards and nabbed him.

Most of us cursed both the general and our army's bad luck. Corporal Hannon was more charitable.

Drawing on his pipe, he said, "I pray to the blessed Mary ever virgin that the good general was able to discharge all his duties to the lady 'afore the dragoons interrupted their pleasuring."

He noted that, like himself, General Lee also was a former redcoat.

The rest of us weren't so philosophical. If the general was caught in a nice warm inn and taken to a nice warm jail, he still was better off than us troops.

"Think aboot it, man," Liddle said. "Aside from shiverin' constant, we are filthy, lousy, flea-ridden and nigh to starving. What good reason have we not tae just gang home and claim General Howe's offer of a generous amnesty?

"But no me," he added, half-defiantly. "Ah'm sticking it oot. All of us what's left is hard men and bull-heided. We manhandled them lobsters, large numbers of them, muir than once, now. An' in my view, we'll be doing it again."

"Yes," I said, "there ain't many of us left. But I agree with you. What's left is choice." Somehow we had a sense of confidence. For some fool reason, we believed our greatest days lay before us.

Not that it made any sense.

Oh, I knew any American was as good as and maybe better than any Hessian or redcoat. But considering that eight thousands of them were trailing only two hours behind a mere two thousands of us...well, it kept us all a bit on edge.

# # #

As my boys and I rolled a boat up the riverbank into concealment it relieved me to see General Washington arrive.

"Push, boys, push!" I said, "and now bring some of those logs beneath the boat's bow so we can keep her moving."

There he was in the gloom watching us from atop that big gray horse, Together they looked like a ghostly statue, snow powdering the shoulders of his blue cloak and building in the corners of his hat.

The general met my eyes and gave a grim nod.

"Ensign Scot. You're still with us?"

"Yes, indeed, Sir. And glad to see you are, too."

As usual, Liddle had to stick in his oar. "On'y the ensign noo is a cap'n, Sir."

The general said, "A captain? Did I not confide that you might rise to such a position?"

I couldn't help grinning. "You did, Sir, only it ain't official. It just kind of happened when the lobsters killed these boys' leader."

He turned the horse and looked back to nod again. "Men." He said, "we have much to do. I pray that The Almighty blesses our enterprises."

When His Excellency spoke so around us, you got the feeling that The Almighty tilted an ear too.

I guess the boys thought so. They fell to laughing and chattering while they kept heaving the boat up the bank,.

Maybe it just heartened them to know that our biggest general remembered a nobody like me.

# # #

Two weeks passed before we saw His Excellency again.

Late Christmas Day his orders gathered all of us uphill from McKonkey's Ferry on the Delaware, less than five miles from Trenton.

We were miserable because winter now had a firm frigid grip on us. Icy northwest wind cut through our rags and pelted us with snow and sleet.

A week earlier the British stopped their campaign and went into winter quarters. So, like most of the men, I wondered why the hell we also shouldn't get indoors and start warming ourselves too.

But here we were, pulling the big Durham boats out of hiding, sliding them downhill to the ford. Trying to avoid noise, we gingerly handed those twelve-foot oars to the boatmen and passed long poles to the bowmen.

In the failing light, a senior officer called a halt and read something aloud to us. It took quite a while, but I remember this part:

> *...the summer soldier and the sunshine patriot will, in this crisis, shrink from the service of his country...he that stands it now, deserves the love and thanks of man and woman...*

That Paine fellow again, speaking directly to our misery and suffering. Huddling there, lips blue and quivering, we grinned at each other.

Those words...*he that stands it now*...seemed to kindle a fire in many of us.

Now we were fording the Delaware again, this time to attack the Hessians. His Excellency personally would lead us. *Amen! Damned right! We'll kill them!*

I was in the third boat to cross. Wind, current and tide drove thick cakes of ice to bang and thump against the hulls. The oarsmen did some very inventive cursing as they rowed and at the same time fended off ice. At least they were able to see the ice, thanks to torches General Greene ordered the advance guard to set up on the far bank.

As our boat grounded, men in the bow jumped right out onto the bank. Those of us near the stern held our cartridge boxes well aloft, going over the side into hip-deep water. It was so cold it hurt. Somebody quavered, "Oh, shiiiit me! Gawdawful cold!"

Fearing the swearing and grumbling would alert Hessians, I hissed, "Quiet, damn you! Move! Move! Move! By God, that'll keep you warm."

It didn't.

Teeth chattering, we splashed from the river, scrambled up the bank and formed into companies.

General Washington's boat arrived. As he clambered ashore, he received two messengers. He snapped. "Damme!"

He announced that two other bodies of Continental troops were unable to cross the river further downstream because the rising tide jammed the river solid with ice.

"Well, General Greene," he said, "we must proceed with our enterprise anyway."

After a quick meeting, the generals' aides circulated with new orders.

His Excellency waved his tricorn at us. "Hasten now! Press on, boys, press on!"

Chapter 31
Trenton

The original plan called for our regiment to join the assault on the village's north side, at the ends of King and Queen Streets.

But because two other Continental forces couldn't cross the river downstream, His Excellency decided his own command would undertake the entire attack.

Our regiment, therefore, received new orders which Captain Pegrim relayed to me.

"Mr. Scot, our regiment still will lead the march to Trenton and yours still will be lead company.

"But instead of attacking, we shall skirt the north end of the village. We'll post ourselves in an orchard to the east. That puts us in place to block any retreating Hessians once the attack begins.

"General Greene has posted guides. They'll trek with you a mile to the east and then due south past the village to the orchard."

As our little column set out, the wind knifed at us. So we trotted. "Only way to beat the cold," Liddle gasped. "Let's try to get the attack over with…fast."

Close to the west horizon, the setting moon dimly lit our path and our puffing breath.

Three guides squatting before a tiny fire awaited us. Without a word one of them jumped up, shrugged off his blanket, shouldered his musket, and led us east along a path beside a frozen creek.

"Thanks," I said.

"For what, Mister?"

"Well, for leaving your fire and leading us."

"Shit, it don't matter none. That little fire warn't all that warm nohow."

As we trotted along the path, low-lying branches whipped and stung our freezing cheeks and ears. People behind me swore furiously.

I gave a harsh whisper, "For God's sake, will you bastards *shut up?*"

The guide said, "You needn't worry about noise around these parts."

"No? So how far do we have to go?"

"Oh, a good three mile yet. You needn't fret 'cause Hessians ain't patrolling this morning. Them green-coated devils gave over yesterday. They be tired out from patrolling and from fighting off ambushes all the past week."

A hour later, with dawn just beginning to show, the guide pointed to our right. "This here be the north end of the town. You see where you are now?"

I was looking straight south down Trenton's main streets, both lined with houses and shops. No soldiers or townspeople were in sight, though breeze was whipping smoke from most chimneys.

"Right. So we just curl along down the east side till we come to the orchard?"

"Right! And please to kill all them bastards you can. Them foreign murderers destroyed my farm and come close to wiping out my entire family."

We moved quickly and quietly, filtering among the apple trees, facing west into the town.

I ordered the men to clean out their musket locks. "I figure they're damp by now. So get 'em dried out, but don't be squib firing until the main assault starts."

As we waited, shivering in the orchard, Captain Pegrim filed in on our right with the rest of the regiment. Now we had a line of almost a hundred sixty muskets to repel any Hessian attack.

The captain slapped me on the shoulder. Through chattering teeth, he said, "My compliments, Mr. Scot. You did a good job to get us here on time."

Hugging myself and stamping my feet, I bowed in reply. I was almost too numb to speak. Just then we heard shouts from the town.

"Hessian sentries, maybe," the captain said. "I think we're about to have some work to warm us."

Deep-toned drums began booming, the Hessian brigade's alarm. Flashes sparkled at the north end of town and the bang and crack of musketry erupted. The drums stopped.

"Mr. Scot, have the boys to fire their pans."

"Yessir, cap'n! Okay, men! Squib fire your locks and then get loaded."

Each man sprinkled a pinch of powder into his musket's firing pan, cocked the weapon and pulled the trigger. Flints sparked and the powder flashed, drying the muskets' locks.

As the men loaded their muskets, a Hessian running towards us stopped and yelled, "*Wer da? Was gibts?*" Who's there? What gives?

I shouted, "Readddddy!"

Whoever he was, he recognized the command and the sound of muskets being cocked. He did a quick turn and sprinted off toward the town.

"Hold fire, men!" Captain Pegrim yelled. "Wait for a real target."

The rattle of muskets now spread inside the town. Full volleys punctuated scattered shooting. The fight appeared to move south through Trenton, spilling into its side streets.

Then came yells and the flash and *whamp* of artillery. Soon after that came cheers.

The captain asked, "What the hell d'ye think is happening?"

"I think these German gentlemen are catching hell," I said. "But...ho! Now what have we here?"

It looked like a full regiment of Hessians had formed up and was coming toward us through the town's little graveyard

"Ready! Presnnnnnt!"

"*Fire!*"

Our surprise volley from the orchard brought the Hessians to a shocked halt.

Their shock worsened. A steady *crack crack crack* from a rifle regiment chopped into the Hessians' north flank. It looked as if a dozen of the foreigners went down.

As we presented our muskets to fire again, a fresh volley blasted from the south into the enemy's other flank.

It was another Continental regiment, firing like clockwork. His Excellency towered over them on horseback, waving his hat and roaring orders.

The Hessian regiment collapsed, bewildered troops bolting and recoiling back toward the town.

Now it was light enough to see a pair of Hessian officers dragging a third who appeared to be wounded.

Smoke from musketry and our artillery shrouded the area so heavily that we missed seeing a column of Hessians double-time past the north end of our orchard.

We later figured maybe three regiments of the foreigners eluded us in the confusion.

None of us really cared, because the remaining enemy troops began surrendering, dipping their flags, raising hats on swords and spiking muskets bayonet-first into the earth.

Jubilant Continentals started capering and yelling. I heard later – though I doubted whether to believe it – that General Washington actually grabbed some officer by the hand and did a quick dance with him.

We had much to celebrate. In an hour of fighting we routed a brigade of professional soldiers, fifteen hundreds of them.

Several of our men – including Corporal Hannon -- sought to join a group of Continentals clustered around several barrels, swilling the Hessians' rum.

Captain Pegrim kicked over one barrel and shouted, "Stop that, damn you! We can't get drunk now. Pour it all onto into the gutter."

They followed his order with grudging bad grace and much swearing.

But nobody stayed angry for long because we'd captured almost nine hundred Hessians.

Later that morning, one of our companies herded them in a hike downstream to Philadelphia.

It was victory, but with costs.

True, our combat casualties were almost nil.

But despite all the jubilation, we still were freezing. Some men who spent the night barefoot now searched corpses for boots to fit their freezing feet.

Others just collapsed, unable to walk because their feet had frozen solid.

Yet others collapsed with fever and died within a day.

Chapter 32
Princeton

No question. The United States of America wouldn't exist had we Continentals not surprised and defeated a worn-out Hessian brigade at Trenton.

Their surrender boosted our confidence and the peoples' belief in independence.

A week later, however, our rag-tag army won the war for American independence.

I don't jest.

It merely took four more years and Lord knows how much death and suffering for Lord North and his pop-eyed monarch to get it through their thick skulls that they never, *ever* could conquer us. After all, we were bulldog Englishmen too.

Victory came January 2, 1777, when God and General Washington humiliated General Cornwallis, the most aggressive of the British commanders.

That same day, we also taught their foot soldiers a lesson I wager they never forgot.

See, Cornwallis staged eight thousand redcoats and Hessians in Princeton. Howe ordered him to attack and destroy us, the tiny Continental Army, camping ten miles to the south at Trenton.

We Continentals meanwhile savored a fifty-degree thaw that God gave us for three beautiful days.

"I canna believe this," Sergeant Liddle said. "'Tis winter, is it not? By rights, we should be shivering of cold. But today I feel like throwing off all me clothes."

"I wouldn't," I said. "You know the weather around here -- bake on Sunday, freeze on Monday. Besides, you don't want to show a naked target to the lobsters today."

Our platoon was ready to fight because we weren't with the rest of the army basking in the sun and digging trenches at Trenton.

Yesterday our regiment marched six miles toward Princeton. Our orders were to support the Pennsylvania Rifle Regiment. His Excellency ordered those marksmen to scatter in the forest along the redcoats' anticipated route.

I brought *Lobster Claw*. We riflemen would try picking off redcoat officers and sergeants at a hundred to a hundred fifty paces. They called it interdiction.

The other men of my platoon carried muskets. Dispersing in squads along the woods, their purpose was stop light infantry flankers when they tried to close in on slow-loading riflemen.

We heard sporadic rifle fire before Cornwallis's advance guard even plodded into view. And, yes, they did indeed plod.

"Here they come," Sergeant Liddle said. "And they ain't marching proud. Or quick."

"I pity the poor bastards," Corporal Hannon said. "Sure and I do. I seen it before." The thaw had transformed the redcoats' route into ankle-deep mud.

"Save your pity," I said. "They'd shoot you without pity if their muskets could reach this far."

"That's not what I mean," the corporal said. "Those lobsters be loaded with sixty-pound packs, plus the Brown Bess and bayonet and forty made cartridges. Good Lord, by the time the rear guard gets here, after them guns and horses an' all pass by, that mud will be so churned they'll be knee deep in it. Ten pound o' mud on each leg, by God."

He was right. The men of the third battalion that passed us already were sinking calf-deep.

And we riflemen made their lives hell.

I drew a bead on an officer on horseback.

Crack!

An instant later he jerked and toppled from his saddle into the mud.

As I stepped back into the trees to reload, Sergeant Liddle called. "He's in a real fix, Cap'n. He just now tried to push himself upright. But he found nought to push upon. His hand and arm just went straight down intae the mud – shoulder-length, ye know? Nothing solid to lever himself up."

One of the Pennsylvania rifles said, "I see him. Heee. Some good Samaritan be dismounting to help. Witness this!"

Crack!

"Got him!"

"Sure did," Sergeant Liddle said. "Pitched him right onto his face."

Fifty feet further down the tree line, Corporal Hannon yelled, "Trouble's acomin'. Flankers racing toward your smoke."

"Okay, boys," Sergeant Liddle said, "Come forward. An' like Ah said, hide yoursel' behind a nice thick pine or oak. Pick off them flankers at twenty paces. Be sure ye aim low."

Their muskets rattled. As they reloaded, Sergeant Liddle yelled to me. "They're done. You riflemen, once ye're loaded, come forrard again."

We did. With *Crack! Crack! Crack!* we picked off as many redcoats.

The war for independence presented many terrifying and tragic moments. I remain forever grateful I never faced the special suffering Cornwallis's men endured during their mud march to Trenton.

Infuriated officers twice ordered full companies to leave the column and assault our section of the woods.

We and our musket skirmishers simply faded back into the forest, moved either north or south and then reappeared to harass another part of the redcoat column.

I've no idea how many of them we killed and wounded. It's certain we delayed them. Our attacks forced their column to stop and attempt to close with us at least three times.

One time our skirmishers and clusters of Pennsylvania riflemen came together to slug it out with the lobsters for almost two hours. Finally, sheer numbers forced us to disperse into the woods.

We re-emerged a half mile away to attack again.

Between our harassment and the mud, it took the redcoats nine damned hours to cover a mere ten miles.

Their advance guard didn't arrive outside Trenton until five in the afternoon. At dusk, those of us in the woods who still had powder and ball sniped at their rear guard which was hardly half-way to Trenton

It was at Trenton, thanks to Cornwallis's stubbornness, that the real butchery occurred.

He should have waited to attack until at least half his force was at hand. But it was growing dark and he wanted his victory right now.

Over the next hour, he launched six or seven assaults against the Continentals' trenches – positions far stronger than those at Bunker Hill, and buttressed by two dozen cannon.

Within ten minutes, Continental musketry and heavy artillery fire shredded every attack, altogether costing more than six hundred men. Their blood and bodies created a scarlet clog on the single stone bridge over which they charged us.

But neither God nor General Washington was through with General Cornwallis.

It was dark when the last muddied British and Hessian troops arrived from Princeton. They began preparing for tomorrow's grand assault that would destroy us.

Meanwhile, The Almighty restored winter. By sundown the gentle south breeze veered and strengthened to an icy northwest blast. We froze again.

So did the muddy roads. Footing became firm.

After midnight, we stole out of Trenton. A rear guard stayed, stoking campfires and repeatedly silhouetting themselves in front of the blazes so Cornwallis wouldn't detect our departure.

The next morning, the British general discovered an empty set of earthworks before him.

By that time we were far into his rear, attacking his own base at Princeton.

Our attack crushed his Princeton detachment, but they were very professional. Despite high casualties, they held us off long enough to evacuate the bulk of Cornwallis's supplies and his military pay chest.

So, leaving Princeton, the Continental Army continued north to Morristown where we established winter quarters.

Cornwallis couldn't pursue. His troops had suffered enough.

All told, we lost about two hundred men to weather and enemy action.

We'd exacted two thousand redcoat and Hessian casualties.

I also believe we permanently erased British contempt for us as fighting men.

Chapter 33
Winter Ills And Drills

Morristown is a tiny place, and it didn't take the Continental Army long to file through it.

Thanks to expired enlistments, our force dwindled to less than the number of Hessians we bagged at Trenton. Little more than eight hundred of us were on hand to commence building timber huts for ourselves.

His Excellency and his staff meanwhile began rebuilding the Continental Army.

It pleased all of us to learn Congress finally decreed that men now must enlist for the duration of the war. That would end the army's grotesque year-end depletion.

In late January, headquarters assigned a draft of four new men to our platoon.

One, Alex Powell, was a scarred, embittered farmer. He was old, too, at least age thirty. The other three – Hugh Davis, Martin Filer and Albert Douglas -- were boys my age or younger.

All showed themselves eager trainees. Powell ached to start killing loyalists, lobsters and Indians. "The bastards murdered my wife and kiddies and destroyed my farm. I want to repay 'em richly."

The three boys, being boys, simply were excited to become soldiers. They even had spent some time marching with the militia. "I can't believe it," Sergeant Liddle told me. "We're ready to start drilling because these lads actually know right from left."

But they came with a price.

Davis wasn't with us three days before he started alternating between chills and the sweats. When he started vomiting, we ordered him to wrap up in his blanket and stay on his straw pallet.

Two or three days later, he claimed to better. "But, hey! I got these red spots on my tongue and inside my cheeks. Should I see the saw-bones?"

We old-timers glanced knowingly at each other. Sergeant Liddle said, "I wouldn't bother. Ain't nothing he can do."

"What do you mean?"

"I think it's smallpox. Ain't anything anybody can do."

The boys turned pale.

"You'll have to be quarantined here," I said, "until all of you are over it. Probably be six or eight weeks."

Powell nodded. "Don't fret yourselves, lad. I had the pox. So did my wife. It's a hard time, but you'll likely survive. You might get some scars like these 'uns here on my cheek, but that's about all."

Two days later a rash appeared on Davis's face, spreading to his arms, hands, legs and body. His rash then gave way to spots which grew into clusters of blisters, some tiny as bird shot, some big as a musket ball.

The blisters on his palms and soles were so painful Davis couldn't close his hands or even stand. The blisters on his back and shoulders made merely lying on his pallet painful. Puss turned the blisters opaque.

"Here, boy, drink your water. It helps with fever."

"Don't want to, Sir. Swallowing hurts like hell."

"Do it anyway. Otherwise you die."

About this time, Fletcher and Douglas showed the same early symptoms. The same thing happened all through the army.

Us old hands had been vaccinated, so we'd experienced a mild form of the pox. It struck the boys with full virulence. The surgeon predicted smallpox would kill one in three. He also said it probably would blind every tenth survivor.

We did our best to nurse the boys and meanwhile built a new shed so that we could burn the old one once they recovered and were out of quarantine.

So the army grew slowly and training proceeded even more slowly. We couldn't train people suffering smallpox. We just had to get them to drink water or tea.

The one problem we didn't have was food. Plenty of it was available all through the winter.

We also received an issue of new weapons, muskets from France. And with bayonets. We pulled them off the wagons in crates labeled *Charleville*. Staff officers pronounced it "Sharluhvee."

We called them "Charlies."

Those of us who weren't ill tried out the new firearms.

Raising one of the muskets to his cheek, Corporal Hannon said, "Well, they're weighin' about like Brown Bess herself. But they'll be easier to get apart. See, they got these bands around the barrels instead of those bloody stubborn pins."

We compared the Charlie's .69 caliber ball to the .75 caliber Brown Bess.

"It don't matter," I said. "I've killed lots a deer with a smaller ball. *Lobster Claw* shoots .45 caliber. It kills deer, and you all sure as hell seen it kill lobsters."

Powell spat, "I care not so long as a .69 ball kills loyalists."

I asked Corporal Hannon to show us lobster bayonet drill.

He grinned. "Sir, are you after bein' serious, then?"

"Of course," I said. "Now that we've got bayonets with these muskets, we should know how to use them as well as the lobsters."

"If you really want to learn," he grinned, "you have a weary way ahead of you." He twisted a bayonet onto the muzzle of a Charlie.

He held the weapon vertically. "Look you how long this weapon now is. So, you see, with a five-foot musket and another foot and a half of blade, I can stick someone afore his sword comes anywheres near me. Now watch!"

He dropped the musket to port arms, stepped back with his right foot, turning his left side to us, holding the musket across his midsection.

Suddenly he danced a step forward, jabbing straight out towards us. He laughed as we recoiled.

Then he danced back, inverted the musket with the butt near his ear, jabbing downward. Then he retracted, jabbing to his right, backed and jabbed upward as if to skewer a man on horseback.

"Now, boys, grab your Charlies and fix bayernets. Ye seen me show how to do it. I'll keep showin' slow-like and give the commands and you can copy me."

Screaming like one of His Majesty's sergeants, he ran us through the basic positions: Port arms. Step back. Guard. Advance. Retire. Double advance. Double retire. High guard.

"Retract the front foot first, dammit!"

Then it was, "High guard! Point! To!" The command "to" meant to return to your original position.

"Low guard! Invert your musket, fer Christ's sake! Butt up, next to your face. Now…*Point!* To!

The drill resurrected some bad memories but Hannon gave me no time to dwell on them.

"Right guard! No! Be jaysus, Mr. Scot! Ye point the bayernet toward his chest not his bloody knees. And all of you, mind that as ye do this, yer coverin' and guardin' your mates."

He drilled the four of us until our arms were limp. But we also came away with a warm grasp of fighting as a team.

That afternoon, we went into the hut with water for our patients. I took along a Charlie with a fixed bayonet.

They all felt sick as hell, of course, and were constantly shifting position hopelessly trying to find relief from the pain.

But nothing excites a boy so much as a the sight of a shiny new gun.

It boosted their spirits when I showed them the weapon.

"Lads, when you're recovered and out of this place," I said, "each one of you gets a brand new musket with a bayonet. And we'll all work together with them."

Davis called, "Hip! Hip!" They all gave a ragged cheer, then fell to coughing.

Chapter 34
Marching Forth

Corporal Hannon drew on his pipe and then spat. "So, do ye say I should desert into them hills in Pennsylvanie?"

"No. I'm not talking about desertion. I want you and your musket with us."

Sergeant Liddle asked, "Then, Rob, whit the hell are ye blethering aboot?"

We were clustered out of earshot at the corporal's guard post enjoying the April sunshine.

I pointed south to the broad swale between two steep ridges. "What I'm getting at that I think the lobsters could come marching through that pass any time -- tomorrow morning even -- and take us."

"Oh, Ah dinna think so," Liddle said. "Army's got much better numbers now. And the sma'pox has well run its course."

Hannon spit again. "Yeah, but the new boys have no trainin' to speak of. They're still learning to load muskets by numbers, and so many of 'em is still weak from the pox..."

"That's why I'm worried," I said. "I think the lobsters could walk right over us. And my point is that if the redcoats throw their net around us, you both stand to hang. So, if they do attack and we retreat I think you both might be wise to scat...to head west into Pennsylvania's mountains. Come back to fight another day."

I felt the British command could pick no better time than April 1777 to destroy the Continental Army.

Granted, our enlistments had risen and our numbers had grown. My platoon now amounted to almost thirty men. Yet perhaps a fourth of them still were weak and a bit wobbly on their feet.

Had Cornwallis been in command, I think the Redcoats would have swamped us that spring at Morristown.

Yet, again, General Howe sat still, giving the Continental Army the precious gift of time.

"I can't figure why they ain't attacked already," Hannon said.

"Well, Pat, you got to remember we bloodied them good at Trenton." Liddle said. "But still..."

# # #

It was at the end of May now. With almost nine thousand men well fed and rested, His Excellency finally marched us south out of Morristown. They told us we were bound for New Brunswick, now a big Redcoat supply base.

"I niver seen such an unsoldierly sight," Hannon told me as our platoon swung into the column.

"I warrant, with all of us wearing scraps of this and that, we look like a band of paupers. Blue pantaloons here, brown 'uns there, all with holes in the knees. Some with stockings, more with none."

"Right," I added, "and threadbare backsides."

Liddle chortled. "Aye, same wi' their coats and shirts of many colors. Minds me of that Bible story the meenister told us at kirk. And all wi' holes in elbows, too. Not a respectical-looking army."

"You're right," I said. "The army looks worse than the militia. But one thing about us, men."

"And what might that be?' Hannon asked.

"We have a wicked sharp sting. The lobsters winkled us out of New York, but never by direct attack. We may look like paupers but after Trenton, I believe His Majesty's generals respect us."

"Right," Liddle said. "And them with all the advantages, too – the numbers, *veteran* numbers, the navy, the food...though, now I think of it, no so much of food. The militia have made foraging a trial for the lobsters."

Private Davis, our first smallpox victim, spoke up. "You're right there, sergeant. Afore Marty and Bert and I joined up, we tagged along with some New Jersey militia against three lobster foraging parties.

"There was only maybe a score of militia firing at them from the woods, but they had near five hundred Redcoats to protect those foragers.

"Once we captured five of their rear guard," Private Fletcher boasted, "and they seemed right happy for it."

"Why?"

"Because they was exhausted from foraging day after day for cattle and garden truck and allus being sniped at by militia and never a chance to fight back.

"Said they allus reckoned to lose four or five men of the rear guard. Said sometimes they'd try to bribe officers so's not to be part of the rear guard. And sometimes they was put in the rear guard as punishment."

# # #

Tattered and rumpled though we Continentals looked, we covered the ground fast. The weather was warm and by now all the boys were walking with a long, strong stride.

But, as usual, we became befuddled about where we were marching, and why.

"I don't understand," Davis said. "We started yesterday marching straight south toward New Brunswick, stayed the night on a ridge. Then we turned east skirting right past Brunswick heading toward Perth Amboy. And now we're turning back north."

"Tis not yours to understand," Hannon said. "His Excellency wants you and your musket in the right place at the right time ready to fire."

"If you say so," Fletcher said. "But I begin to doubt if he knows what the right place is."

"That as may be," Liddle said. Then he pointed, "but for sure *they* ken where we are."

He was calling attention to numerous red dots – British pickets – scattered perhaps a half mile east of us. "Aye, and look," he added. "Beyond them you can make out formed troops – battalion sized, maybe – and they're marching."

We became more mystified because now our route turned west.

"What the hell?" Hannon said. "We're but marching in circles it seems."

That's how it played out. We wound up digging in along the mouth of a rocky gorge facing east maybe ten miles from Perth Amboy. We could smell the salt air. From half-way up the gorge the blue sea was visible along with dozens of ships headed into New York.

The Redcoats spent several days marching back and forth along our front and poking at our lines. We exchanged volleys and they recoiled, tempting us to attack.

And then, June 30, they were gone.

The command ordered our regiment to scout. My platoon was part of the company that crossed to Staten Island and marched most of its length.

Hannon said, "And would you be lookin' at that?"

"Aye," Liddle said. "The lobsters are embarking into a whole bluidy fleet. Look at 'em! Troopers by the dozen, plus frigates and ships of the line."

We started to count ships and had to give up at one hundred because all the masts made the fleet look like a forest.

I asked, "So where do you suppose they're going?"

"Tis a riddle," he said. "But I wager they'll no be headed back to London town."

It was a riddle that over July and August wore out our shoes and boots in hiking more than three hundred stony footsore miles.

Chapter 35
Brandywine

Alex Powell brushed the sweat from his scarred forehead. "Why in tophet," he asked disgustedly, "are we digging way up north away from the enemy. Why ain't we fighting?"

Tossing his hundredth shovel full of earth, Liddle said, "Ain't you heard, Powell? This is mostly how we fight this war. And I aver that spading is much safer work than trading musket volleys wi' Redcoats at thirty paces."

"Oh, we'll fight, Alex," I said. "Just don't know when. Might be the enemy will try sailing right up here. We're building Fort Independence to block Howe's troopships if'n they do show up."

Hundreds of us were digging on a high triangle of land between the Hudson River and the mouth of Peek Creek. The fort-to-be lay just downstream from Peekskill, a little settlement busy with mills of all sorts plus a tannery.

The rest of the Continental Army was busy with shovels at four other sites along this twenty-mile stretch of river. They were building Fort Clinton, Fort Montgomery, a fort at Stony Point and another at West Point.

I was glad we were near Peekskill because we could get leather for new shoes from its tannery.

We needed all the leather we could find because General Washington needed our feet and legs for his guessing game with General Howe.

His Excellency couldn't know where Howe intended to send his Armada — two hundred sixty-some ships bearing some sixteen thousand lobsters and Hessians.

One option could be to sail south down the coast and then up Delaware Bay to attack and seize Philadelphia. It would be cheaper perhaps than marching to the city through a countryside bristling with hostile militia and riflemen.

But the armada, instead, just as well could sail straight up the Hudson River to join with General Burgoyne. Burgoyne had captured Fort Ticonderoga from us and was preparing to invade south into New England.

Howe fostered the uncertainty by keeping the fleet at anchor off New York. So, figuring Howe planned to sail north to support Burgoyne, General Washington marched us fifty miles up the West Bank of the Hudson to fortify several of the river's pinch points, one being Peekskill.

Once we were well underway with our excavations, of course, the contrary happened. Howe's armada weighed anchor and stood out into the Atlantic, meaning Philadelphia was his target.

So His Excellency sent new orders.

Captain Pegrim called our company to attention. "Men, we're leaving within the hour. Bring your picks and shovels and muskets. We're marching for Philadelphia because that's General Howe's destination."

As the men moaned and groaned, the captain came close. "Ensign Scot, be prepared to push hard. To cover Philadelphia, it shall be a forced march of maybe a hundred and fifty miles. We fear Howe's fleet could enter Delaware Bay and fetch north to the capital city faster than we can hike there."

We pushed.

# # #

"Corporal Hannon, I'm sick of looking at your naked heels."

"Ensign Scot, it amazes me you can see my heels through these monstrous clouds of dust."

"Well, why don't you wear your boots?"

"I wish to preserve them, Sir, for the fight. His majesty issued me two sets of brogans. Only one is left and I wish to go into battle well shod."

We needn't have rushed

Howe's fleet took a full month to threaten Philadelphia. It had to sail not only against the Humboldt Current's northly flow, but also against southerly summertime winds. What's more, the armada took an even longer route, passing the Delaware capes all the way to Chesapeake Bay.

"Oooch," Hannon told us. "They'll be a sickly lot when they land. I know. I was on one o' them filthy troopers when we sailed to Boston. It took bloody weeks. And once ashore, it took at least a another week to get your health back and to get shed of all them bugs. Ain't that right, Liddle?"

"Aye, it is. But the lobsters be professionals. Sergeants will snap them into shape soon enou."

I should have heeded Liddle's caution. I forgot his words, though, when Congress announced the news that our northern forces battered General Burgoyne's army at some place called Bennington.

So we felt a bit jaunty on a fine August day when, His Excellency in the lead, we paraded through Philadelphia. Most of the citizens cheered and waved, but many also remarked how disheveled and hangdog we looked.

We looked far better that day, however, than we did two weeks later.

# # #

The battle of Brandywine started as Hessians advanced from the head of Chesapeake Bay. Giving way slowly, we fired from the trees knocking scores of them flat. Then we faded back toward the little river, the Brandywine.

You could say the river was the line in the sand where we wanted to block the British advance upon Philadelphia.

Once again, my platoon – now part of General Greene's division -- was on the far left of our battle line. Just as I remembered at Brooklyn, the Hessians attacked. But they didn't seem all that determined.

"This ain't right," I told Liddle. "Wonder if it's a mock attack, a demonstration."

"How do you reckon that?"

"Well, look, it's late afternoon and they been firing cannon towards us most of the day. Lots of noise. They got skirmishers on the far bank. But no real weight behind 'em. Some of them just shouting. Calling us *Hunde*. Means 'dogs'. Name-calling, for God's sake? Like boys out on a school yard?"

At least this time I was certain no force could forge past my platoon's flank. We were anchored on inhospitable terrain, all sharp little hills with muck-deep swamps between them.

So we stood trading shots with the Hessians.

Late in the afternoon, a tremendous uproar broke out far to the right.

Minutes later General Greene was prancing behind us on horseback. Waving his sword, he bellowed, "To the right, men! Regiments form to the right! Form line! Howe turned our right flank. We must stop him!"

God almighty! Turned us again?

We formed column and scrambled to the right, dodging men who were falling back from Sullivan's and Wayne's Divisions.

We came up and formed our line on the right of a mass of Continentals. Battalions and companies from Stirling's, Sullivan's and Wayne's Divisions were retreating. But grudgingly. They fired as they backpedaled.

Through their smoke we caught sight of a broad two-deep line of advancing redcoats. Behind them many more Redcoat units were massing and deploying, extending to our right.

We fired at the lobsters. Our attack surprised them, but they didn't recoil. With their ungodly platoon-by-platoon precision, they volleyed constant fire at us.

The roar of thousands of muskets deafened me. All I clearly remember was the stink of the powder and how the smoke closed down and cloaked us, narrowing our view. All I could see to do was load, aim and fire.

Through the smoke I caught a brief glimpse of General Washington riding that huge gray horse and waving his sword.

I can't imagine how he escaped being hit. Indeed, I still don't understand how I came away alive.

Oh, sometimes the lobsters fired high, their musket balls rattling through branches above us. By the thousands, leaf fragments fluttered down to carpet the earth beneath us – autumn coming early and bloody.

Thank God we had plenty of ammunition. We used it.

We advanced on the Redcoat line and they advanced toward us. Soon both lines loaded and fired at a butcher's range, maybe twenty paces. Powell grunted and fell. He yelled when Davis tried to pull him to his feet.

Suddenly a team of horses pulling a cannon burst through our midst. The hooves battered Douglas down and I heard bones crackle as the gun's right wheel rolled across Filer, crushing him.

British artillery unlimbered and began blasting grapeshot at us. The first shots were high. Even through musket roar, we heard the clusters of little iron balls shrieking and rattling above us. Then the gunners lowered their aim and began tearing gaps front to back through our ranks.

One blast ripped Davis and Taylor to pitiful tatters. They and fragments of other men lay strewn in a goulash of blood and dust. I think one blast also tore Captain Pegrim apart, for I never saw him again.

Hessian regiments now splashed across the Brandywine, attacking our left as the Redcoats assailed us from in front. Together both forces greatly outnumbered us so we retreated.

But we never run.

We Continentals now knew how to load and fire on the move. We made them pay for every foot they advanced.

Near dusk, we backed into a little village. They kept attacking. With our flanks secured, however we butchered the Hessians and Grenadiers until dark.

With night, both armies moved apart to lick their wounds.

Chapter 36
Losing Philadelphia

As we marched, Hannon groused. "Sure and after a battle, most officers gives the ranks a chanct to settle, like. Sleep, mebbe, or at least get summat to eat and like a sup of rum."

I snarled back. "Stop greeting, you lazy Irish bastard. Ain't any rest for me, so there's naught for you."

Liddle defended me. "Pat, settle yoursel' and gie the lad some time. He's got a bleedin' big job of work like none you ever had afore."

All I wanted was sleep. But because lobsters killed Captain Pegrim at Brandywine, battalion ordered me to command what remained of our company.

Somehow I was supposed to revive the survivors' sagging spirits.

Yes, and I also was required to indent for their food -- and to procure ammunition and new flints -- and to find muskets and bayonets for those lost at Brandywine -- and to integrate eighteen fresh replacements into the company – and to train five of the most raw recruits – and to find an ensign to run my old platoon – and then to write and forward reports about it all.

You could say the regiment scraped the bottom of its barrel by making me a brevet captain. That meant I'd have a captain's work and responsibilities but be paid as an ensign, meaning almost nothing.

At least I knew how to begin.

"Sam, I have a surprise – you're now the ensign who will run my old platoon. Mount a green cockade on your hat."

"And whit did I do to deserve this honor?"

"You survived the battle, Sam. So this is your reward. Wouldn't your father be proud?"

"How would I ken that? I dinna think the man ever saw me."

"Aye, weel, Ah'm sorry," I said. "And now please give your red shoulder strap to Pat.

"So, Pat? That strap is your reward. You're now Sergeant Hannon. Kindly stop your moaning and start training these new bodies."

"How do ye suppose I do that when we're but two days after a big fight and already marchin' again?"

"Just get it done," I said.

His was a good question.

General Washington had the Continental Army converging in four columns toward the upper fords of the Schuykill River. Supposedly we would crush the lobsters as they crossed. That way we'd stop them from capturing Philadelphia.

The prospect of renewed battle roiled my brain and turned my stomach inside out.

But my worries and fears weren't the kind of thing you discuss with subordinates. So instead I told all my troubles to one of the battalion's old captains, Nazareth Robbens, age 27.

"I don't know most of the men in the company," I said. "I've never commanded a company in combat. I ain't clear about where we fit in the regiment."

"Don't worry, Scot," Robbens said. "I seen you in battle afore. You ain't shy and you keep your head. So just have 'em under control 'til it's time -- and then you keep em' firing.

"As for the regiment," he added, "being's how the colonel's also a last-minute replacement, he don't know how or where you fit in neither"

"God help us," I said.

"Amen," he said.

Fortunately, God did.

Two days later our regiment deployed to help intercept General Howe's advance guard, a Hessian brigade.

"Load!" I yelled.

Just as the boys bit open their cartridges, the sky opened upon us.

Rain roared down soaking both armies and our muskets and powder. Any thought of battle ended. The downpour continued into the night, turning the Schuykill and its creeks into rampaging floods.

One of the new recruits yelled to me through the rain, "What do we do, Sir?"

"Lad, we just endure. Can't fight. Can't lie down. Can't start fires. Just keep marching."

"But the mud is calf-deep!"

"Yep! Won't be forever. Keep marching."

# # #

Hannon loomed out of the streaming darkness to announce a minor miracle. "Sir! "Tis an old barn I found for us! Bring the boys this way."

It was a hard shoe-sucking walk to the crumbling building. The thatch roof leaked in places, but not enough to stop us from kindling fires and warming ourselves.

The next morning we learned the floods destroyed much of the army's wagon train, soaking the bulk of our reserve ammunition and leaving us unable to fight.

That forced us to retreat. As we did so, it didn't help our morale to learn that our other army – the one way up in New York – had just compelled Britain's General Burgoyne to surrender his entire force.

The news may have made His Excellency grind his teeth in envy. But without ammunition, we had no choice other than to steal away, leaving the road to Philadelphia wide open for General Howe.

I don't like remembering the next few weeks of disaster upon disaster flavored with starvation and cold.

In a night attack, a lobster battalion bayonetted and killed several hundred men in General Wayne's Division.

Perhaps seeking revenge for that bloody insult, General Washington launched us into a complex attack upon some of Howe's army at Germantown.

His plan required each of our four divisions to take a fifteen-mile night march by separate routes. We were to meet outside the village at dawn and then attack.

Blundering about in dense fog, two divisions never arrived. The fog also caused two of our regiments to fire into each other.

Both fled in panic.

After a costly three-hour brawl, we of General Greene's Division covered the army's retreat. Our platoon was downcast about losing four men. The one hopeful note as we marched away from that battle, was that Hannon seemed unusually cheerful.

"Cap'n, you got to admit our new boys was fairly steady under fire. I have hopes for them now, that I do. 'Tis my belief you learns more in five minutes of battle than in five months of drill."

"True, they did very well," I said. "But we all need more polish. We're still not as efficient as lobsters. Fact is, I noted that during the fight one of the boys fired away his ramrod."

"Aye, Sir," Liddle said. "Yon was one of my recruits, Tommy Blair, the negro lad. Did ye also note Tommy didn't run? He found a new ramrod from one of the deid. Kept on loading and firing like an old hand.

"Now the main thing we need," he added, "is training for our officers. It's my belief you're no reading from the same books."

# # #

Soon after, we marched fifteen miles to winter quarters and began cutting timber to erect huts for ourselves.

A headquarters major rode his horse past our half-built hut and remarked, "The work goes painful slow, don't it?"

I glared at him.

"Yes Sir, because rations are painful slow. My men have had no food for three days. So when a body's had nought to eat, swinging an ax or hewing with an adze goes painful slow."

He flushed. "Yes, well. His Excellency wanted us to winter in numerous scattered camps. Supply would be easier. But Congress mandated keeping the entire command close to Philadelphia.

"Trouble is, farmers hereabouts sell to Redcoats rather than us. But we're trying. Some food should get through soon."

It did. Enough to keep us barely alive when winter really hit. Even so, my company lost eight men to desertion and three men through amputation after their bare feet froze solid and turned black.

At times jeers followed officers as they rode through the camp, men chanting like Jays, "No meat! No meat!" Others took up a different jab. "No food, no soldier!"

"Now and again," Private Blair complained to Hannon, "I got to wondering why General Howe don't just charge up here from Philadelphia and put all of us out'n our misery. We're only twenty mile away, for God's sake. This is just plain damnation."

"No, lad," Hannon said.

"It's Valley Forge."

Chapter 37
The Valley Drills

The portly general abruptly turned on one heel causing his cloak to swirl. "*Mein Gott, mein Gott!*" He shook a massive fist at me. "*Tu es un koddamm eedioht!*"

I felt blood rush to my face. "Sorry, Sir, I don't understa…"

A grinning captain interrupted me. "Beg pardon, Sir. Name's Walker. Ben Walker, of the 2nd New York. I'm General Steuben's interpreter. Uh, sorry, to tell you, but he just said you're a goddamned idiot."

Open guffaws came from enlisted spectators who watched from the edge of the parade ground.

I guess I earned the insult by gawking like a farm boy when ordered to extend the left end of a line of twenty officers – all trying to stifle their own laughter.

The general took a deep breath and came to stand beside me. "*Mon Dieu,*" he said quietly. He gave me a kindly look and a slap on the shoulder. Then, as laughter subsided, he pointed to the interpreter.

The captain said, "Gentlemen! You are the first contingent of officers to be here at General Washington's express command. You'll being trained by Major General the baron Friedrich Wilhelm Ludolf Gerhard Augustin von Steuben.

Someone muttered, "Jesus! This damned Dutchman man has more names than our family Bible."

The captain went on. "The baron will show you how to march and maneuver every bit as well as the enlisted troops he already trained.

"Oh, and General Washington directs me to tell you he has complete confidence in Baron du Steuben -- that, indeed, as the army's Inspector General, the baron outranks all other officers save General Washington himself."

We officers looked at each other in awe provoking more giggles from the gallery of enlisted men.

Among them I spotted and returned Hannon's and Blair's toothy grins.

The general walked back in front of us. He cleared his throat. "*Et mon nom est prononcé Shtoiben no Stoobin.*"

"Gentlemen," the captain said, "the general pronounces his name '*Shtoi-bn*'."

All business now, the general walked back through the snow to my end of the line. He yanked the blanket from my shoulders, grabbed my wrist and pulled my right arm upward to the right. He bent it at the elbow and pushed my palm down against my right belt line. Then he shoved me sideways until my extended elbow touched the left arm of the lieutenant colonel standing beside me.

"So!" he said.

"Then he grabbed my jaw and turned my head to the right.

"*Ainsi!*"

"That means 'This way'," the captain said.

The general nodded to him. "*Expliquer!*"

"The baron directs you to do the same. Turn your heads to the right and point your elbows directly to your right. Now each of you shifts position fore or back so that you all form a perfect line."

Back now at my left side, the general stooped to peer down our line. I puzzled why a major general and a nobleman would do a sergeant's job.

But he was.

"*Troisième homme!*"

"Third man," the captain said to the brigadier general next to my neighbor.

The brigadier inched forward slightly.

"*Bon!*"

The baron trotted back and forth along the line demanding adjustments.

He waved his swagger stick and commanded, "*Officers! Marche en avant!*"

Captain Walker translated, "Forrrard, march!"

We stepped out maybe five paces when Steuben turned red in the face. "*Merde!*" he said.

Then he barked. "*Halt! Koddam HALT!*"

Confused, we stopped. The stubby Prussian shook his head. He rolled his eyes skyward, repeatedly swatted his leg with the stick and sputtered, "*Unglaublich. Ja ganz unglaublich!*"

"I don't understand that," Captain Walker said. "He just spoke German, not French. But I suspect it's not complimentary."

A man called from the edge of the parade ground, "It means 'Unbelievable, quite goddam unbelievable'."

The enlisted people slapped their knees and bellowed with laughter. Steuben rocked his head back and laughed aloud, too. He paused to wipe his eyes. "Hoo!" he said. Then he stiffened up and commanded, "*Noch einmal.*"

The interpreter said, "I do know that one. It means 'once again'."

In a growl, the general ordered us to march and began to call cadence. We didn't know, "*Un! Deux! Trois…*" one minute any better than, "*Ein! Zvo! Drei…*" the next. But the rhythm was unmistakable and we quickly swung along to it.

We spent almost three hours again and again practicing how to march in step. All the while, the baron brow-beat us in guttural French and German larded with occasional English curses.

One minute we all were idiots – the same word in all three languages -- then *Putains* and the next *verdammt Arschlochs*. Except for a couple of Pennsylvanians, none of us was clear about what he meant. But we got the idea.

He demanded that we stride twenty-four inches, not twenty-six, not twenty-three. He fanatically demanded we preserve that elbow-length interval. He wanted a quick march -- one hundred twenty paces per minute, not the stately sixty per minute we copied from Redcoats.

The next day he drilled us for hours on the maneuver called wheeling -- a line of soldiers executing a ninety-degree swing just like a sixty-foot gate.

When I was the line's pivot – the gate's hinge, you might say -- I hardly had to do more than turn my body in slow degrees.

But then when I was the far end of the wheel – the latch rather than the hinge -- I had to cover at lot of ground almost at double-time. In making each wheel, the baron led us, facing us and stepping backward as the gate swung, holding his sword horizontally to keep our line's rigidly straight and to preserve our intervals.

He yelled every minute it seemed, cautions one instant, damnations the next, praises when we succeeded.

As we tried the wheel for perhaps the twentieth time, he shouted in French and Captain Walker translated, "You men must concentrate! You'll have to maintain your intervals while under fire!"

He cursed constantly. But soon I sensed he directed half his abuse at his own frustrations and half of it for the sake of comedy. Blasts of profanity amuse soldiers. He often sounded fierce. But even after one of his explosions, his long nosed countenance usually was humor-filled.

Some of my fellow students became furious with him, but they kept it under their breath. I heard the brigadier mutter, "Undignified, damme, taking abuse from a bloody Dutchman and in front of the troops. Besides, who gives a damn how pretty we march?"

Yep, the abuse was embarrassing. It dawned on me, though, that Steuben's endless nit-picking about pace and stride length had a purpose.

I'd had the benefit earlier of seeing maneuvers by a full battalion of the baron's enlisted trainees.

Granted, most of the men wore little more than rags. No two hats were the same. Some were barefoot in the patchy snow still on the ground. But the tattered soldiers moved in perfect step and held the muskets to their shoulders in rigid alignment.

They marched with the magnificent poise of the best-drilled Redcoats. Then they showed how marching precision is essential to battleground maneuvers.

I became an eager student. Like any good teacher, he sensed my enthusiasm and quickly promoted me up from the ranks of idiocy.

Reflecting later, I told Liddle, "You know marching by itself don't impress me.

"But then -- after what, a week of the baron's schooling? -- that battalion's platoons kept in line and in step as they moved oblique to the right. Sam, those platoons just *flowed* from column into line, and straight as a yardstick. They was smooth as water in a brook gliding past a rock."

"Haud on, Rob. Ah dinna believe it!"

"'Tis the God's truth, Sam! I saw no confusion. No mixed-up orders. No troops stumbling into each other. No shouting. They'd practiced so much, every man moved at the same pace knowing exactly where to step and still keep aligned.

"And then, Sam, they did the reverse every bit as smooth. Right back into column. Not one blessed instant of confusion!

"You know, Sam. With this kind of training, I think you'd say that we Continentals now are becoming regulars."

Sam nodded. "Aye, Ah oonderstand. Sounds like a ship's crew after two months at sea. With that experience, they're all able seamen and need very few orders. Bosun just blows his pipe and calls 'Two reefs in topsails, lads.' And it's us racing up the ratlines and done, quick as can be.

"So, maybe at last the entire army will use the same drill," Liddle added. "No more differences between companies or each colonel changing his own special commands every other day?"

"That's the baron's aim," I said.

I volunteered our company to serve as one of the baron's model units. Once we mastered marching, wheels – the most difficult and critical maneuver – came next, and then formation evolutions. We in turn trained other companies, all to the same commands.

That was only for starters. As we mastered the baron's drill, we also heard he was paring down the strength of some regiments and beefing others up.

"It really frosts some of the officers," I told Captain Robbens, "but don't it make sense to have all the regiments to be the same size? Then whoever's commanding needn't worry about whether Johnny's regiment or Willy's is too small or too big to tackle a redoubt."

"Correct," Robbens said, "I think Steuben has achieved monumental things. The men show themselves proud about marching and maneuvering well."

"We don't have the pretty uniforms," I said. "But we're regulars now…maybe as good as redcoats."

# # #

The army's spirits also improved as, thank God, mid-April arrived with warmer weather. Wagon trains with food also now made it into camp regularly.

Then on May Day we had a rousing celebration. We cheered ourselves hoarse, in fact. Headquarters announced that the king of France had just signed a military alliance with us Americans.

A few days later we cheered again because George III was recalling General Howe to England.

Even more exciting, the new British commander, General Henry Clinton, had received some orders from London too.

He was to ship eight thousand Redcoats from the United States to fight France…in the Caribbean islands.

Chapter 38
Toe-To-Toe

Musket fire roared ahead, maybe a half mile.

It made us all swallow nervously, but Private Blair distracted us.

"Whoops, sergeant, there be another," he said, pointing to a redcoat stretched on his side just off our track, shoulders and chest heaving.

"Aye, boy," Hannon said. "Have pity for yon lobster. That's what a wool coat and a sixty-pound pack does to the likes of him in heat like this."

"It *is* terrible hot, sergeant," Blair said. "Don't you suppose we could rest in the shade for a space?"

Overhearing, Ensign Liddle exploded. "Whit's that ye say? Shade? Do ye mind the baron calling us 'eediots'? Well, boy, for certain, you're an eediot!

"You greeted all winter long about how cold you was. You couldn't be satisfied with straw like the rest of us. No! You wanted blankets! And great coats! And fire, fer the love o' God! You ached for the sun. You *prayed* for the sun. This braw June day answers yer bloody prayers. You have all the warmth you need and you *still* complain!"

By now Liddle had most of his platoon laughing – Blair included.

"Tis time, boy, to keep a still tongue and be a soldier. And mind, keep yer glims open. We're marching toward trouble."

My company was approaching the battle, preparing to file down a hillside spur to a road dotted with maybe thirty inert British and Hessian soldiers.

Our scout, Corporal Dawes, climbed up the slope to meet me. Mopping his sweaty face, he reported, "Several is dead from musket wounds. But most is prostrate from this soggy heat. No fight in 'em at all."

"Thanks Dawes. I think the militia must have shot some of them earlier today when their wagon train pulled through here."

The British and Hessian forces, amounting to about ten thousand troops in a twelve-mile column, were trekking toward New York after abandoning Philadelphia.

Our army followed on the lobsters' heels.

I told Liddle, "We heard General Washington urged the New Jersey militia to harass the enemy column. If they was anywhere as good as us that day between Princeton and Trenton, then it's been a damned hard day for General Clinton."

The rattle of muskets ahead subsided somewhat, but went on steadily. The lobster army itself still showed plenty of fight.

I reckoned we'd soon be in the battle because, for the first time in a week, it wasn't raining.

Afternoon thunderstorms had soaked us day after day, only added to the misery of 90 and 100-degree weather. Today, the sun baked us and caused the surrounding woods to steam.

As we came off the hill, we joined a dozen other regiments of General Greene's division. As usual, I had only a vague impression of what was happening.

I caught a glimpse of General Washington well to the front, silhouetted against the bank of battle smoke. He was on that huge gray horse, riding hell for leather among clusters of Continentals. He seemed to be in a fury, signaling with his sword.

The sight gave the sense that our advance was just in time to stop other units from retreating.

Be that as it may, the troops around him seemed to coalesce into a solid formation.

Then, emerging through the battle smoke beyond them, came a broad treble line of Redcoats.

Just like at Bunker Hill, they marched to the rhythm of their drums.

"They be comin' for us," Liddle said. "An, men, we'll gie them Sassenach devils a hard reception."

The British line looked implacable, rolling toward us like a broad red wave, sunlight glinting on its rows of bayonets. The wave remorselessly submerged the dead and the screaming wounded lying in its path.

In our turn, we silently side-stepped obliquely, moving from column to battle line. Without a hitch we continued our march toward them…muskets loaded, bayonets fixed.

At thirty paces, we halted.

The men in our front rank knelt on their right knee, steadied their left elbows on the left knee, aimed and brought their muskets to full cock.

We in the rear tank, turned our left side to the enemy, raised our muskets to aim and brought our muskets to full cock.

The lobsters halted, and started firing their rotating series of platoon volleys.

As so often happened, much of their fire went high. But a ball thudded into the man kneeling in front of me, knocking him backwards into my shins.

I tilted my musket up and, trying to be gentle, dragged him by the collar back behind my position. It was the negro lad, Blair, clutching his stomach, his dark hands already bloody.

I barely heard him through the volley blasts. "My God, I'm hit, Cap'n. Don't leave me, Cap'n. Please!"

I patted his shoulder, "Don't worry, Tommy. I promise I'll just be three feet away in my position. Got to keep firing at them bastards."

"You promise, Sir?"

"I promise."

Just then Liddle yelped and dropped his musket. He instantly bent to grab it and jumped upright. Blood was flowing through the sweat on his left forearm and hand.

"Tis no that bad," he said when I looked to him. "I can still load and fire."

Though the lobsters' smoke cloud we saw the flashes of more platoon volleys. I heard their shots sometimes thud and sometimes crack into our men.

Then, yelling furiously, the Redcoats charged through their smoke, muskets leveled, to bayonet us.

At one time, the sight of massed bayonets spooked us.

But this day, I don't think any man of my company twitched so much as an eyebrow. Yes, each must have been as fearful as me. But weeks of the baron's drill had built our army's confidence in itself.

We didn't budge.

Our rear rank leveled our muskets and fired with a single shattering bark into the crimson wave. Then the front rank. And then the rear rank. And then the front rank.

Our volleys broke the redcoat wave into a subsiding welter of bloodied bodies and scrambled weapons.

As the second line of Redcoats came into view to renew the assault, we met them with renewed fire.

Meanwhile, our artillery came into cruel play.

Cannons fired into the British line from their flank. Again and again, I saw sudden swirls in redcoat ranks as round shot bowled through their files, tossing caps, muskets and limbs every which way.

So it continued until dark.

General Clinton called it quits. After midnight he and his troops took a leaf out of our Trenton book. They quietly stole away from the field at Monmouth, continuing their retreat to New York.

I didn't see or hear that happen.

We and the redcoats still were fighting along toward dusk when a shot knocked me out.

Chapter 39

Monmouth's Wake

Somebody's cough kept nagging me from my sleep. I tried to cover my ears, but that stung like crazy on the left side.

Then I recognized that it wasn't a cough I heard. It was an explosive sound, something between a grunt and a yell. It came from right next to me – somebody grating out "God! Ohhhh, God!"

I groaned, "Shut up, damn you!"

"Cap'n, izzat you? You're still alive? Ohhhh, *God* it hurts!"

In the dark I recognized Tommy Blair's voice. He was panting heavily and, about every minute, crying for God.

I snarled, "God almighty, will you just give over?" Then I regretted my words. I recalled Tommy had lain there since afternoon with a musket ball somewhere in his guts.

"Tommy, I'm sorry. It's me, Cap'n Scot. Something hit my noggin. Must have knocked me out. I see some torches off aways, I'll see if I can get us some help."

"Cap'n, promise you'll come back, Pleee…ohhhhh, God! The other ones didn't come back."

"I promise," I said. It took me about five tries to get up. I had to toss aside a musket lying on my chest. Then I used my left foot to shove someone's corpse off my right leg. It grunted. Bodies start doing that after a time.

I was so dizzy that standing was almost impossible, so I groped until I found the musket and sort of used it as a cane.

Fortunately, I didn't have to stumble more than fifty feet among other bodies until I encountered a man carrying a torch. He was a nurse and drunk as a lord.

I told him about Tommy and he said surgeons could do nothing for belly or chest wounds. "We jes' kind of set them aside and – *hic* -- leave 'em be until they d- diie in their – *hic* -- own time. Can't do naught for 'em."

I stole his whiskey bottle, yanked his torch from his hand and made my way back to Tommy.

Tommy tried to smile, but the torch light showed his black face to be a contorted sweaty grimace. It also lit up my face.

"Cap'n, you been shot, too? Your ear be hanging down long 'side your neck…Ohhhhhhhh, *God*! Sorry, cap'n, but this hurts so bad!"

"I brought something that'll help." I practically collapsed to to sit beside him. He gripped one of my hands, so I tilted the bottle to his mouth with the other.

Tommy swallowed and immediately coughed the liquor up, screaming at the pain of the spasm.

After his agony eased, he said, "S-s-s-sorry Cap'n. I can't keep it down that way. Sorry."

"Don't worry, Tommy." I tried to make my voice sound soothing. "Let me just give it to you a little at a time. Just take wee sips, Tommy. Soon it'll help with the pain."

So, as the torch guttered out, I had him drink the rotgut sip by sip. After a time it did seem to ease his agony. He thanked me and asked that we be sure to bury him. "Don't want no buzzards and no crows feeding on my hide. Hate them birds."

"Don't worry about that, Tommy. We'll take care of it."

Eventually he seemed to pass out, but then roused himself to murmur, "Cap'n, be sure them sawbones look to the left side of ya face."

"I will, Tommy. So rest now. Sleep if you can."

As he sipped again, he pleaded for me to stay. I stayed.

At last, just as the east horizon took on a faint glow, the whiskey overwhelmed him. He passed out.

I gave him the only mercy I could.

I slit his throat.

Wiping my tears and chugging the remainder of the whiskey, I staggered up and started looking for my company.

# # #

When General Clinton and his lobsters left the battlefield, they also left us all the dead and the screaming, groaning wounded.

So the survivors were in a black mood doing what they could to help wounded comrades and enemies alike.

My dizziness was so bad I could do little more than walk. When I found Hannon, he helped me to a surgeon.

As we walked – well, he walked while I leaned on him -- Hannon told me our company lost eleven men killed outright and eight wounded, me and Liddle included.

"Call it one more dead," I said. "Tommy died just before dawn. How is Sam?"

"Mr. Liddle's wound weren't much more'n a fleabite," he said. "Upper arm. He'll recover so long's it don't go rotten on him."

I took my place in line for the surgeon. About ten he got to me. "My God, boy," he said. "You must have a skull like iron. Now looking at your eyes, I'd say you got a good concussion."

"A what?"

"It's a bruise to your brain, son. Now shut up while I work on you."

It was difficult not to cuss and yell. His needle hurt bad enough as it pierced the skin. But the thread hurt much more as he dragged it through the skin to close a gash extending from the corner of my left eye to past my ear.

"Some redcoat sure plowed a neat furrow on you," he said. "Sorry, but I had to snip away the upper wing of your ear.

"You're lucky you got that big mop of black hair," he said. "You'll want to brush it over to the left so's the ladies won't see that ugly ear hole of yours.

"Now listen," he went on. "For the sake of your brain, you need to rest three, four months before you return to duty. If you can, go home."

"Thanks, surgeon, but I got no home."

Hannon chimed in. "No, but you do have a pretty lady back outside Boston. And that ain't all. Come over here."

He pulled me to a grove of trees near the surgeon's tent. He leaned close and whispered. "Ah, Sir, well it seems like some of the boys had good fortune in looting them dead redcoat officers. Some was real swells.

"So here's your share."

He handed me a weighty little leather purse. It held twenty golden guineas, a considerable fortune, and four gold Louies -- the Louis d'or, a gold French coin, also worth about a pound sterling, twenty-one shillings, actually.

"I figure you and Mistress Fletcher can put this money to good use if'n she'll have you for a husband."

"Good Lord, Hannon, how much...?"

"Cap'n, least said soonest mended. So now here's your old friend." He handed *Lobster Claw* to me. "Sir, fare you well and come back to us in autumn." He doffed his cap in salute and walked away.

I sat my rump on the tailgate of a cargo wagon and squinted at the acres of dead and wounded still to be dealt with. I couldn't help but think about the coins in my pockets. Doing so helped me not think about Tommy.

Captain Robbens stopped to talk. He told me I looked as if I needed a shot of whiskey because and I seemed to have aged ten years.

"Feels more like twenty to me," I said. "But I had one drink earlier and don't feel like having any more. I'm feeling a bit sickly about now."

"I suppose it's always like that after a battle," he said. "This was my first."

"Yeah, it is like this," I said. "But I must point out that this particular time it's different. Someplace down inside I do feel a tiny glow."

"Why's that?"

"Well, for the first time, Sir, we American clodhoppers just went straight head-on against one of the world's best armies.

"We whipped 'em good."

Chapter 40
Interlude

Trying to rest as a passenger in a wagon train of wounded the next day just wouldn't work.

The oxen pulled us steadily enough, but the roads were so rutted that the wagons bounced and jerked constantly, causing the wounded – especially the amputees -- to scream.

I was one of the lucky few, merely suffering dizziness and a headache. My vision was fuzzy, too.

Originally they said we'd go through Philadelphia. I looked forward to seeing the city. I wanted to view what the redcoats had done to it.

My wagon, however, was loaded with New Englanders headed past the city for Fort Mercer on the Delaware River. There they helped us board a fast schooner bound for Boston.

If I'd had trouble walking on land, I practically had to tie myself to the mainmast of the *Martha Mary*. Otherwise I'd have collapsed like a bag of bones.

But during the days, at least, I wasn't confined below decks in a hammock with the rest of the wounded. I have no notion whether sea air helped my brain bruise, but it was refreshing by contrast with the muggy land temperatures.

Even so, the idea of sailing to Boston worried me. I knew the British fleet would be out, escorting thousands of British troops from New York to the west Indies.

Once we cleared the Delaware capes, we indeed saw troop ships, plus ships of the line and frigates, all flying the union jack.

"Paaah, 'tis no worry," the skipper said.

"We're sailin' opposite directions to 'em," he said. "And we're faster nor any king's ship save their mail packets."

"Them packets don't carry guns," he added. "Us neither. We see them. They see us. Each just waves to the other."

He combed fingers through his beard. "Now weeks back," he grinned, "a couple of his majesty's brigs gave chase to us. They even tried some long-range shots at us but hadn't a hope. We sailed rings around them."

It turned to be a quiet voyage. The vessel rocked and pitched with a corkscrew motion, but we never even met with a respectable gale. A week later *Martha Mary* landed us in Boston.

# # #

By the time we entered Boston Harbor, my vertigo was somewhat abated. As I eased down the gangway to the quay, though, I found walking still to be a trial. That together with being on solid ground after seven days at sea made my staggers even worse.

Even using *Lobster Claw* as a cane, my tipsy gait probably led some Bostonians to think I was a drunken sailor.

At a stable, the owner wanted $800 in Continental scrip to sell me Ferdinand, a sunken-eyed, sway-backed old pensioner from the plow.

The stable-owner's eyes gleamed when I offered him three golden Louies for Ferd plus saddle and tack.

After biting the coins to make sure they were gold, he clapped his hand into mine and said, "Done!" He let me sleep the night at the stable and even helped me saddle and mount the horse the next morning.

It was a hot day so I just steered Ferd, but let him amble. I felt a bit guilty about even riding him because I could hear his ancient joints grind and creak. I was suffering enough guilt already about Tommy.

It was late afternoon before we arrived at the Fletcher farm.

It sickened me to see the place. The house was a charred ruin, the upper floor having collapsed into the ground level. The main barn was little better than a blackened heap.

I turned Ferd toward the third building, the farm's original barn -- a small one – where Isaac Fletcher had stored most of his implements.

Still dubious about my balance, I did a slow slide off the saddle and leaned against Ferd for a moment of stability.

Suddenly, I heard Alice scream, "Rob! *Rob!* Tis you! Oh, Rob!" She was half-way between the barn and me, her feet hardly touching ground she ran so hard.

Her screams startled Ferd who backed away from me. I staggered and fell, using the rifle to get back to my feet just as Alice slammed into my arms.

After hugging and kissing me and crying for perhaps ten minutes, she stepped back and slapped her hand against my chest.

"Rob Scot, you never wrote a letter to me! Not one!" Her voice was cold as Valley Forge.

"Well, I'd little time and no idea how to send it..."

"I don't care! I knew not if you was living or dead," she said. "You asked me to bide! You spoke of marriage! And I must ask how I can bide -- or prepare for my wedding -- if I don't know what transpires with you.

"Really, Mr. Scot, in the future you must be more...Oh, goodness! Your poor face! What befell you, Rob?"

I feared my wound and half-chewed ear would revolt her.

They did not.

She yanked off my hat so the sun would show the damage. Frowning, she peered at the side of my face. Then her expression softened as she reached up to gently seize my head and pull my face to hers.

She kissed my eye, the wound and my little nub of an ear.

Tears spilled from her eyes. "Oh, Rob, so close."

I gulped. "Yes, Alice. Too close."

"I think the Lord was with thee," she said. "Come, Rob, leave us go inside." She led me and Ferd toward the little barn.

"This is our house until we rebuild," she said. "It was where Poppa kept all his implements."

"Well I know, Alice. I spent quite a bit of time using the tools from this building."

"Of course," she said, smiling at the memory. "Of course. But mayhap you'll not recognize it now."

# # #

I didn't recognize it.

I marveled because she had transformed half of the little building into a tiny home. The fireplace made one room a kitchen. A hanging blanket partitioned off the other, her bedroom.

"It's bigger than the shed that old man Vandermolen forced mother and me to live in," I said. "And with the fireplace, it's certain to be warm in winter. And, you know, it just *looks* like a home with the pictures up and all."

She giggled and pointed to the two chairs. One a bare rocker, the other cushioned with arm rests.

"The plush chair was my daddy's," she said. "I rescued it just before the house collapsed."

"Speaking of that," I said, "have you seen ought of loyalists or raiders or that Simpson fellow?"

She frowned. "Some of my neighbors claim Simpson was wounded, that he fled south when you men caught and hanged his gang. Supposedly there's loyalists living further west, but they pretend to be patriots."

"It could be they're just waiting," I said.

"Waiting for what?"

"Waiting to come out in favor of the side what wins. And our side will win."

"I know," she said. "But I'm afraid this war will be the ruination of us all.

"Anyways," she said, "back to the chair. It's yours. Please to try it."

I cautiously lowered my backside into the chair. "Ohhh, it's nice," I said and leaned back.

"Alice?"

"What, Rob?"

"Beyond this…" I pointed toward my face… "the redcoats gave me a brain bruise. My balance is getting better, but I feel I should stay seated. Now my eyesight is still a little foggy, too. So from down here, I cannot see you as well as I would wish. I therefore must ask a mighty favor of you."

"Oh, Mr. Scot? And what might that be?"

"I'd be very much in your debt if you'd come over here and sit your beautiful self on my lap. That way I could see your lovey face better. And I could even cuddle you and maybe tell you how much…"

"Like this?"

She perched on my right leg. I reached my long arms around her and pulled her to me, head to my shoulder.

"I was going to tell you how much I have missed you for going on eighteen months now."

"I want to hear allllll about it," she smiled. "But do you suppose you might kiss me first?"

"If you insist."

Chapter 41
Rebuilding

My Monmouth treasure paid for lumber for me to build a two-room addition to Alice's little house...*our* house, she insisted.

"We can call it our house," I agreed. "But 'twas your daddy who stablished this farm. I feel 'twas his doing."

She tossed her head and grinned. "Well, Mr. Scot, his granddaddy cleared the land and planted the first crops, so it be mine by right of descent and I say it be ours by right of marriage. So there!"

"Yes, my lady!" I said as I nailed a new plank into place.

I was getting along well. Headaches had long ceased and my balance was much better.

Though a full week of July, Alice and I stooped, knelt and sweated as we culled the ruins of the barn and house. Sifting the filthy ash and charred timbers cost us many scrapes and cuts. One day she asked ruefully, "I wonder if my hands ever can be white again."

The drudgery paid off, however, because the ruins were a treasury of nails, hinges, brackets and other pieces of metal work such as door and drawer handles.

Oh, yes, and we found time to meet the pastor and be wed, one of her cousins and the pastor's wife serving as witnesses.

Now as I've mentioned, my youth as a virtual slave gave me little contact with women prior to first meeting Alice and her dear departed mother.

So when I saw Alice the first time, I suppose I fell into a state of awe or even worship.

Of course, it was pretty much worship at a distance since I was soldiering most of the time.

I didn't really get to know her, therefore, until after we exchanged our vows.

What a wonderful time of discovery it was for me. She was beautiful, of course, so now as her husband I could take in her beauty with my eyes all I wished. And kiss her whenever I liked.

And her eyes... the things she could do to me merely with her eyes!

I might not like her request for, say, a north window in the new addition. I might say something like, "Seems to me like it'd be more touble'n it's worth."

She could cast those blue pools down and whisper a faint, "Oh."

Or, like General Washington, she could pierce my core with a glare and say, "Oh?"

Either way, argument over.

She could duck her head and slightly thrust out her lower lip in an angelic pout.

I began thinking of myself as Cap'n Putty. I loved slaving for her.

As newlyweds, we also had exciting nights of discovery.

Being inexperienced, neither of us at first really knew quite what to do. But my silken goddess and I taught each other. We learned. Quickly. With fast-growing enthusiasm.

In the mornings, we'd look at each other and blush. Then we'd giggle. I remember one rainy morning I reluctantly stood up from our breakfast. "Well, guess I better get outside there and get to poundin'."

She looked at me innocently. "Mr. Scot, could you not help me with something else, first?"

She led me to the bedroom. "Very well Mrs. Scot," I said. "What do you need?"

"You."

She wrapped her arms around my neck.

"You can do some poundin' in here first."

I started to laugh, but she muffled me with her lips.

It rained practically all day.

# # #

Some weeks later, the last nail went into the final roof shingle just as Alice called me to the supper that I already could smell.

"I'm on the way," I called, tossing hammer and nail pouch to the ground. I jumped the last five feet from the ladder, landing lightly, feeling fine.

She watched from the doorway, but she wasn't smiling. "Rob dearest," she said, "when you arrived in June, you said you'd be going back to the army sometime in September."

"Yes," I said, "if I was getting around well and had my balance back."

"Well, it looks like your balance is good. I'd say building that new room has helped you."

"Of a certainty it has."

She crossed her arms and looked away from me. "So now you'll leave."

"I must." I wrapped my arms around her. "Alice, I don't like this any more than you. But I gave my oath."

"You made vow to me, too, Rob. At our wedding." That statement sliced.

But then her shoulders shuddered and she began crying. Her voice muffled against my chest, "You promise you'll come back to us."

"Of course I prom...what do mean, 'Us'?"

She said, "I'm pretty sure that come spring we're going to have a baby."

"Oh...good heavens, you mean it?"

She stepped back from me. "I'm not for sure yet, but I think so. It's quite an thought to take in, is it not?"

I just stood there and stared at her. "Indeed it is. Never thought before about being a father. Guess it kind of excites me. I'll tell you one thing, I'd never bring up a son the way VanderMolen raised me. Nossir.

"If he's a boy, though, I'd sure teach him how to shoot."

Alice grinned again.

"But what if we have a daughter?"

That stopped me. It made me picture a tiny Alice. "I don't know...but what about you? What about when your time comes if I ain't here?"

"Well, mister, if you are here what would you do? You never helped a woman deliver a baby?"

"Sure haven't. But who would help you?"

She assured me several women in the area helped each other with birthing. She said they had teas and potions that would help in the months ahead.

"The main thing I need from you," she said, "is some letters now and again to let me know how you're faring.

"I *know* you're familiar with quill and ink," she said. "So no excuses or evasions. You can send letters to me care of the Sudbury Apothecary."

# # #

We scrambled in our last week together.

She knew how to load and fire a pistol, and I had her practice for accuracy. I also showed her how to load and fire her father's musket. Once she got over flinching at the flash from the lock, she was a hell of a good shot.

The neighbors in spring had plowed and planted her fields. When harvest commenced they would share the yield with Alice so she would have food through the winter.

I cut and split maybe six cords of wood to see her through the cold months. It was good to have the work because my mind could focus on all she'd given me to consider.

"Rob, if I wasn't expecting," she said, "I'd want to come with you to the army."

I barked, "Never!"

"But I could keep your clothes clean, and darn your socks."

"Alice," I said. "I'll worry about you constant whilst I'm gone to the army. But if you were with me there, I'd be so wrought up about you that I could pay no heed to my men, ninety or so of 'em. Got to make sure they're fed, and armed, and clothed and drilled and, now and then, take them into battle.

"Couldn't do it if you was with me. Just couldn't."

"Well, husband, I dispute what you say, but it don't really matter since I'll be here at home carrying the child.

"I talked a lot with Mrs. Adams," she added.

"Who's Mrs. Adams?"

"She's the wife of John Adams, a very important man in Congress. 'Twas he who helped bring the French into the war for us."

"Oh!"

"Yes, and Mrs. Adams – her name is Abagail -- is a very accomplished woman. She says, and I warn you, that we ladies can do more than just have babies and…" she reached into a carpet bag beside her rocker "…and knit stockings."

She handed me eight pairs of stockings, the kind what reach from above the knee, plus two pair of knit gloves.

"For you in the coming winter," she said. "Since we don't know your birth date, think of them as a birthday gift."

"And a Christmas gift," I said. "And a wonderful wedding present.

"But you, my wife, have been the most wonderful gift of all. And will be all our lives long."

"'Til death do us part," she said. "And I charge you to avoid death for the next thirty, forty years."

I simply said, "Amen!"

We both wept the next morning when I set off on foot for Boston.

Chapter 42
Heading South

When I arrived in Boston, I learned General Washington dispersed the Continental Army to far-separated winter quarters.

His Excellency posted one division to West Point in upper New York and another to Connecticut. The bulk of the army was camping in New Jersey, the site of his personal headquarters.

So, being as how I was a Continental Army captain, I persuaded the skipper of a Boston privateer bearing an army cargo to give me free passage to Philadelphia.

Once we arrived, I learned his cargo was baled uniforms for the Army from France. I simply hitched a ride with the supply wagons making the three-day trek to headquarters. Two guards rode with each wagon.

"Why haven't you men loaded your muskets?" I asked.

The guard grinned and nodded his head. "Oh, nowadays it be a safe trip. All the lobsters and loyalists has locked their selves up safe in New York. Nobody bothers us."

Thanks to the state of the roads, it was a rough trip. But at least the days were warm even though the maples had begun to change. Autumn's crisp approach made me dread the thought of another Valley Forge winter.

We crossed the Raritan River at New Brunswick and paralleled the stream upgrade to Middlebrook – a ridgetop New Jersey town.

Our first hint that we were nearing the town was the faint sound of tunes on the wind. The nearer we got, the louder the music. Once in Middlebrook itself we discovered a tremendous celebration underway.

A band was playing and numerous officers and their ladies were dancing a Virginia reel. General Steuben and General Greene were among the on-lookers. Towering above the crowd, General

Washington and another tall officer were receiving what looked like a ten-rod line of well-wishers.

I asked one of the teamsters, "What's this carousing all about?"

"I got no idea," he said. "Seems like they officers be havin' parties all the time. I just got to deliver this cargo, get some food and turn round and drive my team back to Philly."

I tried to report for duty, but a junior officer named Willard instead urged me instead to sample some punch.

"Nobody's working today," he said.

"Why?"

"Because today, September 22, is a special day for the lobsters. It is the anniversary of the crowning of King George III. Coronation day.

"So, the Continental Army marked this august occasion by dubbing it the King's Damnation Day." Apparently having sampled several cups of punch, he giggled at undue length.

"We all are relaxing," he added, "save for some sentries keeping their eyes glued to the east."

I accepted a cup of punch and he directed me toward a large sideboard laden with meat, smoked fish and small cakes.

Before I sipped I asked, "Only a few sentries?"

"Well, we also have a few patrols down on the plain," he said, pointing toward the densely wooded flatland below us. "We want to make sure the Redcoats are attending to their own revels in New York and not planning anything to embarrass us."

"Well, let the bastards try," I said. "We'll make a day of damnation for every single one of them."

"Oh, well said, Sir!"

Speaking was a lieutenant colonel across the sideboard from me. He asked, "And who are you with, Sir?"

I doffed my hat in salute. "I don't know now, Sir. I've just returned from injury leave."

"Was you at Monmouth?"

"Yes Sir. I had a company in General Greene's Division. But even though I'm commissioned, I'm no gentleman so I fear I be much out of place here. I was just hoping to locate my men and rejoin them."

"Oh, pshaw," he said. "We don't fret so much about such distinctions now. But really, Sir, we must get you into proper uniform."

"Sorry, Sir. I own only my rifle and the clothes on my back." I didn't mention my kitbag full of the stockings Alice knitted for me.

"Sir, permit me to introduce myself. I am Lieutenant Colonel Tilghman."

"Your servant, Sir," I said. "And come to think of it, I believe I recognize you. Did I not see you with His Excellency during the Delaware crossing the night before our Trenton victory?"

"Indeed? And your name?"

"I am Rob Scot, Sir. I was in the third boat across and my half-company led the way to the east of town."

"Then, Sir, we are comrades in arms. All the more reason we must find your uniform."

"But…"

"I speak of the uniforms from France. The French have sent us money, muskets and now uniforms. The French navy aids us too and we may hope one day to have French soldiers and engineers."

He looked up and snapped his fingers. "Ensign Willard!"

"Sir?"

"Do you take Captain Scot to the undercroft and help him find a captain's uniform. Double quick! I wish to present him to General Washington."

"Oh, Sir," I said. "You needn't bother. I have been honored to meet His Excellency three times, I believe."

"Without uniform, I wager."

"Well, yes…"

"Then, Sir, kindly permit the ensign to guide you to the uniforms and then back to me."

# # #

The uniform certainly looked impressive – a heavy blue coat with red facings, white waistcoat and white trousers – full-length, not pantaloons. It was stiff, nowhere near as comfortable as farm clothing.

So I not only felt stiff, but was stiff when Colonel Tilghman said, "Your Excellency, may I present Captain Scot who was with us at Monmouth."

I removed my hat and bowed.

Instead of speaking to me, the general almost grinned. He turned to his wife. "Look you, my dear. I believe this is the young man who threw himself at your feet one snowy night at Boston."

She beamed. "Oh yes, Old Man. Indeed, I remember. You look like a perfect soldier now, Sir. And, how, pray is the lady friend you brought to me and Mrs. Adams?"

"We are husband and wife now, Lady Washington. She busies herself knitting the most wonderful warm stockings. And we may have expectations."

She congratulated me as did the general who immediately turned to a tall man by his side. "General Lafayette, may I present Captain Scot, of Massachusetts."

The general smiled and reached to shake my hand. "Do you know zee baron Steuben?" he asked.

"Yes Sir, last winter I was proud to be one of his most diligent students."

"Well, I wanted you to know I am zee only general in ziss army to 'ave more names that he."

"Indeed? How many, Sir?"

"Oh, zut, I 'ave lost count – zey are Marie-Joseph Paul Yves Roch Gilbert Motier de Lafayette."

"Good Lord, Sir, the baron must be jealous."

He chuckled as I moved on.

As I left the reception line, another colonel spoke up. "Tell me, captain, in which regiment do you serve?"

"Colonel Archer's regiment when last I heard. I canna say how the regiment faired. We was in General Greene's Division and I was unconscious when the battle ended. At the moment, I know not where it may be or whether they still include me."

He smiled. "Do please call upon us at headquarters on the morrow and we may be able to help."

Colonel Tilghman interposed. "I'll guide him from here, Alex. The man's not had a chance to eat a thing, let alone sample the punch."

My impressions of my first meeting with Lieutenant Colonel Alexander Hamilton were nil because that instant I spotted a familiar face in the crowd.

I couldn't believe it. I looked again and shouted, "YOU, by God!

"YOU!" I yelled again.

I dropped my platter and bellowed, "I'll have your bloody hide!"

Eyes wide, Jonathan Simpson spotted me, turned and ran.

I vaulted over the sideboard and tried to sprint toward him. Too many guests were in the way, gawking at me. I couldn't work through the crowd fast enough to waylay him.

Chapter 43
Frustration

In an ungainly, limping run, Simpson was nearing the line of horses when four burly soldiers intercepted me and wrestled me to the ground.

I recognized one of General Washington's personal guards and bashed him on the jaw, but the others quickly pinioned my arms.

"Damn you," I snarled, "he's escaping!"

They ignored my words. They stood me up and turned me to face Colonel Tilghman whose face was brick red, a thick vein standing out in his forehead.

"What the devil are you playing at, Sir?"

"Why the devil have you stopped me, Sir? That man has escaped! He's a loyalist and a murderer. He's responsible for the death of my mother-in-law and the destruction of my wife's farm. Near Sudbury Massachusetts."

"That is a ridiculous allegation," Colonel Hamilton snapped. "Charles Mason is a patriot from Rhode Island who was injured in battle."

I shouted "Absolutely not, Sir! I wounded the bastard two winters ago when he was fleeing from justice and after he murdered one of his own compatriots in order to escape...oh, and, Colonel, his name isna Mason but Simpson! Jonathan Simpson! I submit to you he probably was here as an agent of the crown."

Looking daggers at me, General Washington loomed behind Hamilton. "Can anyone verify these charges you're making?"

I calmed myself and lowered my voice. "Yes indeed, Sir, Captain Dan Marshall. He led our retaliation against Simpson. May these gentlemen release me, Sir?"

He nodded to them and my arms were free.

"Captain Marshall at the time was with the Massachusetts militia. Perhaps you gentlemen remember our group driving cattle to your headquarters after we hanged three of the raiders who were terrorizing the Rutland area.

"Indeed, I do recollect that," Tilghman said.

"Yes," the general said. "And I recall meeting you, young man, several times it seems. Perhaps, Colonel, it would make sense for one of the guard to pursue this Mason or Simpson fellow and place him under arrest. If he is, indeed, what Captain Scot says, then he would fly toward New York, would he not?"

Colonel Hamilton turned to one of the men behind me. "See to it," he said. "At least three gallopers, I would say. Keep an eye skinned for ambushes."

The colonel turned to me. "Until this matter is cleared up, captain, it might be wise for you to remain at headquarters."

"I understand, Sir," I said, brushing soil and leaves from my new uniform.

"As I see it," he added, "Mr. Simpson's or Mr. Mason's flight attests to the truth of what you say. Nonetheless, it would be good for you to stay with us so that we can get your details down on paper."

# # #

The riders came back next morning emptyhanded. I spent three frustrating months with headquarters.

Messengers at last located Captain Marshall, now a major, with a New England regiment in winter quarters at West Point.

I begged Colonel Tilghman to be assigned to my old company at West Point, but he urged me to be patient.

"General Lafayette was impressed by your impetuosity," he said, "and he's thinking he might like to have you as part of his command. At this juncture, however, he doesn't know how big his command will be or where it will be."

I gathered from those words that General Washington hadn't decided whether to keep the army near New York, or to send regiments south to the Carolinas.

That wasn't His Excellency's only concern. After returning from a long visit to Congress in Philadelphia he seemed dejected.

One night I overheard him complain to Lady Washington about how some Congressmen now seemed much more interested in enriching themselves than supporting the troops who defend them.

"'Tis indecent, Martha, how they luxuriate when our own people go hungry. I had to attend dinners where they served scores of courses. Scores, madam! Yet they had no thought for our men. And at a time our money is losing value, they run prices upward just to increase their own gain.

"At first I thought the common folk were our great handicap. But now I believe the merchant class have that honor. They buy Paris fashions for their wives – yes, and their mistresses – and feed with gluttony."

He said much of the problem was that leaders like John Adams were absent. Others, like Sam Adams and Joseph Reed no longer could deliver the votes to support the Continental Army.

I chuckled at her reply.

"Old Man, you worry too much. 'Tis turning your hair gray."

# # #

As least I had one good bit of news as I wrote to Alice.

My Dear Mrs. Scot –
You probably know this already but so far The Almighty this year
blest us with a most temperate Winter. We have rc'd almost no
snow and they tell us the temperature keeps on staying above
freezing, I very much hope it is the same for you at the farm. And I
pray that you are keeping warm for you <u>and for the little life</u>
<u>within</u>. For sure my feet stay warm thanks to the wonderful
stockings that you knitted for me. We have had no battles at all
and very little sickness. But I did see that Jonathan Simpson. He
was at a celebration <u>right here</u> at Gn'l W's Headquarters. When
he saw me his face turned white. Too bad, he got away. We
believe he's now in New York with the rest of the Redcoats and
Turncoats. I miss you very much. If I end up where I requested
mayhap I can visit you come spring.
With all my love, yr Dear Husband

Chapter 44
Attacking The Tribes

I anticipated rejoining my regiment at West Point after completing a lengthy report regarding Jonathan Simpson.

As so often happens, the Army had other plans.

Through late June, headquarters used me as a Steuben-style drill master, browbeating platoons and companies of new recruits into the intricacies of battleground maneuver.

Then at the end of the month, Willard – now a lieutenant in the adjutant's office -- informed me I was one of six captains ordered to accompany a big supply column to central Pennsylvania where we'd report to Major General John Sullivan.

"The general has been preparing an expedition against the Iroquois Indians," he said, "and he needs company commanders."

"I don't fancy fighting Indians," I said. "My war has been with the Redcoats and the Hessians."

"With respect, Sir," Willard said, "your war is a matter of General Washington's choice, not of your own."

I couldn't quarrel with that statement.

"And it so happens," he added, "the Iroquois have allied themselves with the redcoats and have done much damage to us."

# # #

Before we reported to the Sullivan Expedition, Lieutenant Colonel Mifflin of General Washington's staff gave us a run-down.

"General Sullivan now will to settle some scores with Joseph Brant and the other savages and loyalists who have burned and pillaged so many settlements in New York and Pennsylvania.

"His Excellency gave General Sullivan fifteen regiments of infantry and one regiment of artillery – a force of about three thousand men. He desires not merely that we fight the Indians.

"Here! I will read directly from his order."

*The immediate objects are the total destruction and
devastation of their settlements, and the capture of as
many prisoners of every age and sex as possible. It will
be essential to ruin their crops now in the ground and
prevent their planting more. You will not by any means
listen to any overture of peace before the total ruinment
of their settlements is effected.*

One of my fellow captains asked, "Sir, what are the lobsters likely to do when we attack their allies?"

"Probably nothing," Mifflin replied. "They haven't the strength right now.

"The British force in the city of New York is much reduced," he said. "You probably heard that England decided to make war on the French in the Caribbean using eight thousand redcoats taken from New York's garrison.

"Meanwhile, General Washington gulled the British into the fear that we are to launch a new attack into Canada. It is a feint merely, but to find reinforcements, Canada has pulled five lobster regiments from New York's garrison.

"In short, gentlemen, the redcoats can defend and hold the city of New York, but they haven't power to obstruct our attack on their allies two hundred miles away on the frontiers.

"We expect to pretty much have a free hand in dealing with the savages."

# # #

General Sullivan had divided his command. My comrades and I joined his troops on the far side of the Pocono Mountains.

Sullivan's second, General Clinton – now a brevet major general – took the other half of the command into west central New York.

My orders put me in charge of a company of light infantry leading the New Jersey Brigade. My men were new to the army itself, but most had served in the militia. Even better, they were tough farm boys, so setting a hot pace through Pennsylvania's stifling forests didn't bother them unduly.

Once we joined Sullivan's force, the next three weeks were little more than a march because the Indians fled before us, abandoning their villages. Per General Washington's orders, we immediately put all their wigwams and all their crops to the torch.

I became disgusted to learn that a surveying crew was with the company which followed mine.

Even as we went about starting fires, they set up their transits and began recording their readings.

"You've surveying the lands so Congress can know what's out here, right?"

"Well, Cap'n, that's supposed to be why we're along. But if I've got it aright, I believe there's some in Congress wants these meets and bounds recorded so as to take over this Indian land for their own."

"How 'bout you? You want some of this land?"

He started shaking his head.

"Nossir, Cap'n! I ain't about to bring no wife and kiddies out here. Just watch! After we're gone them devils will come back. They'll slaughter any white folk on their land. Can't blame 'em, neither. Nope! Not me."

I fretted that our actions might provoke counterattacks, but none occurred. Even so, I kept scouts well out front and to our flanks as we moved through those endless wooded hills.

The scouts often sighted Indians…but only tribal scouts, never war bands.

One of my scouts, Lucas Jones, was an old hand on the frontier. "I seen a pair of them first thing again this morning," he told me. "They was kind of bold, just staying there until I got a few rods from them.

"One of 'em shook his musket at me and then faded into the trees. And I seen lots of tracks, all of 'em pointing west. Just like the other settlements we seen, the whole village just up and fled from us."

"When?"

"Can't say. A week? Yesterday, maybe. Ain't rained of late so can't tell for sure, but they're all fleeing…women, children, old folks, and warriors."

In fact, it never rained during our expedition.

By parching crops in the fields, the drought helped us burn a destructive path. Smoke from our blazes cloaked the countryside so we coughed constantly.

At night the sky glowed red, not only from our crop fires, but also far to the north. Maybe as far as New York the night sky also glowed red.

We reckoned the glow reflected fires that Clinton's force set in burning their own paths of destruction.

Chapter 45
Adoption

Meeting no resistance at all, we worked our way north.

Actually, we burned our way north.

In mid-August, We took our only prisoner.

Johnson called to me just after he and I passed through another empty settlement. Troops coming behind us began kindling the fires.

"Cap'n! Over here! We finally got us a Indian prisoner, but she ain't worth much."

I dismounted and he led me off a trail to point out an Indian girl who looked maybe eight years old. She was squatting beside the body of a very old white-haired woman.

I asked, "Hey, sorry. Was she your mother?"

The girl stared into the trees, showing no awareness of us.

"Acts sick in the brain," Lucas said. "Probably oughta knock her in the head. Otherwise, she'll just grow up and start shucking out more Indians."

"For God's sake, Lucas, I'm not killing a child. Maybe she can be brought up with white folk."

He nodded. "Didn't think of that. Could be she'd be make a good servant for some family."

"A slave, you mean?"

"Yep. I seen some Indian slaves. Had to be whipped now and then. Pretty stubborn, but I hear they are very hardy and can be hard workers."

I said, "Lucas, I know what you're talking about. Used to get whipped myself."

He stared at me.

"I was indentured starting at about this girl's age," I said. "Got beaten quite a bit. It made me stubborn, now I think about it.

"Know what?" I said. "I think I'll just bring this little squaw along with us."

"She's a bit young," Lucas said. Then he leered at me, "But in six years or so I'll reckon she'd give you some sport."

I glared at him and he chuckled.

I grasped the girl's hands and pulled her to her feet. She glanced at my face. "Drink?" I asked, extending my canteen to her. She just looked at it.

When I pulled the cork and pantomimed tilting the vessel to my mouth, my meaning dawned. She nodded her head, took the canteen and drank deeply.

She wiped her lips with her hand, met my eyes with hers and gave another nod.

Taking her by the hand I started to lead her to my horse. She pulled her hand away and turned back to look at the body. She spoke a few words – I supposed a prayer -- and returned to me, tears coursing down her cheeks.

She watched as the troops moved from wigwam to wigwam, making sure each was alight.

Because the weather was dry, the outer bark shells first went up in flame, smoke and flying sparks, leaving behind glowing skeletons that were the wooden frameworks.

She didn't sob, but her tears flowed again. I tried to divert her by slapping my chest. "I am Rob. Rob!" Then I pointed to her. "You?"

She wiped her eyes and frowned. I repeated the exercise. This time I pointed to my chest. "Rob!" Then I pointed at her and raised my eyebrows.

Another nod. She ducked her head and whispered something like "Dissi."

I said, "What?" I cupped my hand behind my ear and asked "Whaaaaat?"

Lucas, who had been watching us, snorted and walked away. Behind him, fire began roaring across a nearby corn field..

The girl followed Lucas with her eyes. Then she gave me a glance and said, "Name *Diindiisi*."

"Oh, you speak English."

"Little," she said.

"You hungry?"

She frowned, so I patted my stomach. "Hungry? Food? Do you want to eat?"

This time I got a vigorous nod. "Eat! Yes!"

I brought out an oil cloth pouch from my saddle bag. From it, I handed her two corn cakes – Pennsylvanians often call them corn pones -- and two strips of beef jerky.

She gripped one of the jerky pieces in her snowy teeth and yanked off a bite. It took about three minutes for her to wrap herself around the jerky and corn cakes. She pointed to the canteen, "*Nebe?*"

I passed it to her and she drank again.

I poured a puddle of water into my palm, pointed at it and said, "*Nebe?*"

She gave me a nod and a slight smile.

The smoke and flame spread toward us. Riding double, the girl clinging to my belt, we followed Johnson and the scouts to the west, upwind from the fires.

As our troops emerged from the village, they spooked several deer which went bounding toward the hills to the west. We also began receiving a noisy protest from a gang of angry Jays.

"Oh!" the girl pointed to the birds. "*Diindiisi! Diindiisi!*"

I pointed to her and said. "*Dindeese?*"

"No!" she said firmly. "*Diindiisi.*"

"From now on, child, I'm calling you Jay."

# # #

General Clinton's New York contingent linked up with us in Sullivan's force at Fort Tioga just south of the New York frontier.

A member of Clinton's staff spoke Mahican, one of the Iroquois tongues, so I persuaded him to speak with *Diindiisi*.

After speaking with her, he told me her dialect differed from his. Nonetheless, he learned that *Diindiisi* was nine summers old and an orphan.

The dead woman with whom we found her was her paternal grandmother.

She said the grandmother sickened and collapsed during the evacuation of the village.

Having no parents or other family, the child stayed with her. When the girl awakened at dawn two days later, the old lady was dead.

Not knowing where the villagers had gone, *Diindiisi* – Jay as I shall call her hereafter -- waited by the body, reconciled to being killed when the white invaders arrived.

Chapter 46
The Newtown Assault

After resting, we troops in Sullivan's and Clinton's combined force crossed back north across the New York frontier.

For those of us who'd been with Sullivan, Clinton was a source of curiosity. One of our lieutenants asked General Sullivan whether General Clinton was any relation to the British general of the same name.

"On that question," Sullivan grinned, "I shall defer to General Clinton himself."

Clinton, a peppery gentleman with a lantern jaw, said "Thank you, Sir, I certainly wish to clarify that matter."

He cleared his throat. "Before the revolution," he said, "I was a lawyer practicing at New Windsor in New York.

"That redcoated officer who happens to bear my family's name and who currently commands the hostile forces occupying the City of New York is no relation at all to me – not of *any* kind whatsoever.

"To avert any further confusion, I'm wish to point out that I am plain old Brigadier General Johnny Clinton and he is Lieutenant General Lord Henry Clinton."

All of us laughed. And then we moved out on the next leg of the expedition.

As before, we encountered no resistance.

But then, as we approached a riverside village known as Newtown, a rifleman from Clinton's advance party came trotting back to us with news.

"Looks to us scouts like the Indians is fixing to ambush us," he said. "One of our boys got up in a tree and claimed he seen a breastwork dug clear across the toe of that big hill." He waved his hand toward a massif in our path.

The hill, thick with pine and oak forest, was steep and high. It extended northwest maybe a mile, the river flowing parallel to its south face.

We could barely see Newtown itself, a cluster of Indian dwellings nestled maybe a half-mile distant betwixt the river and the hill's south slope.

The rifleman went back to report to the generals and I sent Lucas Johnson and two other scouts forward to reconnoiter the area. Meanwhile, I took Jay back to headquarters and ordered one of the horse holders there to watch after her.

The scouts were back in an hour.

"'Tis breastworks for sure," Johnson said.

"Looks like they dug it chest-deep and maybe a half-mile long. They got it all covered over with branches and brush so's you can't see much. Main thing, it blocks us from moving directly along the river to the village.

"Way I see it," he said, "we should fire at the breastworks. Keep 'em occupied. And then we ought to send troops around to the right to climb that hill's north slope. Once our boys gain the crest they either can come down and attack the breastwork from behind or they could just go down t'other side of the hill to hit the village."

It took them almost four hours, but that's exactly the plan Generals Sullivan and Clinton concocted.

Of course, it didn't work out quite that way. It's been my experience that battles never do.

About mid-afternoon, we of the New Jersey Brigade and Hand's Rifle Brigade began demonstrating against the breastworks.

The artillery regiment, finally with something to do, began slamming grapeshot into the woods at the base of the hill, slashing down all manner of trees and brush around the breastworks.

"We ain't really hurting them," Johnson told me. "They're hunkered down in their trench."

"Maybe," I said, "but it looks to me like some of 'em are in a panic. Between cannon shots, I'm seeing people jump out from behind the breastworks and flee uphill into the woods."

At least that's what I thought they were doing.

Meanwhile, Clinton led his New York and New Hampshire regiments along the base of the hill's north face. Then they started to climb.

Whoever commanded the Indians must have seen Clinton's flanking movement and twigged onto his intentions.

So what I thought were Indians running away from artillery actually was large number of warriors improvising their own ambush.

The way I heard it, those who climbed the hill formed up in the woods and attacked headlong into the front and flank of the 2nd New Hampshire as it crested the hill.

Johnson was the first among us to make out what was happening. Pointing toward the hill's crest, he said, "Cap'n, see the gunsmoke up there? Them Indians are hitting Clinton's boys."

The same realization dawned upon the rifle brigade and the rest of the New Jersey brigade, so we quit demonstrating and charged to attack into the toe of the hill.

We far outnumbered the Indians within the breastworks.

I felt personally outnumbered, however, when a screaming six-foot warrior vaulted from the trench swinging his war ax at my head. I managed to block the blow with my musket barrel. The impact slammed the weapon out of my hands but a soldier behind me shot my attacker.

Another Indian leaped at me thrusting a long knife toward my midsection. I seized his wrist and we teetered at the edge of the breastwork.

I'm strong, but the grease and sweat on his arms enabled him to slip my grip. I desperately grabbed his wrist again and again he wrested it from me, managing a good slash to my forearm.

Flinching, I fell backward into the trench. He landed on me, fury contorting his face. I grabbed his wrist again, but his strength seemed to double and he was using all his weight to push his blade toward my throat.

Johnson rammed his bayonet into the base of the Indian's skull. As he yanked the blade from the corpse, he gave me a sour grin. "Strong, ain't they?"

"Yes, by God, they are. Thank you for my life, Lucas."

He nodded. As I recovered my musket, a little knot of warriors, two of them wearing British red coats, the others naked to the waist, ran up the trench toward us.

Two of my men fired their muskets. None of the rest of us was loaded so we barreled into the Indians with our bayonets.

Two of them ran, and a third hurled his war ax into our midst. Our charge broke up the rest of the attack which seemed to be a delaying sacrifice, to enable other warriors to retreat.

With them, a stream of Indian families hot-footed it along the river, abandoning the village. A small group of Indians armed with muskets retreated too, but slowly. They were a well-disciplined rear guard.

We didn't pursue.

Our men just got busy setting fire to everything.

Jay hissed at seeing my arm. She removed the surgeon's wrapping from the wound and hissed again. She disappeared for twenty minutes, returning with a large piece of honeycomb. After slathered honey on the gash, she used needle and thread from my housewife to stitch the wound.

As she stitched, I was the one doing the hissing.

Meanwhile, the surveyors unpacked their equipment and began work. They informed me the next morning that the hill overlooking the now-charred village was six hundred feet high.

Chapter 47
West Point

The battle of Newtown was the only real fight during the entire Sullivan Expedition. Compared with the Brandywine or Monmouth battles, it was little more than a two-hour skirmish.

Yet it gave me the scare of my life which still looms large in my nightmares.

I often awaken sweating…but with the grateful realization that a slippery demon warrior about to slit my throat is only a phantom.

Despite the lack of combat, the expedition probably was the most important Continental Army campaign of 1778. It certainly accomplished General Washington's strategy.

It nearly destroyed the Iroquois people.

Because we obliterated their food and destroyed their homes, the Iroquois fled by the thousands to Canada.

The way I heard it, the unprepared British did what little they could to feed and shelter the surge of refugees. Unfortunately, those families had the misfortune to arrive in Canada at the same time as one of the meanest winters on record.

A great many did not survive to see spring.

By 1780, however, a good many of the surviving warriors – now animated by pure hatred -- did exactly as the surveyor predicted. They filtered back through the forests of New York and Pennsylvania and as far south as Virginia and the Carolinas to murder whites who settled on or near their original villages.

But as a major military force supporting the British army and its loyalist allies, the Iroquois no longer counted

# # #

After the Newtown fight, the Sullivan expedition burned north into the villages of western New York's finger lakes region.

I left the force to head back toward civilization.

The Newtown fight left us with several wounded men, leg amputees, too badly injured to stay with the expedition.

And I had Jay in whom the Continental Army had not the slightest interest. Since her people had disappeared, my choice either was to abandon her in this forest wilderness or to look after her.

I applied to command the platoon which would accompany the wounded in wagons. Early in September, we turned east toward a fort on the Hudson River called West Point.

At first, the travel was rough, torturing the wounded because the rutted game trails were difficult for wagons. But the further east we progressed, the wider and smoother the tracks became.

At first, Jay was stone-faced, seeming withdrawn and depressed. After our first few days, however, she willingly copied me in pronouncing and learning English words.

My clumsy attempts to pronounce the Iroquois equivalents first puzzled her and then elicited wry smiles. Then giggles.

When I deliberately exaggerated my mispronunciations – especially trying to say *pejoshkwe* for horse -- she actually began laughing.

I also pretended special difficulty with *wawackee*, meaning deer. When I came up with *wuwalkuh,* she shook her head, laughing "Rob! No! No! No!"

Kakai for crow made sense to me because it seemed to imitate a crow's call. Likewise, when pronounced quickly, her name, *Diindiisi*, sounded much like an alarmed bluejay.

In the same way, her people named the owl for his call *Kokokoho.*

Some of the wounded men played along with our language game, at times almost convulsing Jay with laughter. She also began acted the clown with her own mispronunciations of English.

A certain warmth began to grow between us. I think she grasped I was trying to lift her spirits.

"Jay," I told her, "I wish I could explain how I was orphaned when I as about your age. Some day you'll know enough English that maybe I can tell you.

"But I'll say this much right now little girl, I'll do all I can to ease your sorrows rather than add to them like that old bastard VanderMolen did to mine."

One of the wounded men told me, "Don't worry, Cap'n Scot. I think she a'ready reckons that you're looking out for her. My little girl knew that about me 'afore she could even talk."

"I hope you're right."

"I am," he said. "Children know where they stand with their parents."

# # #

When at last we arrived at West Point, I had a happy reunion with Sergeant Liddle and the newly-promoted Sergeant Hannon.

Hannon tried to charm Jay by bowing and proposing to kiss her hand.

She snatched her hand away, but gave him a coquettish grin, flicking her eyes sideways at him.

"Ooch," he said, "though she's but a child, she's already after bein' a charmer. Mark my words, Cap'n, in a few years you'll have to be standin' guard to keep the young lads away from this lovely little girl."

Both men seemed downcast because of bad news.

"The lobsters havena been up to much here in New England," Liddle said, "but they, the loyalists and the bloody Royal Navy captured two big seaports in the South – Savannah and Charleston. Now we hear they're raiding inland."

The cities' names meant little to me, but the sergeants said officers such as General Wayne, the West Point commander, were depressed about it.

"Mind you," Liddle said, "the general of late has boasted a bit, just like us troops. About two months back we assaulted and captured the British fort at Stony Point fifteen miles south of here on the Hudson.

"We attacked at night strictly with the bayonet," Hannon added, "and, don't you know, we so surprised 'em that we compelled four times our number to surrender.

"They was crying 'Quarter! Dear Americans, quarter!' I heard 'em, that I did."

"Aye, we captured muir than six hundred lobsters," Liddle said. "And the next day, we and our lobster prisoners together leveled that entire blessed fort. They were a mighty rum lot as ye might say because they had sweat so much when workin' to build it."

"Well," I asked, "what's to stop them from doing the same to you?"

Both men exploded in laughter.

"This West Point place ain't no little earth mound like Peekskill was, no nor a Stony Point fort."

The two sergeants said that the fortress called West Point was immense and complex.

"You haven't seen 'em yet," Hannon said, "but we've got redoubts with artillery on every road from the south.

"And the main fort has four 240-foot walls with a twenty-foot ditch before 'em. Plus we've got buried powder magazines, food and water for eight weeks and barracks for six hundred troops. Real brick barracks, would you believe?"

"Aye," Liddle added, "any lobster trying to attack us is going to find himsel' whacking at a hornets' nest."

"Well, what about the lobster ships?"

"Well, o' course, we've got artillery on the river. But, ho! you ain't seen the chain, now, have you?"

They explained that the entire fortress and its outworks was established adjoining a narrow S-shaped turn in the Hudson River. And lying across the river at its narrows was a gigantic iron chain, six hundred feet long and kept at the river's surface, being stapled to massive floating tree trunks.

"We'll be hauling it all into shore here in a week or so," Hannon said. "Otherwise winter's ice pack would destroy it.

"But meantime, any of His Majesty's ships coming up here would have to tack, and practically stop when doing it, to turn and sail west into that river bend. And that's where the chain lays."

"Aye," Liddle added, "and dinna forget yon timber boom that's floating but thirty paces downstream from it.

"So the whole time they'd be trying to turn through the wind and batter against the boom and chain, our artillery would be pounding them."

"How big are the links in the chain?"

"Ah, Cap'n, 'tis a braw, ponderous thing. Each link is two foot long and is a bit over a hunderdweight.

"T'would wreak desperate oonderwater damage to any of His bloody Majesty's frigates trying to sail through it."

Chapter 48
The Hardest Winter

As Jay and I and our horses crossed the Hudson on a ferry, we gawked at the tidal current breaking over the massive chain and boom.

Then we started riding due east.

"Where we go?"

"Our home and my wife," I said.

It took some work to explain the word "wife" but when I demonstrated holding a baby in my arms, Jay nodded and her big black eyes lit up. "Understand."

We faced a six-day journey from West Point to Boston's environs. And from its start, the trek was pure misery.

Though it was only early October, the weather was cold and windy with overmuch of rain and sleet.

We didn't have the clothing to handle what nature swirled around us. Knowing Western Massachusetts abounded in loyalists I had no intention of seeking shelter in people's homes.

Fortunately, *Lobster Claw* brought down two big deer and we reversed their uncured hides to serve as rain capes.

When I started gutting and skinning the first deer, Jay jumped right into the task with me. She not only was better than I at skinning, but she also was the more clever at separating sinew to serve as laces.

As we rode, we resumed our word games. I had a hard time remembering that *wajak* and *wonkis* meant muskrat and fox. But I had no trouble with *waboz* for rabbit. In fact I found myself wondering. The English and Scots use the word "hare" so I couldn't help asking myself whether early colonists might have created the word "rabbit" by borrowing from the Indian "waboz."

We regretted rarely catching sight of *Kizis* or *Tibik-kizis* – the sun and moon – but *Makwa*, the bear, and *Esiban,* Mr. Raccoon, alarmed both of us when they scented our kills and spooked our horses.

The further east we progressed, the more I worried about how Alice might respond to Jay...or, for that matter, how my Indian daughter might react to my wife.

I estimated we were perhaps five miles from home when the first of winter's savage blizzards struck us. It seemed to me that we had a good bayonet-length of snow on the ground by the time we arrived at the Fletcher farm.

It wasn't the snow that bothered us so much as the knifing north wind which numbed our bodies and faces.

As we approached the little house, the door opened and Alice came out. She squinted into the wind and pointed her musket at us. "Keep your distance!"

"Alice! It's Rob! Can you let us..."

She dropped the weapon, ran through the snow toward me screaming, "Oh, Robbbb!"

I dismounted in time to hug her.

As the wind whipped at us, she looked up at Jay still on her horse and ordered, "Inside! Inside, 'afore we all catch our deaths."

# # #

Jay and I thawed ourselves by turning front to back again and again in front of the fireplace.

Teeth chattering, I said, "Alice, please to meet Jay. She's an orphan..."

She scolded, "Yes, Mr. Scott, she's a frozen orphan. You ought not have had her out in this weather." She enfolded Jay in her arms. "Welcome, child. Welcome!"

Jay looked puzzled, then she smiled at me over Alice's shoulder. She said something I didn't recognize and pulled away from the hug. She placed her palm on Alice's stomach and gave a big smile and again said something.

Alice grinned. "Yes. Baby."

I got my coat and deerskin back on. "I've got to tend to the horses. You gals fix us some dinner."

By the time I returned, frozen again, I could hear them chattering happily. Alice was busy explaining pan, kettle, pot, plate and spoon. Jay was responding, I suspect, that Indian women cooked much the same food with exactly the same implements.

After supper, I fixed up a pallet for our guest and then Alice and I retired. We snuggled in each other's arms, happy and warm as the wind howled outside.

The storm petered out the next afternoon and we looked out to see blinding sunshine on huge snow drifts. Neither Alice nor I could remember so much snow at all, let alone so early in the season.

The scenery, or perhaps the icy cold, seemed to depress Jay who began a sort of discordant humming.

Alice looked a question at me.

"I don't know," I said. "I think it could be kind of a funeral song for her folk. Without their homes, this kind of weather would be deadly."

"Why without homes?"

I explained what the Sullivan Expedition had done in New York and Pennsylvania.

"This horrible war," she said. "We all seem to lose."

She went to drape a comforting arm around Jay's shoulder. The gesture reminded me of the night we first met when Alice tried to comfort her newly-widowed mother.

Despite *Diindiisi's* sorrow, October marked the beginning of the most wonderful – if hardest -- winter of my life.

Alice was beautiful as her pregnancy advanced. With Alice's help, our orphan steadily learned more English. Jay mastered the alphabet and began to learn reading and writing.

She seemed to glow with pride the day she printed her original Iroquois name. Soon Alice began calling her *Diindiisi*. Eventually, I did too, though I stuck with Jay as a teasing nickname.

As Alice's time approached, the three of us engaged in long discussions about names. Were the child a boy, I held out for

MacDonald, to honor my foster father, and the first name Isaac, after Alice's father.

I didn't care much about girls' names, but Alice and Jay certainly did. Finally I seem to recall they settled on Mary and Otsi'tsa, her people's word for flower.

It turned out they'd have to wait on that one.

For in mid-March – just as the worst of the drifts melted so I could fetch a neighbor lady to help – Alice brought our son into the world.

Master Isaac MacDonald Scot appeared to me to be an ugly squally little mite. I had the wit to act pleased and to praise his beauty – even though he looked ugly to me.

Because Alice labored for nearly twenty hours, she was utterly spent. Jay was a tremendous help to her in the next weeks, shooing me from the little house so she could cook and feed and care for my wife.

Chapter 49
The Southern War

I anticipated rejoining my regiment at West Point, but in late May none other than Sergeant Liddle banged upon our door.

"You again, Sam! I get the horrors when I see you. What now!"

"Oh my captain, you maun coom tae Boston with me. A guid part of the army is heided south."

"South? To where?"

"Ah don't ken the place. Somewhere in the Carolinas. But they need us regulars to help recover from some disasters."

"What disasters?"

"Well, as you recall hearing, the lobsters captured Savannah in South Carolina last year.

"So now this spring they captured Charleston, another big port in South Carolina. Worse yet, we heard that along with Charleston, the lobsters also netted a whole American army *and* its bloody general.

"And the victor was our auld friend Cornwallis – him what we scourged so bad along the Princeton-Trenton gauntlet."

"Oh." I said, "and now they want us to put some salt on that bird's trail?"

"We think that's how it's to work out," Liddle said. "First, though, General Gates has been put in command in the south, so he gets his shot at the lobsters."

"That sounds good," I said. "It may be they won't need us. Remember Gates it was who captured a whole British army up north at Bennington and Freeman's Farm."

"The same," Liddle said. "So mayhap this summer he can do to Cornwallis what he did three years ago to General Burgoyne."

"Then why in hell do they need me? I kind of had it in mind to retire with my family."

My words shocked Liddle. "How can ye say that, Cap'n, after filling in all those enlistment papers for people to serve the duration? Sir, you're just like me -- a Continental Army regular until we kick the redcoats out of the United States."

# # #

My dawn farewell a week later to Alice, little Isaac and *Diindiisi* was the most painful moment I've endured since my mother's lingering death.

After Sam arrived, I took an entire six days to wallow in my family, the last afternoon holding a pig roast for all of us, including the neighbor midwife and her husband, and Sam, of course.

As I turned the spit, I smiled at the memory of warnings men gave me during the Sullivan expedition when I spoke of Alice's pregnancy.

"Laddy, ye know, don't ye, that once the babe is at yer wife's breast, she'll have little place nor time for you. Mothers work awfu' hard to keep them infants alive through the first year what with croop and colic and rashes and all. So, the missus got no energy for no rompin' at night, neither."

It didn't work out that way. Alice, to be sure, focused her entire being on our son. But, for that matter, so did I. And I found it a wonderful daily sight to see Alice nursing Isaac when I came in from the fields.

Being a stout, healthy, noisy little brat he made me proud.

Our Indian daughter helped tremendously with the infant so that at night Alice at least could snuggle with me, murmuring most sweetly.

That last morning, however, in the midst of her last hug, Alice dropped all tenderness. She crisply ordered, "Captain Rob Scot, I charge you to write to me regular."

"I promise I will."

"Yes, and you can start right after you arrive in Boston."

Diindiisi came to hug and kiss me.

"My father, I charge you come home safe."

"I shall. Bless you, my daughter, and I beg you please to look after your brother and mother."

As we rode away, Liddle said, "Cap'n, you have become one fortunate man."

"True, Sam, though right now I am dreadful sorrowful."

"Of course," he said. "Ah tell ye, if 'tis in my power, one day Ah'll return you alive and whole to your family. And I'll seek the assistance of that disgusting Irishman, Patrick Hannon."

"I'm thanking you in advance, sergeant."

# # #

We spent a busy month assembling troops on our old Bunker Hill battleground uphill from a now-rebuilding Charleston. I actually found time to write two letters – one to Alice and one to Jay.

As time came to depart Boston, I groused to Liddle that our little company of eighty would suffer a miserable voyage to North Carolina.

"Oh, dinna fret," he said. "Mayhap, some of you'll get sick because a schooner can be lively when out to sea. But, Cap'n, it'll likely be a fast passage, perhaps only a week or so."

"So I'll be heaving my guts the whole time."

"Ah doubt it, Sir. Not after the first day or two. But even then ye'll be fortunate compared to what our enemies go through.

"Imagine five hundred redcoats crammed in the belowdecks bilged stench of one of them rotten auld trooper ships.

"Those ships' hulls are so overgrown with weed and barnacles," he explained, "that they canna make muir than five knots. And if the wind be contrary, then they must sail a zig-zag course, tacking a dozen or muir times a day.

"A schooner is twice as fast as a Royal Navy vessel and needn't tack so often 'cause she sails much closer to the wind. And when the schooner does tack, why with that fore-and-aft rig, it takes hardly three minutes compared to maybe thirty minutes for one of them square-rigged troop ships.

"Oh, yes, and if the puir lobsters are lucky, they have leave to go up on deck for fresh air maybe one hour each day. Otherwise, they live just like prisoners below decks in them hulks.

"So, yes, you might get sick," Liddle said, "but you'll have fresh air most of the time. And when we land, you'll be up and about the next morning right as rain.

"When lobsters coom ashore from a month in a slow convoy, they can hardly walk. They need a week or muir to recover. Some might never recover."

"But won't their navy try to stop us, Sam?"

He gave a short bark of a laugh. "Cap'n they may wish to, but that's all. Oh, aye, the British Navy claims to rule the ocean waves and even the Hudson and East Rivers.

"But His bluidy Majesty's fleet – which this year also needs worry about the French and Spanish fleets – hasn't the ships to control our coastal waters or our small ports. Yankee schooners sail back and forth between New England and Virginia and the Carolinas all the time with damned little Royal Navy interference."

# # #

As Sam predicted, our schooner landed us after five days at sea. We came ashore at New Bern in North Carolina. I was grateful for our fast passage, but once on land, I wanted to get back aboard and return north.

Boston in June often is sultry, but to someone like me from Massachusetts, North Carolina's heat and humidity were staggering.

"I can't believe it, Sam. The temperature is near 100 degrees and it's *foggy*! I'd far rather be on a vessel at sea enjoying the breeze."

"Aye," he said, mopping at his face, "and Ah hear it becomes even hotter in August."

Beyond complaining, we had much to do -- getting ourselves and our supplies ashore, oiling our rifles and muskets and protecting made cartridges from mist and dew.

Above all, we got busy locating other arriving Continental Army units.

Chapter 50
Carolina Torture

Our orders were to catch up with General Gates' army of regulars and militia that already had opened its campaign into South Carolina.

In the next ten days, we hiked inland about a hundred fifty miles to a tiny burg called Cross Creek. By the time we arrived, I believe my blood was thinned enough that the soggy heat didn't smother me quite so bad.

The rain was another matter.

It either poured or misted most of every day. As we sloshed past some of the natives they said we'd arrived at the height of the rainy season. "Leastways," one of them crowed, "y'all won't be getting' much sunburn right now."

The downpour, however, was only part of the problem. For the first two nights in North Carolina, flooding made it hard to find places to sleep.

We still were splashing along about dusk when one of our young recruits, a lad named Peter Jones, summed it best. "I swear before God, sarge, them sailors let us off that schooner *way* too early. Fact is, they never really landed because I believe we still are in the ocean. It's just too shallow for ships and too deep to walk."

"Jones!" Liddle snapped. "Hush your damned greeting. Aye, 'tis swampy here, but that's all. We just got to keep going and we'll be out of this onto dry ground afore long."

Jones's buddy, Private Willy Billingham, couldn't keep his gob shut. "Awwww sarge, I wager there ain't no dry ground in this place. And how we gonna sleep? You can't get no shut-eye laying in a foot of water."

The third grouse in the group, Zach Saddler, a quiet young giant, told us he wanted to apply for a transfer to the Dry Tortugas.

"Where's that?" Billingham asked.

"Don't know," Saddler said. "Heard about it from a uncle what's a seaman."

"What did he tell you about it?"

"Nothing," Saddler said, "I just like the name. Dry Tortugas. Sounds mighty appealing."

We were lucky to find and bed down upon an elevated road graveled with ground-up sea shells. First, though, we had to kick away numerous serpents who slithered onto the roadway to escape the flooding.

But even with the copperheads, water moccasins and rattlers gone, I can't say we rested, because that's when the biting bugs swarmed.

Now when we walked, the critters were content to whine or buzz in our ears. We were accustomed to that. Mosquitos were all-to-familiar companions on our marches in New Jersey and New York.

But Carolina mosquitos had some nasty little allies.

Maybe the worst were midges. Those tiny blood-suckers massed at the corners of our eyes, mouths and nostrils and took up housekeeping in our ears.

"I don't know," Billingham said. "Maybe the black flies are even worse. The devils slurp your blood wherever they find a speck of bare skin they can rip open with a sawblade. Bastards!"

The bugs gave us a choice.

"At night," Jones said, "we can cover ourselves with our blankets and lie there sweltering and getting no sleep.

"Or we can throw off the blankets," Billingham added, "and be unmercifully needled and getting no sleep."

I will agree that of a morning, the men in our company looked like walking misery. Red-eyed and haggard, they scratched constantly at skin pebbled with tiny pink bumps intermingled with half-inch crimson welts.

Some folk we met sold us sure-fire remedies to keep the bugs away. "Just rub it on ya skin, soldier boy, that keeps them little suckers off."

After he tried one of the nostrums, Jones agreed that the potions were successful – in making money, that is, for the people selling them. "They made lots of money," Jones said. "And the bugs kept getting lots of blood."

We encountered an aged Indian who informed us, "Onliest thang that keeps off noseeums and flies be bear grease."

Billingham asked, "Do you have any bear grease?"

"Yep."

"Can you sell us some?"

"Don't have enough."

"Well, where can we get it?"

"Kill you a bear."

# # #

At Cross Creek we joined a slowly growing assembly of Continental regulars. General Gates hadn't waited for us, having marched a week earlier into South Carolina to take the fight directly to the British.

We enjoyed a reunion with Patrick Hannon, now the topkick of another light infantry company. He complained about recently having to peel strips of fragile skin dangling from his face.

"Before the rains came, the sun down here was cruel to us fair-skinned folk," Hannon groaned. "I niver knew that smilin' nor yet frownin' could be so painful."

He grinned. "It forces me to take an occasional tincture of the baby's hair."

"The what?"

"Oooch, it has many names. A wee sup of the cruel. Some calls it *uiscebrou.*"

"You mean whiskey?"

"Yes, the same."

Liddle asked, "Now, Pat, be it the sun or the pain-killer what's makin' you stagger so."

"By the saints, Sam, I believe 'tis the sun."

"When it's cloudy and rainin' thus?"

"Well…"

# # #

A dark-skinned man with a rifle joined us. "Gennlemen, may I interrupt? Name of Jimmy Tolliver. A militia lieutenant."

"Welcome, lieutenant. I'm Cap'n Rob Scot. Bein' as how I'm a rifleman 'tis always a pleasure to meet another."

"Thank you, Sir," he said. "I'm with a militia troop what's honored with guiding you newcomers. And I wanted to advise your sergeant that while a lot of fellas in these parts do favor drinking corn, if'n the bugs has chewed them so bad as you Yankees, they'd slather on some goose grease…and on sunburn, too."

"Goose grease?"

"Yessir, it's what our mommas do with small children afore they get a good tan like I have now."

Liddle asked, "The grease makes you tan?"

"No, sergeant, it just eases the itch and the burn until old sol leathers you. And after that you ain't quite so appetizing to the bugs."

"Makes sense," Liddle said. "We often got real serious burns when at sea in the tropics. And we spread a lot of goose grease on 'em."

"Lieutenant," I said, "we heard tell that bear grease keeps the bugs off."

"Cap'n, that's an old Indian remedy. Pretty good, they say. Trouble is, ain't many bear around these parts. T'other trouble is that after a few days the smell gets so bad it keeps away not just bugs but ever'body."

"So, Jimmy" I asked, "have you seen much of the redcoats?"

"Indeed we have, Sir. Once the lobsters captivated Savannah, they seemed to feel they had conquered South Carolina. They got even worse after they took Charleston.

"So they set up little garrisons all over the colony, to protect the Tories and loyalists.

"Well, some South Carolina folk didn't see it that way no how. People here always fight among themselves anyway – Church of England folks agin' the Presbyterians. Baptists and Presbyterians agin' each other, all of 'em hating the Catholics.

"Some loyalists rose up about the time of Bunker Hill and the Whigs crushed 'em. But now with lobster support, the loyalists keep cropping up.

"So some of us from North Carolina been circulating over there doing our best to make life hell for the lobsters and loyalists."

"It sounds kind of like a patchwork," I said.

"Well it is," Toliver said. "But lately, some loyalists quit feeling quite so loyal. We started spreading the word that British generals wanted to recruit their sons for service as Hessian soldiers."

"No!" Hannon laughed. "Sure and I can't believe they'd do that!"

"Oh, warn't true," Tolliver grinned. "Our invention. But the story sure stirred up lots of folk. Then that tale kind of dovetailed with General Clinton's move."

"What was that?"

"Well, the British offered amnesty to anyone who had rebelled at first and then thought better of it. Then Clinton offered to parole those people who rebelled again' the crown. A lot of them accepted the parole and just quit the fight.

"But then just a month ago or so, Clinton revoked the parole for anybody who doesn't join up and fight for the king. Otherwise, they're to be treated as rebels in arms again' the king and be immediately hanged.

"That came as a hell of a shock to a lot of folk who figured they were protected. After that, Clinton returned to his headquarters in New York leaving Cornwallis to handle the mess.

"I got no sympathy for Cornwallis, but revoking the parole really riled people who wanted to be neutral. Now they worry they might either wind up dangling from a gibbet or serving with Hessians.

It ain't helped the King's cause much that lobster and Hessian troops steal a lot of grain and cattle from folks hereabouts."

He took a deep breath.

"Worse, sometimes."

"How do you mean, Sir?"

"Well, there's this big troop of mixed cavalry and infantry called Tarleton's Legion. It's a band of Tories and redcoats led by a lobster colonel.

"The legion scouts and raids for Cornwallis. Sometimes it just murders, like it did my own family. I hope one day to meet personal with Colonel Banastre Tarleton."

I was about to say I hoped he would, too, when Private Saddler came running to us.

"Cap'n! We just heard it from a messenger. Cornwallis has defeated Gates. Place called Camden.

"The messenger said the Redcoats captured quite a few of Gates's troops and sent the rest running, and Gates along with it."

"God help us," Hannon said.

Chapter 51
Marking Time

The news of Gates' defeat was crushing for us...and it kept getting worse.

Out of a force of four thousand men, Gates – the hero who captured Burgoyne and all his regulars -- lost almost half his own troops in casualties and captures.

Also making the rounds was a tale that Gates himself didn't merely retreat but that he fled all the way to Virginia.

"The way I heard it," one of the rumor-mongers told us, "is the cowardly old bastard would be in Maryland if his horse hadn't died under him."

The story caused Sergeant Hannon, never a calm sort, to turn pale. "Sure, and hearin' about that redcoat victory hits me just like it did when the lobsters captured New York..."

"Stop that talk right now, Pat!" I snapped. "We don't want our troops giving up hope and deserting like they did back in '76."

He raised his shoulder and ducked his head. "Well, Cap'n," he pleaded in a harsh whisper, "with our southern field army so badly beaten, what the hell are we going to *do*?"

"Sergeant," I said, "if you'll take a deep breath and remember, we lost Brooklyn and New York but then we scored lots of small victories of our own. Remember Harlem Heights? And seems to me we scored a pretty good-sized victory over Cornwallis himself at Trenton. Remember *that*?"

Liddle looked up with a grin. "In fact, Pat, we ended up making life so hard on the redcoats that they've just stayed stoock in New York and never venturing forth, right? We been through this before," he added. "We can do it again. So buck up, boyo!"

Toliver said, "It surely is bad news. But we don't need Gates or his army. There's plenty of fight left down here."

I asked what he meant.

"We militia – sometimes they call us partisans -- been harrying the lobsters in South Carolina ever since they arrived two years ago," he said. "Our people stay out of sight and, when we can, we strike around their outposts and attack the convoys that supply them. We also hit their foraging parties.

"Besides that," he said, "we got two other commanders down here with a lot more sense than most regulars."

"Who?"

"One is a fellow called Thomas Sumter, a militia brigadier general. They calls him the Carolina Gamecock. He just purely lives to fight. Been wounded twice, but he and his men keep the fight going all over the hill country to the north.

"Last month, Sumter and his boys attacked the British outpost at Hanging Rock up there. In the end, they couldn't capture the place, but during their attack, they killed nearly two hundred lobsters for a dozen of their own.

"The other commander is a fella name of Francis Marion. He's a farmer just like Sumter. In fact, they practically was neighbors afore the lobsters burnt their homes.

"Anyhow, Marion is a Continental regular. I believe he's a lieutenant colonel. Did a lot of fighting in the Indian wars. He's a sickly-looking little duck, but he knows what he's doing."

"So he wasn't serving in Gates's army?"

"Hell, no! Gates don't want anything to do with either man, see, 'cause their troops don't salute or wear pretty uniforms. Neither Marion or Sumter goes in much for marching or ceremony. And the way I hear it, Sumter just plain don't like taking orders from anybody, neither.

"Anyhow," Toliver told me, " I have worked with Marion. For the past six months, he has kept stirring the pot all over the south part of the state.

"He's been such a trial for the British that they call him the Swamp Fox. That's because he and his boys – militia, Whigs, anybody what's got a horse and is willing to fight – hide in the swamps and harass the British and loyalist outposts."

"With much success?"

"They ain't captured any outposts. But the way I hear it, Marion and his boys drive Cornwallis wild. They wear down his troops by destroying wagon trains that supply the lobster outposts.

"They also destroy mills that loyalists and lobsters need. They burned up all the boats along the Santee and Pee Dee rivers. Then Marion arranged for teams of riflemen to pick off redcoats and Tories trying to cross the fords.

"It's gotten so the loyalists and the British daren't send a party nowhere without a big escort. The lobsters we capture claim to be whipped from all their marching and countermarching."

I said, "It sounds to me just like it was in New Jersey and New York."

"Well, then, you know this kind of fighting," Toliver said, "Marion's men operate on horseback. Local folks tip them off to targets. They ride out, strike, and get back into the swamps in just a few hours. Cornwallis's people can't never find 'em."

"Where do we find the colonel?"

"Right now, without horses, you don't. He's at least a week-long hike from here, over in the swamps along the Pee Dee River. We all best stay here for now until we see what develops."

# # #

A few days later, the other officers and I were briefed by a major from headquarters.

"Men, it gives me pleasure to report that, contrary to many vicious rumors, General Gates did *not* flee to Virginia.

"Right now he's headquartered just over the line in North Carolina, at Charlotte. He's trying to rebuild the army. For now, we're under orders to proceed in that direction. Looks like about a hundred thirty miles west – an eight or nine-day hike."

It turned out to be a bit longer. We couldn't march directly west to Charlotte because of so much flooding. Instead, our guides took us northwest to Salisbury where we could cross the Pee Dee, and then head southwest to Charlotte.

But at Salisbury, a giant general named Dan Morgan halted us and took charge.

I'd glimpsed Morgan when he led a band of riflemen at Bunker Hill and saw him again at Monmouth. But this was the first occasion I met him up close.

I'm taller than most men, but the general towered over me.

"Sir," I told him, "it seems to me that mayhap you could look down on General Washington himself."

His hard face broke into a broad smile. "Yep. I'd say by three inches or then some. I'm six foot seven."

I chuckled when he leaned to me with a pretend confidential whisper, "I always stoop a bit when I'm around His Excellency. He don't like to be shown up."

Morgan was like that, often joking not only with officers but also privates in the line. My chat with him came after one of his staff, a Major Ledger, directed us to camp around Salisbury.

"We have scarce provender here," the major told us, "but there's practically none to the east in Charlotte, so General Gates required that we send no troops to him. He said they would starve."

"So just how do you go about building an army," Private Jones whispered to Private Saddler, "if you got no food for new troops?"

Liddle said, "Shut up, youngster."

# # #

August gave way to September, cooling and drying us…and making us nervous.

Major Ledger confided, "We keep hearing reports that this is exactly the kind of weather Cornwallis wants. Much easier on his troops.

"Supposedly, he plans to lead his army, about eight thousand men, in an attack into North Carolina. They say he plans on moving right through Charlotte and then Salisbury."

"Well, if that's the head lobster's plan," Billingham said, "it seems to me like we're camping in the perzactly the wrong place."

Major Ledger looked furious at the comment but Liddle stepped in

"Nahhh lad," he said. "This be the *right* place. If Cornwallis tries to attack here we'll get athwart his column and whip his arse just like we did on the road to Trenton. Ain't that right, boys?"

We all nodded and grinned.

Later when we were alone I asked Liddle, "D'you really believe that?"

"Nope, Cap'n, not when they so outnumber us.

"But we dinna want these bairns becomin' scared to death, now do we?"

Chapter 52
Revival!

Instead of invaders, mid-October brought us exciting and positively reviving news.

I called my company together. "Men, I told Sergeant Hannon something like this would happen – just like Trenton back in '76. Should have made a wager with him.

"Cornwallis sent a Tory force way up into the hills about a hundred miles northwest of here. Wanted to get better control of the area. It was a big troop, about eleven hundred men, and a lobster colonel was leading it.

"Well...a lot of riflemen came out of those mountains, took on the Tories and trapped them for the kill at a place called King's Mountain.

"About nine hundred of them riflemen surrounded more'n a thousand Tories. Killed three hundred or thereabouts and the lobster colonel, of course. They captured eight hundred more...all for the cost of twenty-eight militia dead."

The company exploded in cheers. After the noise subsided, Sergeant Hannon yelled, "Hey lads, it ain't the king's mountain any longer! What say, maybe we ought change the name to 'Patriot Mountain' or how about 'Whig Mountain'?"

It took a while for the cheers to die down again.

I believe the cheering would have lasted much longer had we also known that the King's Mountain victory forced Cornwallis to postpone his plan to invade North Carolina.

Within days, two other items of exhilarating news heartened us.

First, Congress fired General Gates.

At the same time, we learned George Washington appointed Nathaniel Greene to command the entire Southern Department.

"Men," I told our company, "this news is as good as King's Mountain. Sergeants Hannon and Liddle and I have served under General Greene. He's earned a reputation of being thrifty with his men's lives and generous in food and supplies for them. Things are going to start looking up."

Of course, when the general arrived he didn't have much of an army to command.

Thanks to Gates's defeat back in August, the army was down to fewer than a thousand men. And because supplies were so scarce, our troops were scattered in both Carolinas.

The general arrived in December, delaying in Virginia to badger Mr. Jefferson, the governor, to start sending supplies to us. He also left his second-in-command, General Steuben, in Virginia to organize the supply flow.

Once in North Carolina, General Greene also contacted Colonel Marion and Brigadier Sumter to include them in his plans and to ask their suggestions.

We light infantry from Massachusetts, however, didn't get to see the new commander.

Late in December he gave a quarter of his army, including us, to General Morgan with orders to maneuver along the Carolinas' common border.

Calling ourselves Morgan's Flying Army and attacking wherever possible, we three hundred men moved as fast in those hills as our legs could carry us.

As we moved, our numbers grew.

News of King's Mountain brought militia and some veteran regulars to us. So did Morgan's reputation as a brawling fighter and a friendly, back-slapping leader.

Veteran companies from Virginia arrived at our camp almost daily. So did Carolinians along with militia and riflemen from the hills. Also joining us was a tough little cavalry unit led by a Colonel Washington, a distant cousin of General Washington.

By the time we welcomed in the New Year, our little army had tripled to nearly a thousand men. The weather was cold and we often had to hike through a shallow snow cover. The cold bothered southerners but those of us from the north found it exhilarating compared to a Carolina summer.

Spies informed us General Cornwallis ordered Tarleton's Legion to stalk and destroy us or, at the very least, to keep us separated from Charlotte where Greene concentrated his men.

I can't speak for anyone else, but the men in my company, even the brand-new enlistees, were itching for a fight.

Colonel Washington's dragoons informed us in mid-January that Tarleton's force was hot on our tails, camping but six miles away.

Single-handedly, I think, General Morgan readied us for the British assault. The general was half-crippled by rheumatism, but nothing was wrong with his brain.

He staged our little army in three sections, a screen of skirmishers in front of a line of militia which, in turn, screened a third line composed of regulars.

He first explained his battle plan to us officers then detailed us to make sure the men understood. "I want them to know every particular of the plan," he told us, "so that when our lines retire there will be no panic."

We did exactly as he bid us.

"Boys, when they attack," I explained, "our company will be in the first line as skirmishers."

Jones, Saddler and Billingham glanced at each other with widened eyes.

"We will bleed them with three volleys. Then we'll retire squad by squad back to the second line…they'll be about a hundred fifty paces to our rear.

"The second line will bleed them again. Three more volleys. After that, the second line will fall back to the third line.

"Now, men, the lobsters won't see the third line. It'll be behind yonder ridge. So they'll come tearing over that crest chasing what they think is a broken enemy. Imagine the surprise when we give them ten or fifteen volleys."

"That will finish the job!

"One more thing, boys. When I say retire, I mean we walk – understand? *Walk!* We walk backwards, with a loaded weapon, firing when need be and then reloading. We keep facing our enemy. No running! That only encourages the lobsters and dispirits your own comrades."

I wanted to settle in for a good night's sleep, but worry about tomorrow kept me awake – along with occasional bursts of laughter.

The laughter was General Morgan's fault.

He spent much of the evening limping from camp fire to camp fire cracking jokes with the men and grousing comically about his aches and pains.

He also explained his battle plan over and over to the men. He slapped their backs and told them how proud their sweethearts and parents would be after the victory.

# # #

I explained to you that we won the revolutionary war way back in 1776.

The king and his ministers, being bull-headed folk, just wouldn't believe it.

They finally saw the light in 1781...after we bludgeoned their forces straight three times.

Chapter 53
The Legion Attacks

The year's first British defeat started just after dawn January 17 at a place called Cowpens in South Carolina.

We staged ourselves on a broad meadow. It sloped upward from a scattered woods to a low ridge at its north end. Locals called it Cowpens because they used it as a pasture where they penned herds during cattle drives.

Maybe Colonel Tarleton reckoned he could drive us like so many cattle.

He opened his attack by sending fifty green-clad dragoons to break up our skirmish line in the wooded end of the field.

Somebody yelled, "I see 'em coming! Make ready!"

As the saber-waving horsemen cantered into view, I raised and cocked *Lobster Claw*. Kicking up mud and snow, the dragoons looked huge and unstoppable

I settled my sights on a rider bent forward over his steed's neck.

My rifle and twenty-some muskets cracked in our first volley.

Wounded horses and men screamed as we reloaded in the gray smoke. Sawing at the reins, the surviving dragoons regained control of their panicked, whinnying mounts, turned and galloped south out of range.

"Hey," Hannon jeered. "What a lovely sight we're seein', lads, them lobsters showin' us their backs and horses' tails.

Maybe a dozen dragoons lay writhing in the snow while a half-dozen horses rolled and kicked in agony, coating themselves in churned mud.

I asked, "What do you think, Pat? Infantry next?"

"Bloody right," Hannon said, "Likely light infantry. Sure, and they'll be too spread for us to rely on volley fire. Every man must pick his target."

We waited fifteen minutes before the next attack…a line of mixed light infantry, dismounted dragoons in green, lobsters in red and some Hessians in green.

They were practiced skirmishers, keeping well apart, often dashing from tree to tree, moving much more rapidly than an ordinary infantry line.

"Okay, men," I called, "mind that you attend to their officers and sergeants first."

My first target was an officer who either didn't realize he was within range or he thought to impress his enemies with his courage.

Maybe he was just stupid.

He marched erect at rigid attention in plain view looking like a toy soldier, even resting his sword point on his shoulder.

"Watch this," I called to Hannon. "I'll get him at a hundred paces."

"Oooch, you'll nivver do it."

Liddle chuckled. "Just watch!"

Crack!

The ball spun the officer and he collapsed onto his side. Another man went to look at him and turned away.

Several of the dead officer's comrades yelled and fired toward us, their shots whacking among the tree limbs above.

Jones yelled back, "Very, very bad shooting!"

Liddle snapped, "Shut your gob, lad. Dinna let them know your position. They fired 'cause they want the smoke. Makes them harder for us to see. So take care to stay behind your tree."

"Oh!"

"Right, heed your own aim and shooting. Remember to aim low. Fire at their knees."

"Yes, sergeant."

Tarleton's skirmishers now were coming into musket range.

"Right, men," I yelled, "time to pepper the lobsters."

Irregular firing broke out along our line, as one man after another spotted a target and pulled his trigger,

Tarleton's men returned our fire and kept pressing toward us. As they took casualties they slowed, but they kept coming.

One lobster startled us by leaning to shoot from behind a nearby tree. His shot notched a branch just above Liddle's head.

"Ouch!" Liddle yelped.

"Sam," I asked, "are you hurt?"

"Naa, just some splinters hit the side of my head."

Saddler spotted the redcoat's jerky reloading movements and fired, producing a scream then cursing, "Damn you, you shit!"

"First platoon," I called, 'Tis time to retire. By squads now. Take them, Pat, and be careful."

"Right, Cap'n, Sir. I'll see you soon."

As the sergeant led First Platoon to the rear, we did all we could to redouble our fire to keep the lobsters' heads down.

They, of course, knew exactly what we were doing. They tried to rush closer, the better to pick off our people now moving backward over a hundred fifty yards of wide-open meadow.

The distance must have seemed like miles to Hannon and his people. Yet when I glanced back, they were well spread out and nobody was running. Their conduct filled me with pride. Nothing takes more courage than to retreat at a measured pace when under fire.

Next came our turn.

"Backward, men, and steady!"

As we backed perhaps fifty feet from the tree line, three lobster skirmishers came running to kneel near our old positions. When they raised their muskets to pick us off, my fear magnified the bores of their weapons, making them look enormous.

I took aim but several shots rattled from behind us, knocking two of the redcoats backward. The third jumped up to shelter himself behind a tree.

Hannon had kept a squad kneeling in the field to cover us.

As we loaded, fired and moved backward past Hannon's team, I called, "Thanks, Pat. We appreciated your help."

Billingham said, "Sorry, Sir, Sergeant Hannon was hit and killed." Saddler nodded in confirmation.

Beside me, Liddle stopped and choked, "No!"

I grabbed his sleeve, "Come on, Sam. We must get to the line. We'll mourn him later."

He looked at me furiously, then nodded. "Come on, men!"

We made our way to join the second line, militia ranked two deep in four regiments spread over almost five hundred yards They had their muskets at port arms, looking steady. And ready

The main British attack now emerged from the woods in six regiments. Moving in line, shoulder-to-shoulder, bayonets fixed, they swept up the slope towards us.

They looked impressive, their drums rumbling, the soldiers bellowing a deep "Huzzah!" about every three steps.

Our orders were to scream back at them with frontier war whoops we imitated from the Indians. I found that the "Yip! Yip! Yip!" screeches relaxed and even emboldened us.

Jones, though, found it difficult. "My God, will you just look at the lobsters?"

Liddle turned to him, "Hey, they look unstoppable, right?" Billingham and Jones both nodded.

"You're wrong!" Liddle yelled.

"They are but men, just like Pat Hannon. One musket ball is all it takes.

"Now Jones? Billingham? Saddler? All of you! Remember the plan! When the orders come, three volleys. Take out their sergeants and officers, and then we retire behind the ridge."

All of us turned left sides toward the advancing redcoats.

We raised our weapons and cocked them.

Chapter 54
Victory!

We took aim when it seemed the lobsters looked so close that we could have spit on them.

General Pickins, the militia commander, bellowed "FIRE!"

Three hundred militia muskets went off in a single shattering thunderclap.

At a range of fifteen yards, heavy musket balls devastated the front of the British line, bashing scores of redcoats backward into their comrades, knocking down many in the second line.

With my ears still ringing, I barely heard the surviving redcoat officers and sergeants shouting. "Steady there! Get up! Face yer front. Close in! Close in, damn you! Forrrrrward!"

The redcoats resumed their advance, staggering toward us over the tumbled line of dead and writhing wounded.

Twenty seconds later we delivered another sheet of gunfire, stunning them once more. But, being professionals and veterans, they recovered and fired a volley in our direction.

Firing uphill, most of them shot above us, just as at Bunker Hill. The blast was shockingly impressive – enough so that it caused some of our militia to start backing to the rear early.

Beside me, Billingham jerked, dropped his musket and fell to all fours. He coughed a huge gout of blood and collapsed to his side.

Jones' eyes goggled. But he and Saddler automatically ripped open cartridges to prime their muskets, and then grounded the weapons to feed in powder and ball.

As we officers and sergeants reloaded, we kept bellowing, "Steady! Steaaaaady, men!" In my ringing ears our voices sounded as tiny as childrens' cries.

Most of our men managed to reload. We leveled our firearms and blasted them the third time, wreaking havoc again.

As the redcoats sagged and recovered, we backtracked up and over the gentle slope of the ridge.

Once there, we sprinted to the side, passing from the front of General Morgan's last line -- five hundred Continental regulars on the reverse slope, muskets loaded and cocked.

We aligned ourselves on the right flank just as the yelling redcoats poured over the crest of the ridge.

They ran into pure hell – murderous rolling volleys from their front and, as we got into position, volleys ripping into their flank, fire they couldn't return.

We and the Continentals held them for five minutes them in that wicked cross-fire.

Then something occurred that we'd never, ever seen before.

The Continentals fixed bayonets and charged right at the lobsters.

And the redcoats broke.

Some fled, others dropped their muskets, fell to their knees, raised their hands and pleaded "Quarter! Quarter!"

I peered about, fearing that Tarleton's dragoons might yet charge. sabering their way into our flank and turning defeat into victory.

It didn't happen.

I didn't learn until later that at the climax of the battle, General Morgan ordered Colonel Washington to charge with his dragoons into Tarleton's rear.

That melee ended the battle, Tarleton himself barely managed to escape with his own dragoons.

In less than thirty minutes, thanks to superior generalship, we had destroyed Tarleton's Legion, amounting to roughly a quarter of Cornwallis's army.

Tarleton left behind more than a hundred dead and eight hundred prisoners, many of them wounded.

It was the first British defeat of the new year – actually a rout.

Chapter 55
Aftermath

A headquarters officer told me General Morgan was so elated over Tarleton's rout that he picked up a little drummer boy and kissed him on both cheeks.

Liddle and I didn't feel like celebrating.

By late morning, while our troops busied themselves looting the dead and collecting weapons, the two of us went back out onto the field to find Pat Hannon.

It took time. Battle had strewn a great many corpses across the pasture.

Some lay stretched full length, arms outflung, as if taken down from a crucifix. Others lay curled as if sleeping. Yet others showed gaping wounds where the soft lead balls had torn bellies, legs or chests wide open.

Pat lay on his right side, right arm pointed south, head resting on that arm. His eyes were half-open, but his expression was one of puzzlement, as if curious why we were digging the grave for him.

It took us an hour or so to lay Hannon to rest.

After we shoveled earth onto him, I tried to pray. "For Patrick Hannon, who I recall said he was from Sligo in Ireland, blessed be his soul…"

A voice startled us.

"Beggin' your pardon, Sir…" We turned about to see a British corporal lying behind us. With a groan he sat upright. "I suppose I was stunned during the brawl but, any roads, I may be knowin' the words ye need. I heard officers say them so many times."

"I don't know about that," I said. "He was a Catholic."

"By now his church don't make much odds, do it?" He gave a sardonic smile. "For months we been buryin' 'em all – Catholics, CofE, Methodists, the Kirk – using the same words. It don't matter to the dead."

I nodded. "Well said, corporal. Please to go ahead."

He tried to stand, but his bloodied left leg wouldn't support him. "No disrespect, Sir, but I best say it from down here. I think it goes this way…"

He cleared his throat. "Unto you Almighty God we now commend the soul of our brother, and we commit his body to the earth; earth to earth, ashes to ashes, dust to dust, in sure and certain hope of the resurrection into eternal life."

He faltered. "Then, Sir, there was summat about '…earth shall give up her dead.' but I'm sorry, Sir. I'm still a bit mazed. Can't remember no more."

"Thank you, corporal. Better than I could do."

Liddle and I lifted the redcoat from the ground. With his arms over our shoulders we walked him up the slope toward the line of wounded waiting outside a surgery tent.

"Corporal, I have a question for you."

"What's that, Sir?"

"We saw a lot of redcoat dead and wounded. Seems to me your uniforms and equipment looked worn."

"Oh, beg pardon, Sir, but our kit is bloody well ruined. They ain't issued any us new kit since long afore last summer, an' we been marching and fighting most all the time. Coats got holes in 'em and boot leather's about worn through, toes coming apart at the seams. A lot o' muskets are bad worn, too.

"We say it's all Clinton's fault. He hates General Cornwallis and he's hoardin' all the new kit up there in New York, whilst we do all the fightin' down here. We don't feed very well, neither.

"Fair's fair, Sir," he continued. "Can I ask you a question?"

"What's that?"

"If a body was to just take leave, as you might say, to disappear from the army and stay here, would he need permission of the likes of the Lord Lieutenant, or a squire, or some such to get a piece of land?"

Liddle laughed, "Corporal, we dinna have lords or their like here. Ye want land, ye go out on the frontier and just clear it and use the trees to build a place. That's what most of these folks around here done fifty or a hundred years ago."

"You're having me on!"

"No," I said. "That's why we're fighting this war. We don't want Parliament or King or a House of Lords running our lives.

"You get your leg patched up, you can do just like some of those Hessian prisoners done already – they just settle and become American. Starting up a farm ain't easy, we hear, but we've seen them doing so."

"Right," Liddle added. "But ye just got to be on guard that the Indians don't come along and kill you. Some of them get right touchy about white folk moving onto their land."

As we seated him in line, a wounded militia sergeant barked, "Why you bringing a goddamned lobster among us?"

"Shut your gob," Liddle snapped. "He isna lobster now. He's just another wounded soldier who helped us praying over our mate. Let him be or I'll see you wind up worse hurt than you are now."

A messenger trotted up and told me to report for an officers' meeting at headquarters. I left Liddle to look after our prisoner friend.

# # #

Morgan started the meeting saying, "You all did well today. And please don't forget," he added, "to give all laud and praise and honor to your men. They earned it. Steady, they were. Most steady. The militia do well when we use 'em right.

"Men, this is the second time in ninety days Americans destroyed one of General Cornwallis's forces. Our victory will dispirit loyalists in the Carolinas.

"I believe Cornwallis will have grave difficulty getting more support from loyalists. Moreover, I wager the loyalist support he does have will diminish. Thanks to our deeds this morning and those riflemen at King's Mountain, people more and more will gravitate to us."

He warned us, however, not to underrate Cornwallis, whom he said was the most able British commander. "He's worth three of Clinton or Howe," General Morgan said. "He's energetic, determined and a damned clever soldier. In all candor, I admit that frightens me."

I raised a hand. "Yes, Captain."

"Sir," I said, "I just finished talking with a prisoner who complained that their uniforms and other equipment are in bad repair. He said the food's scanty. We saw quite a few muskets with split stocks that they tried to staple together.

"He also spoke of bad blood twixt Clinton and Cornwallis."

General Morgan nodded. "We hear that," he said, "but don't let it fool you. Cornwallis's troops may be hungry and their equipment worn. But they're the most hardened soldiers in the south and they still outnumber us.

"Cornwallis will be after us and after General Greene with every means at his disposal. We must be very careful and – if I may – very agile in the weeks ahead."

"For now," he said, "we must march and march fast to effect a union betwixt General Greene and ourselves."

He paused.

"Gentlemen, we can have no carousing about this victory. Some day we all shall celebrate. But for now, we must refit and move. We must have our scouts out yet today and our main force marching tomorrow morning.

"General Greene is somewhere seventy or eighty miles east of us. He won't know of our victory for two days. Cornwallis probably will know tonight.

"If Cornwallis keeps us separated, his army -- being bigger than either of ours -- could defeat one and then the other and I fear our cause is doomed.

"But if we can combine with General Greene, I feel we can give his lordship and his redcoats a drubbing that will save our nation."

Chapter 56
The Foot Race

In the wake of a battle, even the unwounded victors feel battered and exhausted. So I shrank from the idea of marching, let alone forced marching.

But that's exactly what General Morgan demanded of us

"We must march northeast and we must march fast," he said.

"We depend on you light infantrymen to be always on our right, acting as a permanent guard against surprise. That means you may need to be a flying skirmish line.

"We must direct our army's efforts to see if we cannot safely veer east in order to join up with General Greene. Meanwhile, we know Cornwallis will make it his business to keep us from doing so. If he can, he will bring us to battle."

Eventually we who comprised Morgan's Flying Army did succeed in uniting with General Greene's Army.

Not by flying, though.

It took us a march of almost two hundred fifty miles from Cowpens in South Carolina, northeast across North Carolina to Boyd's Ferry on the Dan River in southern Virginia.

No, that's wrong. It wasn't a march.

It was a month-long aching, dragging slog through ankle-deep mud resulting from unending icy winter rain.

Yet though we all hated how the rain chilled and soaked us – and though we ached for the sun's warmth -- we also were grateful for the rain.

Twice along our route, downpours transformed rivers – the Catawba and the Yadkin -- into raging torrents that delayed the redcoat army which pursued us.

Twice, Cornwallis was forced to halt his pursuit several days waiting for the floods to subside.

Still – even though General Morgan allowed us only six hours a night to eat and rest – the redcoats almost caught us. For, just as General Morgan warned, Cornwallis was indeed was an energetic, enterprising soldier.

Even knowing his troops were half-starved, worn-out and sometimes feverish, Cornwallis decided to speed his pursuit by travelling light.

He ordered an enormous bonfire to destroy every wagon and tent in his army, plus all surplus clothing and even the officers' amenities such as beds. Beds and chairs burned especially brightly when splashed with brandy and wines.

The only things Cornwallis saved from the blaze were his ammunition and hundreds of supply train horses.

He mounted two soldiers on each horse and headed north, trying either to catch us or to wedge his force between us and Greene.

For every twenty miles we covered along the viscous Carolina paths, the redcoats were able to travel twenty-five.

During occasional dry spells, we set up hasty ambushes to back off some of his advanced patrols.

Still, when we crossed into Virginia, it was the surprise of our lives to find the bulk of Cornwallis's army hanging on our coattails.

Even after God's floods saved us from Cornwallis, the mass of lobsters was only four miles distant when -- finally united with Greene -- the last of our rear guard crossed the Dan River.

As we crossed, we destroyed every boat in sight, forcing the redcoats to give up and retreat south.

That same night, a horse patrol brought us a lobster deserter who looked about as gaunt as a scarecrow. He told us Cornwallis's men were near starvation.

"I heard the Gineral be taking the army back down inta North Carolina to a place wi' food. They calls it Hillsborough like. Our sar' major said it's only – *only!* – a fifty mile hike.

"Well, I'm wanting none of more marching, not wi' me boots wrapped in twine cause the stitching be falling apart. I'm done wi' this bloody war, I can tell you."

# # #

In Virginia, we also rested and refitted.

I think I slept about twenty hours before Liddle prodded me with his foot.

"Time to rise, Sir. Ye need your tea. The commanders is coming up with a new mission for us."

"Good God almighty, sergeant, what is it this time?"

"Oh, Ah think ye'll love the news, Cap'n. Soom of these Virginia regiments is startin' tae join us now, so we're going to come aboot, as ye might say."

"What do you mean?"

"Cap'n, we'll reverse course. Ah hear that General Greene believes we now outnumber Cornwallis. Our army little has grown while Cornwallis's has shrunk, and Cornwallis is getting no help at all from the loyalists.

"So now, we're going back into North Carolina to chase lobsters."

# # #

Cornwallis's army left Virginia February 13 and we light infantrymen followed. A week later. Greene's full army marched back into North Carolina.

It wasn't exactly a chase.

Greene and Cornwallis seemed to sidle back and forth, almost sparring like boxers at the start of a bout.

We light infantrymen on both sides formed kind of a thunder cloud between the two armies, often striking sparks.

We'd spot a company of lobsters and they'd take potshots to keep us away. The next day, Cornwallis's people might approach and we'd fire our rifles telling them, "Stay back, damn you."

The first real fight exploded February 25 when our cavalry, led by Colonel "Light Horse" Henry Lee, located and charged a gathering of Tory militia.

In ten minutes his sabers butchered ninety loyalists and slashed two hundred fifty others, ending any further local loyalist recruiting for Cornwallis.

Yet Pyle's Massacre, as they called it, only seemed to goad the British general. He now headed west from Hillsboro and General Greene moved his army south.

Though my company was only on our army's periphery, the pace of movement told us something big was coming. And Greene's army kept growing.

Now augmented by fifteen over-the-mountain riflemen, my company at last had a full complement of ninety.

The new men were a self-contained squad run by one Judah Morton, a rail-thin full-bearded fellow who was independent as a hog on ice. I asked if he was a lieutenant or a sergeant.

"We ain't got sich," he said. "I'm just the best shot so I'm kind of in charge. Now mister," he added, "we 'uns dasn't cotton to drills or marching or orders from outsiders, neither."

I asked, "Why did you join us, then?"

"That's on account of we wants to kill loyalists and redcoats. And because your fella Greene says if we want to kill them we got to work with you light infantry people."

"Well, Mr. Morton, if you want to kill with us, then we do have some rules."

"Like what?"

"Like we riflemen in this company do our best to get along with the musket boys. When we're picking off distant targets, they protect us from lobsters who get in close.

"Our motto is that we all try to be good to one another. And we follow my orders. I don't give too many of 'em though."

We haggled for some time. He became a bit hot until I suggested a shooting contest.

"What range? What targets?"

"Well, I don't know about range," I said. "How about we just find us some redcoats and see who does best?"

He gave a big grin.

That same afternoon, we spotted a five-man patrol of lobster horsemen – maybe some of Tarleton's survivors.

We took turns, Judah shooting first. I got three cavalrymen and he hit one plus one horse.

"I'd call it a draw," he said. "But that *Lobster Claw* of yourn is a hell of a raffle. And you're a good shot, too. So we'll do like you say, Rob, if you don't get too loud and uppity about it."

"Deal."

Chapter 57
Another Drubbing

On March 13, we received orders to proceed to Guilford Courthouse, a village maybe thirty miles south of the Virginia Line.

In an officers' conference next day, General Greene outlined a battle plan similar to that of Cowpens. We would allow redcoats to attack us through two collapsing militia lines, then counterattack with a final line of regulars and artillery.

The first line would be Carolina militia, novices to stand-up battle. Forming the second line would be militia who also were Continental veterans plus some veteran militia from Virginia.

Veteran Continental regulars would comprise the third.

"I don't like the ground," I told Liddle. "'Tis wooded -- heavily wooded and brush-choked near the village. Also the approach looks far longer and wider than Cowpens."

He nodded. "The lines will much further separated," he said. "Looks to be three hundred to five hundred yards between…a long, frightenin' way for militia amateurs tae retreat while under fire."

# # #

We had no choice, of course, and at noon March 15 the first redcoat column hove into view on a lane running through the center of our three lines.

Cornwallis spent a half hour positioning Highlanders and Hessians on his right, light infantry and grenadiers on the left. Three light cannon banged at us with little effect. Our four 6-pounders fired back, accomplishing nothing that we saw.

With a barked order, the British line stepped out toward us, drums beating, approaching in that deliberate, implacable-looking pace.

"Aye, lads, they do appear formidable," Liddle growled to the men, "but dinna ye forget, they're but men. Yer Charlies' musket balls will stop 'em deid."

When they were a hundred paces away, a second order came. The front rank of the advancing line leveled their muskets, pointing that glittering bayonet hedge directly at us.

The sight of those long blades was too much for a good many militia. Dozens fired their muskets and fled. Yet others scampered without bothering to shoot. Chasing them were hoots and catcalls from the bulk of their comrades, who stood fast.

As the Redcoats came within fifty yards, almost a thousand militia cocked their weapons and fired.

That massive volley blew large gaps in the advancing enemy ranks. As the militia began reloading their weapons, the line came on another dozen paces.

It stopped to fire its own volley.

The redcoats then charged with a deep-throated yell, hoping the militia wouldn't have time to get off a second volley.

But it did. The second volley ripped further gaps in the British ranks, stopping the charge dead.

Officers and NCOs rallied their men. "Close in, damn you! Face your front, ye stupid git! Now, grenadiers! Charrrrrrge!" The Redcoats stepped over their dead and wounded to charge again.

Then they stopped in surprise.

The volley's smoke faded away to reveal no enemy. The militia had disappeared.

Another line of rebels stood three hundred yards further away, muskets at the ready – much too far away to charge, so the march resumed.

Watching through the trees from the third line, I told Liddle, "I can't believe those lobsters' courage. I don't see how they can keep coming after taking fire like that."

"Aye, and knowin' they'll soon receive another? But mind you Rob, 'cept for the bluidy Hessians, lobsters and highlanders be our cousins. We're of the same land and stock. The army is their life and their home. In their boots we'd be nae different."

"I suppose."

From my vantage, Cornwallis's advancing troops suddenly disappeared in a quarter-mile bank of gray smoke. The splintering roar of the volley came to our ears an instant later.

The second line of militia had fired its first volley. Twenty seconds later they fired another, and then backed toward us in good order

Unbelievably to me, the British line came charging into a third volley. With that, the set-piece butchery dissolved into utter disorder.

As the British advance reached heavier woods near the village, opposing lines of men became struggling knots of bellowing adversaries fighting in the brush and among the trees.

Dozens of little melees mingled Hessian green, American blue and Scot and British red, as they shot and stabbed and clubbed and clawed at each other.

Nobody retreated, but the more numerous British advance pushed the militia back into our third line.

Liddle yelled, "We canna fire volleys intae that mob! We'd be killing our own."

"Right! We've got to charge into it and break up the lobsters. Come on, men! Bayonets, butts and boots!"

We piled into the attackers, converging on what seemed to remain of the British line's left flank.

Grenadiers – the biggest and strongest of the British troops – turned to meet us. They were grimy, white crossbelts gone tan with dust, tattered red coats either faded pink or maroon with mud.

But those things didn't matter.

The grim-faced redcoats fought like madmen, stabbing at us with long, wicked bayonets. A big scowling grenadier attacked me with the same stamping lunge I first saw six years earlier in Jan's house. "Ye'er deid, you fookin' Yankee!" He lunged too far, though, losing balance when steered his blade past me with my rifle's fore end. I slammed *Lobster Claw's* butt into his skull, retracting too late to avoid somebody else's bayonet tip ripping along my right ribs.

Before the Hessian could fully skewer me, Saddler jammed his own blade into my assailant's face. The scream was one of dozens echoing around us in the next five minutes.

I heard occasional shots as someone on one side or the other found a clear target. Otherwise it was all growling, grunting, screeches of agony, thudding, howling, "How's about two foot o' cold steel, you lobster shit!" cursing and furious shouts, "Ye bluidy whoreson! I'll do you noo!"

It came to a roaring halt when cannon blasted grapeshot into the brawl. It looked as if giant brooms swept bloody five-foot lanes through the brawl, shredding Americans, redcoats and Hessians alike.

The cannon fire broke the fight apart. Sides separated and we regulars felt free to resume fire – but independent shooting, for volleys could just do no good either in the dense woods area or the little village.

We found out later Cornwallis himself ordered his artillery to fire indiscriminately into both his men and their enemies.

We withdrew, leaving the battlefield to the lobsters. To keep the enemy at bay, we fired as we retreated. They fired back just to repay the insult.

The boys in the company looked to me to a bit depressed.

"Lads," I said, "I don't see this as defeat. We really bloodied the redcoats today. I'd say we inflicted a lot more casualties on them than they did on us."

I should have kept my gob shut because that's when a lobster ball came flying through the trees and knocked me flat.

Chapter 58
Recovering

I came to with Saddler holding me half upright and Liddle pouring water onto my face.

"Stop that," I sputtered.

"What happened?" I asked. "It feels like a damn horse be setting on my chest."

Jones held a misshapen musket ball before my eyes, "This thing hit you...*whup!*"

"Aye, we figure it to be a parting shot from the lobsters," Liddle said. "Mayhap a spent round or ricochet off'n a tree. Hit ye in the left breast. Knocked ye cold."

Saddler said, "How you feelin', Cap'n?"

"I have felt much better." I gasped, "It's hard to breathe. Must have knocked the wind out of me."

"We maun get ye tae the surgeon," Liddle said. "We looked. The ball didn't go in, but it put a mighty bruise on ye. Could have hurt yer heart. Surgeon ought tae give it a careful listen."

That was easier said than done.

The surgeons from both armies – eight of them, all told – were dealing with thousands of wounded soldiers. By the next morning, me still waiting my turn, amputated limbs lay in fly-buzzing mounds outside each of the hospital tents.

The dead still lay in long lines where volley fire killed them..

From my seat on a tree trunk next to a hospital tent, I watched troops from both sides walk among those lines of bodies.

Some of the walkers collected weapons to be turned in, I suppose, to armorers.

Others were looting both the wounded and the dead.

Yet others seemed to search among the casualties for wounded friends whom they could carry to hospital tents, as Saddler and Liddle had done with me.

At the tents, surgeons and assistants sorted us wounded into three categories.

The largest category seemed to me to be those who'd die soon. Though they were moaning with pain – by now they no longer had the strength to scream – they received no care at all.

The next category included those who possibly might survive if a shattered arm or leg were amputated.

Then there were those of us who might recover and be able to return to the ranks.

I fell into the care of a worn-looking Hessian.

When I pantomimed labored breathing, he impatiently pulled at my coat and shirt. I removed them painfully and he pressed his ear first to my chest and then to my back. Then he repeated the process.

"*Herz ist verletzt*," he said.

He poked the bruise and I flinched. "Like so, ja? Very bad. Rest now."

I frowned and shook my head. "I don't understand."

With a sour look he snapped "*Übersetzen Sie!*" to another man also in garments soaked and blackened with blood. "*Sie mussen sich ausruhen. Wochen, vielleicht monatelang.*"

He barked "*Raus!*" at me. Then he turned and rapped out, "*Nachester!*" beckoning impatiently to someone outside the tent flap.

The interpreter handed me my shirt and jacket.

"You must get out now making room for another man. Herr Doktor Schulte says your heart is serious bruising. You must rest weeks, maybe months.

"Now get out!"

Chapter 59
The End Nears

I didn't know it at the time, of course, but I wound up in an ideal position to watch our country's victory appear over the horizon.

So that I could *ausruhen* – rest, as the doctor ordered -- I was assigned to Baron Steuben's headquarters on the James River, fifty safe miles upstream from Richmond.

My duties at first involved little more than recording Major Ben Walker's translations of reports and letters the baron always dictated in French. Walker was General Steuben's interpreter from Valley Forge training days

But though my work was light, headquarters wasn't restful. Guttural French and German shouts mixed with English oaths burst minute-by-minute from the baron's office. "*Das Verdammte Arnold! Il est un souci constant pour nous. Bloody batard*! Fucker!"

With equal fervor, the general often damned Thomas Jefferson, Virginia's *stupide und dumm* governor.

Major Walker grinned and shook his head. "The baron frets most about General Benedict Arnold," he told me.

"That traitor's destruction of docks and factories around Richmond and other towns cuts into supplies for General Greene. The baron worries Cornwallis might move up here from North Carolina and join Arnold. Together they'd outnumber Greene.

"As for Governor Jefferson" he said with distaste, "he's a small-minded man. He refuses to give our troops help even though it would help him and his state."

At first, even my copy work tired me. It often was hard to sleep, too, because the baron worked well after midnight, often bellowing furious curses in his frustrations.

Eventually, though, three strolls a day helped me. By late May I could walk a brisk mile or so. As my stamina improved, Walker sought my help with intelligence gathering.

This meant regularly questioning scouts who kept tabs on Arnold for General Steuben. The major and I forwarded intelligence to General Washington outside New York City and to Count Rochambeau, commander of the French regiments now arriving in Rhode Island.

It was a nerve-wracking time for us. With only two militia companies for headquarters security, we could do nothing to stop Arnold's destruction of ports and plantations around Richmond.

General Greene was too far away to help. His regulars were sweeping up the redcoats' outposts near South Carolina's coast, three hundred miles distant.

"I suppose this is good news," I said, reading a new dispatch to the major. "General Washington has ordered Lafayette to join us in Virginia with twelve hundred regulars. His orders are to defeat Arnold and, if possible, capture and hang him."

The major whistled. Then he and I carried the news to the baron. "I don't see that Lafayette can handle Arnold," I said. "Arnold might be a goddamned traitor, but he's a very energetic, able soldier. Certainly more experienced than Lafayette, I think.

"Sir," I added, "in all candor I believe when Lafayette arrives, he'll attract flies."

"Ja," General Steuben laughed. "Fliegt mit red coats, eh?"

"Yes, Sir. Cornwallis will tear up here and take over Arnold's command. They'll greatly outnumber Lafayette. Cornwallis will try to defeat Lafayette first and then go after Greene with a superior force, maybe four or five thousand men."

The baron, previously so worked up about Cornwallis, now mystified us. "That maybe would be good,"

"Sir, I don't understand," the major said.

General Steuben shook his head. "*Das machts nichts.*" He waved us away in dismissal.

In the outer office, Major Walker told me, "The baron must know something we don't."

In truth, General Steuben didn't seem worried even after Cornwallis did come chasing into Virginia after Lafayette – not even when that incursion forced us to pack up and move our headquarters fifty miles south to the Roanoke River.

Fortunately, Lafayette eluded a Cornwallis trap. After that, Lafayette followed Cornwallis's force, always avoiding battle but always harassing and nipping at the Briton's heels.

In August, Cornwallis moved his weary forces to the British naval base at Yorktown. He put his troops to work digging trenches, underground shelters and a series of redoubts.

About then two important secrets came to light at our restored headquarters.

First, the baron informed us Cornwallis and his commander, General Clinton in New York City, despised each other. They were utterly opposed about what to do.

So they did virtually nothing.

Then the baron told us Washington and Rochambeau sent several thousand French and American regulars marching through Trenton and Philadelphia to Chesapeake Bay.

There they were to embark in boats and small ships for the 240-mile voyage down the bay to unite with Lafayette in Virginia. Also due soon was a French naval squadron bearing siege artillery.

Transporting that army was possible thanks to a miracle: a French fleet defeated a British fleet, giving French warships total control of Chesapeake Bay.

I wasn't there at the time, but General Steuben told us about it. "When General Vashinton hears French ships win, he…'ehr tanzt!"

"What, Sir?"

"Oh, damme! Il a dansé et agité un mouchoir!"

Major Walker grinned. "The baron said that when hearing of the French navy's victory, His Excellency started dancing about and waving a handkerchief."

"General Washington? No!"

"*Jawhol! C'est vrai*" the baron said, nodding and his eyes alight with amusement. Then he poked me. "*Et en public!*"

So, while allies could be shipped to us in Virginia, nothing at all could be shipped to support Cornwallis's forces at Yorktown.

Greene's army arrived to join us in early September, and I was able to rejoin my old company.

"Boys," I said, "the way we count it, we have almost twenty thousand troops, regulars mostly, surrounding Cornwallis. He had maybe nine thousand men. Those lobsters are all sewed up with no hope of escape or even getting supplies. We've got him under siege. This is victory."

General Washington fired the first American cannon on October 9. After that, the roar of fifty-some cannon forced us to shout to each other.

It became worse the next day when French batteries of thirty-five cannon joined the bombardment.

The British fired back for a time, but our shelling soon put their artillery out of action.

My enthusiasm about the siege dulled a bit the afternoon of October 14.

That's when His Excellency granted Lieutenant Colonel Hamilton to command our battalion in capturing Redoubt Number Ten.

Chapter 60
Redoubt No. 10

Colonel Hamilton summoned me about 5 and gushed that our battalion and the French battalion wouldn't attack the redoubts in full darkness after all.

I sputtered, "But I've already told…"

"Captain, it won't matter. They're arranging a diversion."

"Oh? What diversion…Sir?"

"At precisely 6:30," he said, "the French will raid a British redoubt over to the west side of Yorktown. They also plan quite a lot of howitzer fire. With the enemy's attention pulled away, we will attack at 7 and achieve surprise. It's fairly dark by then anyway."

"Surprise? Sir, we cannot surprise them!"

He stiffened with anger, but I give him no chance to speak.

"Sir, you and I are three feet apart and we can hardly hear each because of the cannon fire. How will a raid on the far side of the fortress divert *anybody's* attention – or added artillery fire, for that matter?"

He gave me a hard look. "Captain Scot, those are our orders. Are you prepared to carry them out?"

"Yes, but by God, now I must make changes. There'll be no cover of darkness for the four hundred of us to sneak to that redoubt…which is what your major told me this afternoon."

"What changes?"

"Too many to discuss now…Sir."

"Look, Captain Scot, as the designated commander of this attack…"

"Colonel, hear me out. I've soldered going on seven years and I know my business. But if you assigned me to run His Excellency's headquarters for one hour, sheer disaster would ensue. Likewise, for you to reorganize this attack…"

Colonel Hamilton suddenly rose sharply in my estimation. He gave a big grin. "I understand completely. You plan. I lead."

"Yes Sir."

I ordered Corporal Saddler to recruit four more ax men and then discussed the plan with Sergeant Liddle.

"Mayhap the laddie got the time changed so scribblers could witness his heroics. Tae lend credulity, ye might say."

"Likely," I said. "But there it is. So, here's what I propose…"

# # #

It was fifty paces from our trench to the abatis, the fence of sharpened trees ringing the base of the redoubt.

Our signal to attack came when the artillery fired a series of signal rockets.

Their lights suffused the land in a ruddy glow and seemed to catch the attention of the men in the redoubt.

Our ax men emerged from the trench, walking gingerly toward the redoubt. They were almost there when a sentry spotted them. A double flash and bang erupted at the redoubt's crest.

We took this as the signal for rest of us, led by Colonel Hamilton, to climb from the trench and trot to the redoubt.

Saddler and his fifteen men didn't try to chop down the fence. They simply dropped the ax heads between the abatis points and yanked the logs out and down flat to the ground.

God, trotting toward the redoubt was terrifying! You visualize that the instant you find a gap and start climbing that slope on all fours, a redcoat will fire his musket down into your skull. If he misses, he'll spike his bayonet into you before you can even raise your own musket. If you make it to the top, their cannon will disembowel you and you'll die on your back, feet at the crest, head half-way down the slope

The colonel leading, we surrounded the redoubt and screamed like banshees and wild Indians.

As the ax men ripped open gaps in the abatis, we scrambled to get up the redoubt's sloping sides.

I didn't see the colonel, but Saddler – shoulders broad as a barn – clambered up the slope ahead of me, swinging his ax as if it were light as a toy.

He bashed aside a bayonetted musket. The disarmed lobster fell to his knees, arms raised in surrender. Saddler split his skull and moved on.

A musket went off beside me. With my ears madly ringing, I slashed my saber blade diagonally through his face, shoved him aside and chopped into the shoulder of another lobster reloading his musket.

I had to parry a bayonet which an American soldier thrust at me. I roared, "Careful, you fool!" Recognition dawned in his face and he turned to disappear into the smoke.

I glimpsed Liddle bayonetting an artilleryman who was about to fire one of the cannon.

"Come on!" I screamed, running toward a knot of redcoats near the center of the redoubt.

The colonel got there ahead of me, slashing with his saber at a line of bayonets – a fool's suicide move. Yet the redcoats, seeing several score of us emerge onto their hill, began dropping their muskets. Other troops crested the slope behind them, their butts and bayonets shattering any resistance.

Some lobsters yelled, "Quarter! Quarter!" Saddler was about to chop another kneeling redcoat when Hamilton sprang in front of him.

"He surrendered, man! Spare him!"

The ax man looked ready to strike the colonel when I shouted, "Saddler! Hold! 'Tis over. We've won."

"Aye, we have, Saddler," Liddle called, "ye dinna need the ax."

The colonel, whose hat was missing, opened a masked lamp beside one of the cannon.

He pulled his timepiece from his waistcoat and looked at its face. He was ashen and his hands were trembling – the same as most of us, Saddler included.

"Captain," the colonel told me, "This was a simple affair. It took a mere ten minutes."

"A simple affair," I said. "Please come with me, Sir."

"Where?"

"We must tour the battle ground."

"Why so?"

"Sir," I said, "At battle's end, a commander must report the results to headquarters. That report must include the butcher's bill. We must tot up the numbers of dead and wounded…on both sides.

"Oh, and, Sir, our wounded might appreciate a word of thanks from you."

A fifteen-minute tour gave Colonel Hamilton a look at the cost of battlefield glory. It sickened him.

Epilogue

At the price of forty-two lives, our little victory won widespread fame for Colonel Hamilton.

He used that notoriety well. I needn't go into his role in creating our constitution and how he almost single-handedly salvaged our new nation's finances.

More important, our success – together with the far more costly French capture of Redoubt No. 9 – forced General Cornwallis to surrender his army to George Washington four days later.

On October 19, Cornwallis's worn and sickly troops grounded their arms and marched down a lane comprised of French troops ranked on one side, Americans on the other.

I'd have felt sympathy about their humiliation atop suffering ten days and nights of constant shelling.

Being such hard-bitten professionals, however, they were insulting about our own ragged appearance. Our boys give as good as they got, so that jeers and insults flew back and forth like shrapnel. The French troops simply looked on in contemptuous amusement.

Maybe the boys would have been a little more charitable had we realized that American independence now was assured.

Our Yorktown victory forced 'is gracious fookin' majesty's government out of office.

Replacing it was a new cabinet headed by a prime minister wanting to end the expense, the bleeding and the war with the United States of America.

Still, the conflict dragged on two more years with minor bursts of fighting – minor except for the civilians and soldiers whom it maimed or killed.

In the end, Benjamin Franklin negotiated with London what turned out to be a most beneficial treaty for the United States.

The British military, however, took its sweet grudging time in leaving, not departing Savannah and Charleston in South Carolina until July and December, 1782.

The royal army didn't evacuate New York City until eleven months later.

At the end, Colonel Hamilton sent me a very gracious personal letter thanking me for my "wise counsel" in leading to "my victory" – meaning his victory – at Redoubt No. 10. He wrote that if I desired to retain my commission in the Army of the United States I should not hesitate to call upon him.

I deemed it wise, first, to discuss that matter with Alice. And Jay. And young Master Isaac MacDonald Scot.

Jay writes that he expresses very strong opinions.

Other Books by the Author –

Brought To Battle
A Novel of World War II

The Green Hell
A Novel of The Army's Pacific War

The Trail Through Hell
A Novel of The Army's Pacific Victories

Chosun
A Novel of the Korean War

A Corporal No More
A Novel of the Civil War

One, Two, Three Strikes You're Dead
A Brad Powers Mystery

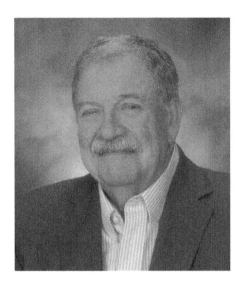

About The Author

J. Scott Payne is a retired newspaper reporter-editor who began his career in the 60s at the *Kansas City Star*.

His professional life involved covering city hall and the police beat where he got to know dispatchers, cops, dicks, judges, chiefs, ambulance-chasing lawyers and sheriff's deputies, and two four-legged officers with long gleaming teeth.

He later served as a counterintelligence investigator with the U.S. Army in Korea, Vietnam and, worst of all, Washington, D.C. It was duty requiring basic journalistic skills. You ask. You listen. You write. Just the facts.

Journalism nowadays seems to call for a different skill set: you join the reportorial herd and never let facts get in the way of current political narratives.

Scott and Jane live in a West Michigan college town. We feed and watch birds and are entertained by fights – or perhaps play – between their short white terrier and their long black cat.